ANYONE BUT ME

A NOVEL OF HAITI

BRUCE KIRKPATRICK

ALSO BY BRUCE KIRKPATRICK

Fiction

Hard Left

The Resurrection of Johnny Roe

The Carnival Chemist and Other Stories

Non-Fiction

Lumberjack Jesus: How to Develop Faith Despite Pitfalls, Roadblocks, Stupidity, and Prejudice

Raising God's Gen Z Teen: 33 Strategies to Teach Teenagers Self-Reliance, Confidence & Responsibility

For Cheryl and Sherman Balch

BEFORE DAY 1

Paul

"You're spending Christmas where?"

"Haiti," I answered.

"Wow. Haiti. That's...bold. When are you leaving?"

"December ninth."

Abigail walked around my apartment, meandering. She'd never been here before. I'd cooked her a late breakfast for our third date. The relationship was still new, but the possibility for it to turn into something real was there. We'd shifted from casual conversation to careful candor in just days. Like me, she was mid-thirties and never married, having focused on her career in marketing.

"Wait. You'll be gone...right before Christmas. Oh, that's too bad. I thought we could do some cool things together over the holidays. Get to know each another better."

She didn't sound upset. Maybe a little disappointed.

"Yeah, sorry. That does sound like fun. This trip is just something I need to do."

I liked this woman, but I didn't know her well. We'd met at a party. Later, I'd invited her to stop by my bakery, and I treated her to a croissant and coffee. Out second date was dinner at a hole-in-the-wall Italian restaurant with killer lasagna.

"We were going to go to that decade dinner right after Christmas. Is that still on?"

I vaguely remembered something like that, but said, "The what?"

"The decade dinner." Her whole face smiled. "You know, to welcome in the new decade, the tens? The twenty tens? Remember?"

Now I did.

"Oh, shoot. I completely forgot. I'm sorry, but no, I can't make it. I'll be gone about a month," I said.

"Wow again." Her eyes briefly met mine and then skipped away. "A month. That's a long time. What's this all about? What will you be doing?"

I didn't exactly know, so I hesitated a few seconds before I answered.

"Uh, there're lots of reasons I have to...want to... make this trip," I finally said. "I've been thinking about something like this for a long time. Being able to dig down deep into myself and see why I'm really here."

"Here? Here, like where we are? Here in Cincinnati?" she asked, scrunching her eyebrows.

Now I smiled.

"Ha, no," I answered. "Here on Earth. Like, what's

my purpose? Am I just running a bakery and making money and...getting to know you? Or is there something bigger?"

"Bigger than getting to know me? Inconceivable," she said, laughing.

I liked the way she could laugh at herself.

I couldn't even tap into all the reasons I'd signed up for the trip and was having a hard time trying to describe my feelings even to myself. I didn't want to be evasive, and since we'd only met a few weeks ago—and I enjoyed being around her—I pressed on.

"Okay. Let me try to explain this. Give me a sec," I said as I collected my thoughts.

I looked toward the kitchen. It was a mess, and if Abigail noticed, she might laugh at that, too. I'd cooked breakfast, but I never cleaned as I went and used more pans than were probably necessary. Two of the kitchen cabinets were half open, and the cupboard, with a black and white checked curtain pushed back to the left, displayed a concoction of boxes, spices, glass jars full of pasta, sugar, and flour, plus two shelves that were a mishmash of ingredients needing to be organized.

When I didn't offer anything, she asked, "What about the bakery? Who's gonna run that while you're gone?"

"Well, we'll close for Christmas week, and then Johnny and Jose will fill online orders and the contracts. They'll be fine. We've let people know we're going to take a short holiday break." I had that part of the plan covered well enough.

"I'll be gone a month. Thirty days, exactly," I continued. "I know it's a long time to be away, but I got... mesmerized by this opportunity. I'll be observing, working, learning. I don't really know exactly what all it entails. I just need to go. To experience it all. I can show you the brochure."

She looked directly at me. It was the first time I noticed her eyes shifted from green to hazel depending on the light. "You're doing fine explaining it. Go on."

I told her about the organization I'd be serving with and the orphanage they ran. I didn't know all of the details, but I mentioned how long I'd been contemplating a trip like this. I'd talked to the director, and he drew out of me an interest in "experiencing the poor" as he called it.

"I'm impressed that you signed up not knowing all the details." Abigail leaned against the counter and tilted her head. "That tells me you're adventuresome, a little daring. Very impressive."

She came closer and gave me a little hug. "Be careful, though. That sounds scary to me."

I caught a whiff of her perfume. Subtle and nice, a flowery scent. I looked down at the worn hardwood floor. "I have to admit, it sounds scary to me, too."

We spent the next half hour talking about Haiti and its history. I'd been researching the country to prepare for my journey and was amazed at how little I knew. Then we covered what she'd be doing over the holidays and how much time she'd spend with her family. I poured her another cup of coffee as we cleaned the kitchen.

While she dried the frying pan, she looked at me

and said, "I like being with you, Paul. You're fun to be around. And I'm excited for your trip. I can't wait to hear about it when you get back."

Warmth filled my chest, and again I sensed the potential for something beyond casual dating with Abigail. "Thanks. The feeling's mutual."

"Do you realize how this trip could change your life? It really could, you know?" Her gaze was tender and understanding.

"Yep," I said. "I'm getting that feeling, too."

THE DAY BEFORE DAY 1

Paul

I TOSSED MY BACKPACK ONTO THE WINDOW SPOT and tried not to grab the seatback in front of me to slide across the row. I knew how that annoyed people who were already seated because it annoyed me. The gate attendant said the flight would be full, and a long line of anxious passengers were already queued behind me, so I did my best to get to my seat quickly. Before I stowed the backpack and settled in, I grabbed a few things. One of Paul Farmer's books about Haiti, a copy of my itinerary, and the brochure. I fumbled with the air nozzle above me as I felt perspiration break out at my hairline. Then I unzipped my Pauly's Bakery hooded sweatshirt. It was worn and beat up, but I loved that my name— Paul Whiteside—was printed across the left side. Pride of ownership, I guess.

The short journey from Cincinnati into Miami

would arrive late afternoon, but I hadn't booked a same-day connecting flight to Port-au-Prince, so the final leg would be tomorrow morning. Even though I was committed to my decision, this leap into the unknown produced anxiety I didn't like. I'd noticed over the past few weeks a slight buzz in my brain—nothing that I could pinpoint physically, just nervousness that was constant, a humming just below the surface but strong enough to disrupt my sleep and keep me on edge. When I took a deliberate look at my hands, something I did four or five times a day, they weren't shaking, but I always felt jittery, like the barista had slipped three or four extra shots of expresso into my latte. I took a few deep breaths and stretched my neck muscles—left, right, up, and down—to try and loosen the constant constriction.

I distracted myself by watching the other passengers as they shuffled down the aisle. Button-up shirts and suits made the business travelers easy to identify. Young adults and young families were more intriguing. What was each person's story? What awaited them at their final destinations? Were they happy and fulfilled, or did they wonder, like me, if there was something more to life.

Finally, everyone was buckled in, and we took off. As the plane leveled off at cruising altitude, I shifted my seat back and closed my eyes. All those questions I'd been asking myself for the past few months resurfaced. Why was I making this trip? Why was I leaving the bakery business I'd owned for ten years for an entire month? I couldn't remember taking more than a week off in any year that I'd been in business. And that was only because Dad had a heart attack and Mom needed help caring for him. Even that time we went to Mexico with the church group, I hadn't been gone a full week. Now, I'd committed to a full month. Thirty days in a foreign country. What was I doing? And why?

I opened my eyes wide and tried to shake myself out of this thinking. I plucked the brochure from the seat-back in front of me and opened it up. It was a simple trifold printed on a standard size glossy paper. I gazed at the few photos of Haiti, slightly blurry from a mediocre printing job, depicting several scenes of people in poverty. One photo showed a young, shoeless child in a garbage-strewn street holding something I couldn't identify in his hands. The background of the photo faded away quickly, leaving the reader to believe that the garbage was never-ending and probably filled with ... whatever kids looked for in piles of garbage. Taking a deep breath, my nose burned and bile stung the back of my throat, as if I'd caught a whiff of what that street must have smelled like to that young child. The stench of something rotten, something gone bad. I wiped my nose with my sleeve and swallowed hard.

Maybe that's why I was going. To smell that street. To stand in that trash heap. To experience the poverty and desperation on that boy's face.

The title on the front of the brochure always stopped me and made me think. *The Experience of Becoming Poor*. The perfect beginning to the story, like a movie title that summed everything up.

I'd read the brochure probably fifty times. Many of

the phrases were seared into my brain. Every time I reviewed it, the words spoke directly to me, like it was written specifically with Paul Whiteside in mind. I couldn't remember hearing the voice of God, not audibly, ever in my life. But those words, combined with the photos, evoked an emotion in me that I couldn't explain any other way than to say: That must be God talking— maybe I should be listening. But why was he talking to me? I hadn't figured that one out yet.

The first time I saw the brochure was after a Sunday service at church. A dozen or so missionaries had set up tables in the courtyard to attract support and donations. I meandered through, but at the time I didn't have much extra money or any inclination to serve in some far-off country. As a baker, I worked long hours and had rent and overhead to cover each month. My job and business consumed me.

One six-foot folding table had ten or fifteen brochures from different groups randomly positioned without anyone behind it ready to pounce on walkers-by. The others weren't really pouncing, but they were aggressive, so I avoided getting too close. I studied the brochures, my gaze meandering from big, glossy ones to business cards, to postcards, and finally to one stack of trifolds with that photo of the little boy. The boy's eyes stared directly at me. A burst of laughter from one of the tables in the courtyard distracted my attention for a few seconds. When I glanced back at the table, I saw that little boy again and fixated on him. I tried to glance away, but I quickly returned to the image of the boy. That child nearly hypnotized me. I grabbed the brochure, found an empty step on the stairs that led to the parking lot, and began reading.

Now, on the plane, that headline jumped out at me again. *How can God fill you with all He wants for you...if you are already full and satisfied?*

What did God want for me?

I'd been trying to answer that question since the day I first saw the brochure. I liked to think of myself as already doing what God wanted of me. I took care of my parents as much as I could, fulfilled my passion—my God-given passion? —for my career by running the bakery, and contributed to charities when I was able. Lived life without bitching and moaning. Adulting, as one of my buddies called it.

I figured I did more than most people. My heart warmed when I served pancakes and sausage at the homeless shelter. I'd helped the staff develop a menu and procured much of the food when they served their Saturday breakfast. I didn't always tithe but contributed to the church and at least a half dozen non-profits that sent requests every year. I treated people well, for the most part. I didn't swear, at least not often and mostly not in front of other people. What else was there?

I knew people that prayed more or served more or gave more money, but I was only one man. I was doing the best that I could, wasn't I?

Still, I'd been wrestling with that phrase, *full and satisfied.*

A slight poke from the older guy seated next to me got my attention. He pointed to the bottled water and bag of peanuts the flight attendant extended toward me.

"Thanks." I nodded to the man.

He didn't look me in the eye, but continued to stare at nothing, lost in whatever was pumping through his earphones.

I skipped over the *full and satisfied* phrase in the trifold, but the next headline prompted more questions than answers, exactly as it had over the past several months.

How can God use you for His plan for your life...if you're so busy with your plan?

Did I even have a plan? I always thought I did. Community college, culinary school, the bakery, marriage, kids maybe. Then the back end of the plan faded from view, like the horizon you can't quite make out on a hazy day. Most people were like that, weren't they? Well, maybe not Elon Musk or Jeff Bezos, but most other people.

That little boy in the brochure caught my eye again. The distended belly, a sign of malnutrition. The garbage. No shoes. And those eyes. Always those eyes.

Why would God let THIS happen to His people? A better question would be: Why would you? God didn't neglect this place. You did.

It was as if the brochure read: *You did, Paul.* I closed my eyes and felt a sting, the one that comes right before tears. I managed to suppress it and opened the bag of peanuts, nibbling them one at a time. I opened the water and poured it into the cup of ice. I took a couple of sips and rattled the ice.

That phrase—*God didn't neglect this place, you did*—was the clincher. The first time I'd read it, I called the number on the brochure. A voicemail message in a voice with a Caribbean accent said something like: *If you're reading our brochure and looking at that little boy, you're halfway to Haiti. Leave your phone number, and we'll see if you qualify to make it the rest of the way.* The voice wasn't trying to sell me. I appreciated that. So, I left my name and number. That was six months ago. The buzzing in my brain started a few months later.

But the brochure didn't just berate. It beckoned. I wasn't shamed into going to Haiti, to spend a few weeks and make the world a better place. I had never traveled internationally—well, if you didn't count Mexico—and now I was putting my life on hold, going to a place that scared the willies out of me, doing something I couldn't comprehend or understand.

Maybe it was God beckoning.

I read the headline one more time: *How can God fill you with all He wants for you...if you are already full and satisfied?*

Weren't you supposed to be satisfied with life? Fulfilled with a good job or career, family and friends, a few extracurricular activities to keep the juices flowing, the adrenaline spiked as much as you could handle? Active, passionate, engaged in life. Satisfied, happy.

But I wasn't completely satisfied. I never had been. I wanted more from life. Most times, I didn't even know what that meant. Weren't you supposed to want more? For me, it wasn't always more money, prestige, or power. In fact, at an early age I sensed I wasn't built for those pursuits, and I wasn't motivated by any of that. Maybe I was even a little afraid of what working toward any of those three would actually entail. But I couldn't define what else I needed or wanted.

I glanced back at the brochure.

If you were to empty yourself of all the junk in your life—pride, pain, scorn, hate, ego, grudges, regrets, trivialities—what goodness could fill up those empty spaces?

I'd started a list of the things in that first group. Pain, grudges, regrets. I didn't have to check the notebook in my backpack to review those. The girl I'd met at culinary school, Eva. How I ached for her even now, but I'd never had to nerve to her ask out. The grudges I'd held onto from all those guys in high school that battered me constantly from ninth to eleventh grade about my looks or my weight or my glasses or my...anything. The disappointment I saw in my father's eyes when I talked about the bakery, like it was one of the lowest, least professional jobs I could ever hold.

I took a deep breath, drained the diet soda, and grabbed my phone for a little soothing music. I didn't want to think more about pain or regrets. I'd had enough of empty spaces. Maybe Haiti could fill me up in some way. With goodness.

There isn't anything wrong with dreaming, God, is there? I drifted off to sleep, listening to Bob Marley's slow reggae.

Later, the faint shriek of the tires as they touched down and the landing lurch reverberated through the cabin, waking me. When the plane finally arrived at the gate, I sat in my seat while other passengers hurried to depart. I stared out the window at the baggage handler as he maneuvered the machine to unload the plane. When a flight attendant finally spoke to me, I looked around, noting I was the last person on the plane. I nodded, grabbed my backpack, and trudged down the aisle.

I checked in at the Miami hotel where I would spend my final night in comfort before that final leap into the unknown.

DAY 1

Paul

THE NEXT DAY I WALKED DOWN THE RUSTED, portable stairway from the plane that had brought me from Miami to Port-au-Prince. The heat of Haiti engulfed me like a sticky and humid August day in southern Ohio. But this didn't look anything like Ohio— and the hot, piercing December sun in Haiti was far from any sun I'd seen in Ohio. I could feel its intensity on my scalp as I made the short walk to the terminal, but my sunblock was buried deep in the backpack along with the insect repellant and all the other medicines I'd read about before the trip, including various intestinal remedies. I was mostly prepared—even got a tetanus shot—physically at least, but deep down I had no idea if I was ready or not.

I followed a dark-skinned man's wave to all of us to

come toward him and saw several passengers from the plane enter the terminal.

When I stepped through the door, I stopped breathing for a second as the chaos of the building hit me. The baggage claim to my right was roped off, so I figured I'd have to go through customs before I picked up my suitcase. I couldn't read any of the signs as I scanned the crowded room that apparently housed everything at the airport, including vendors. I listened but didn't hear any English being spoken, just a cacophony of sound at a fever pitch coming from every direction. A mixture of excitement, tension, and what felt like panic reverberated off the walls directly into my ears.

A slight jab in the ribs got my attention. I turned to see the same dark-skinned man pointing to a line of passengers waiting at what I assumed was customs. I fell in behind a passenger I recognized from my flight.

"Chaotic, isn't it?"

I turned around to see an older man dressed in shorts, a colorful tee shirt, and a sun hat. I nodded. "Sure is."

"Ever been to Port-au-Prince before?" the man asked, a gentle smile on his suntanned and wrinkled face.

"No, my first time."

"Well, they'll get you through customs pretty quick, and then you head over that way to get your bag," he said, pointing back to my right. "But don't let anyone take your bag from you."

"What do you mean?" I asked.

"They'll grab your bag like they're helping you or like they're assigned to assist passengers with bags, but they really just want a tip to take your bag out of the building. No need for that, just keep hold of it. You got somebody picking you up?"

"Yeah, I'm supposed to look for a sign with my name on it."

"Good, good," the man said, nodding his head. "You don't want to jump in some random car. Never know where that's going to end up."

Queasiness hit hard. I stuffed my sweatshirt into the backpack and rolled up my sleeves. A few ceiling fans lazily pushed air like they'd been doing it for years, but they didn't help the suffocating atmosphere.

"Don't worry. It sounds and looks a little worse than it probably is. Just got to get used to everything being different from...wherever you're from."

"Cincinnati," I replied.

"Yeah, you're not in Cincinnati anymore, Dorothy."

I took several deep breaths and reached for my water bottle.

"Good luck. Looks like you're next," the man said, pointing to the customs official beckoning me to step forward.

"Thanks. I'll probably need it."

After I cleared customs, I moved on, only to wrestle my bag away from several aggressive men who smiled and pointed outside just like the guy in the customs line warned me. Then I walked the gauntlet of a small corridor outside that connected the terminal building to the street outside the airport. The corridor looked to be about twenty-feet wide with a chain link fence on both sides. It seemed like every foot of the fence—maybe thirty or forty yards long—was occupied by men waiting. Some had signs, some smoked, others sidled up to me, trying to help with the bag. I just kept shaking my head and looking for my name on one of the signs.

As I got to the end of the corridor, I turned back around, thinking I must have missed the sign. I scanned the area again but was not inclined to head back toward the terminal. The dust from the street stung my eyes as I fished my sunglass case from the backpack. More men with more signs extended to the street, so I trudged toward the traffic and the sound of cars in chaos. Honking horns and loud motors assaulted my ears. Belching exhaust fumes added to the dust to attack my eyes and nose.

Just as I was about to return to the terminal and begin the journey down the corridor again, I noticed a slim black man in sunglasses holding a sign that read "White man."

I gestured to the man to get his attention and said, "Do you mean Whiteside? Paul Whiteside?"

The man looked confused, like he didn't understand English. He rummaged in his jeans pocket and pulled out a slip of paper.

His eyes widened, and he looked at me with a slight bow. "Oh, my, oh my. Yes, yes, Whiteside. Mr. Paul, I am so terrible sorry, I make terrible mistake. Whiteside, yes, Whiteside, please yes, come with me." He went to grab my bag, and I gripped it even tighter.

"No, no, I take. Please. Please. Don't tell Mr. Dessi. Don't tell Mr. Dessi," the man pleaded with me.

I had the entire brochure memorized and recognized the name Dessi. "Okay, okay. Lew Dessi, right? You've come from Mr. Lew Dessi to pick up Paul Whiteside, is that correct?" I wanted to make absolutely clear he was leaving the airport with the right person.

"Yes, yes. I write name wrong on de sign. Mistake, mistake, please forgive me and please don't tell Mr. Dessi. He fire me."

I took a deep breath. And another. "Okay. Let's go."

Later that Evening: Paul

"GOOD EVENING," THE TALL, GAUNT MAN SAID AS we all turned from hushed conversations in the room adjacent to the kitchen where we'd been waiting. cropped haircut framed sunken cheeks and an intense, penetrating stare that continued to move slowly and deliberately around the room. He held our eyes with his, shifting his gaze from one person to the next without saying a word. Some of us looked away before he did. He looked Haitian to me, but I didn't know.

"My name is Lew Dessi, although that's not my real name, and I will be your host for the next thirty days. If you make it that long." Again, no follow up; he just left that statement hanging in the air, sinking to the floor like a dead balloon.

"Why aren't you using your real name?" asked a

middle-aged guy with an expensive haircut. To me, it looked like he dyed his hair, too. Not quite natural.

Dessi looked at the guy with what I could only surmise was a bit of disdain. He stared at him long and hard, more than I felt comfortable with. A few others looked away from the stare-down. The guy held his gaze, defiant, raising his chin even higher.

"Mr. Dean, correct?" Dessi inquired. "Ron Dean?"

"Right you are," Ron Dean replied.

"First, I will answer your question. Then I will tell you why I do not appreciate the question," Dessi began. "My first name, Lew, is abbreviated from Lieutenant, because I am a lieutenant in God's army, of lower rank, but not the lowest. Dessi is taken from Jean-Jacques Dessalines, who led the Haitian revolution in 1804 and became our first ruler of the independent nation. Lew Dessi. You all may call me Mr. Dessi until you earn the right to call me Lew."

Sounded logical to me, and as I looked at the small group gathered in the room, no one offered further inquisition. Dean still looked skeptical.

Mr. Dessi wasn't finished. "The reason I do not like your question, Ron Dean, is the insolence with which you asked it. You want to know my real name, but you have not earned the right to ask the question. Of what concern is it to you? We have much to accomplish in the next thirty days and not enough time to get bogged down in pursuits that will not produce results. But the question shows me that you will need extra work. I am willing to work with you—to a point, but not beyond. It remains to be seen how far that point will take you."

He looked away from Dean and moved to circle the group. "I am willing to do everything in my power to help you all with the mission that carried you to Haiti, to me, to this room on this evening in December 2009. I will be your guide, your confidant, your confessor, but I will, under no circumstances, treat you as the spoiled Americans that so often come to our door. You all will work hard here, harder, I suspect, than you have ever worked in your life. Not just physically, but mentally and emotionally. You have begun this journey with something in mind—and we'll begin to discuss that with each of you tonight. But that something will change over time. I can guarantee that and not much else."

I noticed a practiced pattern to his speech, like he'd done this many times before. His posture almost rigid, he didn't speak with his hands and with only a slight Caribbean accent.

"Some of you will relish the change, grab hold, and make a difference in the world, or maybe simply the world in which you operate. Some of you will not last more than the first week or ten days. You'll quit. You'll come up with a perfectly rational reason for quitting—you'll probably blame me—and you'll have wasted perhaps your last chance at redemption. The others? Well, you'll be somewhere in between. Which, as I have observed over my years, may be perhaps the worse place to be. No man's land, no woman's land. Stuck in the middle. On a sandbar. Immobile. Dreadful, indeed."

Dessi looked down at a dilapidated three-ring binder, flipping pages. I looked around. I assumed we were in the dining room, although the narrow table had been pushed to one side and the mismatched wooden chairs were gathered haphazardly facing Mr. Dessi. Everything in the room looked worn and tired. The cinder block walls had been painted—probably long ago —and now exhibited a faded, light-blue cast. The floor, although mostly clean, consisted of long, wooden planks, worn down over the years, then abruptly morphed into faded, yellow linoleum at the start of the kitchen at the far end of the room. A few hand-painted signs—one that read *Make a Change in Yourself, Make a Difference in the World*—adorned the walls.

I quickly counted ten people in the room. A few I'd met briefly between the time I'd been dropped off after repeated pleas from my driver not to mention the misspelled name card at the airport and this gathering. I'd been shown to my room by a light-skinned black woman named Andrelita, who now stood off to Dessi's right, hands folded in front of her, head bowed slightly. I remembered her name because I made her repeat it several times and even spell it.

I'd asked Andrelita a slew of questions, but I soon figured out that she likely had limited ability to understand English. She answered me in French several times, *merci, merci*, which I knew meant thank-you but often wasn't the right answer to my question. I also got *Due time* once or twice. She never looked me in the eye and quickly left me in the spartan room after simply pointing to the bed, the chair, and the bathroom down the hall.

"Thank you for your patience. You will learn much about patience in Haiti." Mr. Dessi again commanded the room, the corner of his mouth lifting in the barest of smiles. "We will begin with introductions."

"Many of you have met Andrelita," Dessi continued, first stating that the young woman, a light-skinned Haitian in her late teens or early twenties, worked for him and only him. "She is here to serve you, but you are not to ask her to do anything for you that I have not approved. She is the perfect servant, and you would be wise to observe and emulate her because part of your training will be learning to be a servant."

Andrelita bowed deeply from the waist to the group, head down, extending and holding the bow beyond what I'd thought was normal.

I glanced over at Ron Dean, quietly but repeatedly tapping his pencil on the unopened notebook in his lap. The woman sitting close to him at the table was looking at him, not Dessi.

"Next, may I introduce you to Mirlande." Dessi pointed to a woman standing at the back of the room, arms folded across her body.

She was older than Andrelita, probably in her thirties, with ebony skin and coiled braids. Mirlande nodded slowly and smiled but exhibited none of the subservience of Andrelita, her posture straight and proud. Her smile masked something I couldn't quite place. Not disdain or dislike but nothing even close to sincerity. Maybe it was the way she bared her teeth, like she was ready to growl but tried to smile instead. She had nice white teeth—big and strong and straight. Remarkable, really.

"Mirlande runs the small school and orphanage here

on the property," Dessi explained. "She will help you with your assignments, your life in Haiti outside of these walls. She has been with me for a very long time and will be invaluable to your experience here. You may trust her implicitly." He looked at Mirlande with his piercing green eyes, holding his stare as the room grew quiet, still, like the Earth had stopped rotating for a split second.

They continued to stare at each beyond my comfort level, a sort of battle of the wills, it seemed. The spell, if that's what you'd call it, was broken by who else but Ron Dean.

"What assignments?" he asked.

Dessi shifted his stare to Dean, and after what seemed like thirty seconds but was probably a lot less, he shook his head. "All in due time, Ron Dean. Let's continue the introductions. Please state your name and answer this one—and only—question: Why are you here?

"And since Mr. Dean would like to dominate the room, which tells me more than any formal introduction could, we will let him begin." He motioned with his hand for Dean to start.

"Yeah, right. I'm Ron Dean, and this is my wife, Gloria. We're from—"

"Stop." Dessi's voice was too loud for the small room. Dean turned toward him, his mouth open. "You will have to learn, Ron Dean, to listen and to follow instructions if you are to survive this journey. I am already beginning to doubt that. I'm sure your wife is quite capable of introducing herself." He nodded at the blond woman to Dean's right. "Now, your name and why you are here. Only that. Start over."

Dean's expression told me people rarely spoke to him that way and when they did, he didn't like it much. His jaw set, lips pursed, he said, "Ron Dean. I'm here because...I believe," he glanced toward his wife, "that it's the right thing to do." He relaxed in his seat, his gaze never leaving Dessi.

Dessi made a note in his binder and then looked up. He nodded again to the blond woman. "Mrs. Dean, I presume?"

"Yes, I'm Gloria Dean. And I just..." Her voice caught like she was holding back emotion, ready to cry. She patted her chest softly. "Sorry. I have been reading and studying about Haiti for several years and thought I just needed to be here. To understand. To see if it was possible that I could do something...to help. In some way. I don't know how." She raised her hands in front of her, palms facing each other about six inches apart, and then dropped them to her lap in a gesture I took as part surrender, part frustration.

"No understanding is a perfectly fine position from which to begin. It allows for understanding to eventually present itself," Dessi said. "If you begin with knowledge you believe to be substantial, there is little room for learning."

Mrs. Dean took a tissue from her pocket and dabbed at the corners of her eyes. I noticed a huge diamond on her ring finger. She was dressed in blue jeans and a simple cotton shirt, but I could tell she didn't shop at Target.

Dessi turned to a young woman seated at the far side of the room. I guessed she was in her mid-twenties.

She spoke up quickly. "Hi, I'm Annie. Annie Segura. I want to work with the children here because —" she stopped and looked at Dessi.

He gave her a single nod, which she took to mean she should continue.

"—because I work with kids back home, in a daycare, and my heart broke when I learned what's going on here. Yeah, that's me."

"Thank you, Annie," Dessi said. "When God breaks your heart for something that breaks his, you can choose to ignore it, but you can never forget it." He pointed to the back of the room, and everyone turned to see what he was pointing at. The exact phrase he just uttered was hand-painted on a small wooden sign posted on the wall.

I completely missed the next introduction, another woman who looked to be about the same age as Annie Segura. I was too busy trying to figure out what I was going to say when my turn came around. I made a mental note to seek out the young woman and apologize for not remembering her introduction. I tried to focus on the next one.

"Yeah, I'm Luke Himes. The first time I came to Haiti a few years back I helped build a few tiny houses for an organization. I'm here this time cuz I'm thinking I got lots of skills that this country could use but got no idea how I might fit in."

I checked out Himes in his old work boots, a dingy pair of shorts, a faded tee shirt, and a baseball hat. He probably hadn't shaved in two weeks. I immediately liked his smile and casual demeanor, though. I figured in another life, we'd be friends, maybe buddies. He looked about my age and spoke with an ease that defied his scruffy look.

Suddenly, all eyes were directed to me. Dessi was looking at me with a faint smile.

"Me?" I asked.

He nodded.

"Oh, sorry. I'm Paul Whiteside." Then my brain went blank. Nothing. I couldn't think of a thing I'd rehearsed only minutes before. Sweat broke out over my entire body, like my body temperature had jumped ten degrees. The room was waiting, but patiently.

"I saw that little boy's eyes," I finally said. "On the brochure. You know the one? Yeah, you all saw him. I couldn't take my eyes off him. I don't know why I'm here and I have no idea what I'll learn. And I'm pretty sure I don't know what a broken heart even feels like. But I just had to be here. Maybe to find out about all those things. Maybe."

Dessi smiled and nodded his head knowingly, as if he knew exactly what I was talking about.

Until then, I hadn't noticed I was up on my feet. When did I stand up? I plopped down, a little too quickly, and almost missed the chair, having to balance myself awkwardly to right myself in the seat. I heard a snicker and quickly looked at Ron Dean, catching him looking away and trying to suffocate a smile. Dessi, however, said nothing.

"Mr. Waterman, I saved the best for last. Please..."

Dessi gestured to an older white-haired man sitting next to me.

"Thank you, Mr. Dessi. I am Alan Waterman. I'm looking for my legacy. What I will leave this world when I pass from it. I am hopeful that I will find it here. In Haiti."

He had a pencil-thin mustache and perfectly combed white hair. His skin was taut, especially for a man I guessed was pushing eighty. He had placed his hands at his chin, his forefingers forming a steeple. I remembered that old children's game I'd learned in Sunday School—here's the church, and here's the steeple, look inside and see all the people. Alan had the finely manicured hands of a man with the time and the means to have finely manicured hands. Rich guy, I assumed.

"Thank you, all," Dessi said. "Now, let's discuss the accommodations and a little about tomorrow when your real journey begins."

What a diverse group of people. I hoped I'd fit in. But it was too soon to tell.

The same evening: Mirlande

I'D SEEN THESE SAME PEOPLE IN THIS SAME ROOM many times over the past ten years. Different names and different faces but always the same. They all looked pampered, spoiled by their American lives. I hadn't even heard their stories yet, but they all had stories about themselves—mostly about how hard their lives were, how they'd struggled, survived, made it through dark times.

They had no idea what life on the edge was all about.

Dark times? These people didn't know dark times. No, they didn't know what it meant to be hungry, for Lord's sake. Look at them all. Every single one could lose twenty pounds and still look healthy and privileged.

I listened as Lew went over some of the precautions he stressed—don't drink the water or you'll pay the price; be careful of the food sold on the streets, but don't be so careful that you miss the experience. By tomorrow, most of these people would forget what he'd just said, and I'd be the one hammering it into them day after day, at least for the first week. By then, some would be on airplanes back to their lives of comfort. The rest? I knew if they made it through the first week, they'd—probably —stick it out for the full thirty days.

I smiled to myself when Lew fielded a few questions about what their $3,500 fee included. How he got these rich Americans to fork over that amount of money for what little he offered them I never figured out. Fools and their money are quickly separated. My saying, not Lew's. He was always searching for the best in people, even as he kept up this intense outward appearance. Tough guy mode. And I had to admit to myself, he was a tough guy—for the most part. A little too soft-hearted, but steely when he had to be.

"You'll be provided two meals a day, breakfast and supper," Lew said. "You will be gone from this house most every day, so lunch is on your own. Mirlande can point you in the right direction for food—and caution you what not to eat."

I did my best to smile when they all turned around to look at me. Lew kept telling me I had to be *polite* and *accommodating,* but it wasn't my nature. I showed them my teeth, my very best feature.

Then Lew launched into his God speech. He kept preachin' it, gotta respect him for that, I suppose. It's who he was. I never questioned his sincerity, just his religion.

"We use the descriptor, God, in this house," Lew began. "To us, it's the right word. A higher power. A supreme being. You may refer to Him or Her as Elijah, Mohammed, Jesus, Jehovah, Yahweh, Allah, Spirit, or Father. We will not disparage you if you prefer another name. Or no name at all. The name doesn't hold the power. The spirit does."

As he continued on and on, I tried to guess who in the room believed in this American God Lew kept talking about. Hard to tell before you got to know them, but my sense was the *blan,* the white dude who called himself—can you believe it?—Whiteside was a believer. He believed in God, for sure. Like when he couldn't take his eyes off the little boy in the photo. I knew Lew had staged that photo. Staged, not faked. The little boy lived not far from here, and he was always out roaming the streets in the garbage. I was always asking where in the world his mama was, and he never knew. Life in Haiti was tough, terrible at time, but I never understood why the children had to suffer so much. Shouldn't we take care of the children first, before we take care of ourselves? Broke my heart.

I looked at Gloria Dean taking notes in the cheap little notebook Lew gave them all. She probably believed in this God. Although, as I peered at her fingernails, I had to admire that manicure. Maybe God provided the means to get that. She probably had a new one every week. I looked down at my own hands, no fancy nails, worn down, callused. Nails and skin both cracked. I didn't have fancy girl hands; mine were like everyone else's here in Haiti—workin' hands. I shoved them in my pockets.

I wondered how Gloria Dean would react when her fancy girl nails had dirt under them, and she couldn't find any soap to get them clean, and she spent half her day in that tiny bathroom room, crappin' lunch out for hours. I wondered how much she'd love her God then. Or keep trustin' him.

These people had no idea. Tomorrow when they got their "assignments," life would hit them smack in the face, splitting apart this holier than thou, do-gooder journey they were on into a thousand little pieces.

I always enjoyed the second day the most.

DAY 2

Paul

WE GATHERED THE NEXT MORNING AFTER breakfast in the same room as the night before. I got up my nerve and approached the young woman from last night where I blanked out and missed her introduction. She was sitting close to Annie, and I noticed they were both wearing tee shirts, jean shorts, and sandals. They could have been sisters except Annie was stocky and broad-shouldered; the other woman slender with a nice figure, long-legged, and toned.

"Hi, I'm Paul Whiteside," I said, directing the intro to the other woman. But picking up on excluding Annie, I said, "You're Annie, right?"

She nodded.

"I'm Ashley." The second woman had a cute, easy smile.

"Did you two know each other before coming down

here?" I asked.

"Nope," Ashley said. "Just getting to know one another."

Then, nothing.

"Kinda spartan accommodations, aren't they?" I tried again to keep things moving.

"What'd you expect? It's Haiti," answered Annie, with a disgusted look.

I didn't know if she was disgusted with me or Haiti. "I guess I didn't know what to expect. And still don't."

"It does seem rather intimidating," Ashley offered, a life preserver thrown to a drowning conversation. "I've read a lot about Haiti, but I guess you never know until you experience it firsthand."

"You ain't seen nothing yet," Annie said, throwing more water on the drowning.

"Have you been here before?" I asked.

"No, I'm just saying. It's the poorest nation in the Western Hemisphere, so it just stands to reason that it's gonna be hard, is all." Again, the condescending look. She was going to be hard to work with. Just saying.

Dessi appeared, and as if he'd heard the conversation from afar, he said, "We are changing up that description, Miss Segura. In this house, we say: 'Haiti is the first free black nation in the history of the world.' Has a much stronger and positive emphasis, wouldn't you say?"

Not waiting for an answer, he walked over to his seat and the three-ring binder.

"I really like that," Ashley said with that same smile, stroking her long, blond hair.

Annie squinted at nothing in particular and appeared to consider a big dilemma. Maybe she'd learned something new. I know I had.

Dessi rose out of his chair and stood at attention in front of the room. He said nothing, but the room quickly became silent.

"We just had an interesting conversation over here," he began, pointing to the three of us. "One member of that group described Haiti as the poorest country in the Western Hemisphere. I'm sure you've all heard or read that description before. It seems to be the fallback position of the global press when they can't come up with anything new or original. And although it very well may be accurate, it certainly does the people of Haiti a great disservice." Dessi's voice was matter of fact but grew louder on every word. "It describes us in words of poverty and despair. It brings about notions of pity and inevitability. Like we have always been—and always will be—poor. It labels us as a nation at the bottom, and if repeated enough, saturates the conversation with an oily black sheen. A devil sheen."

The room grew even more still. Annie looked down at her sandals, moving one foot in slow circles. I picked up that Dessi included himself as Haitian. I'd wondered about that because his accent was much different from Andrelita or Mirlande.

"Perhaps none of you will do anything to change the direction of the global conversation about Haiti. It is a very tall order indeed. As you will learn. And I will teach you. But...perhaps"—he scanned the room slowly, briefly resting his glance on each of us—"perhaps one of you will do just enough to move the needle, so to speak. Like a subtle, slight shift on the rudder of a ship to make a complete change in direction to the final destination. It is possible. It would only take one of you."

As Dessi studied his binder, Ashley meekly raised her hand. He didn't notice, and she patiently kept it in the air.

Finally, he looked up and said, "Yes, Miss Tanner?"

Ashley Tanner was her name. Why hadn't she said so? I'd noticed the generation behind me never introduced themselves with their last name. Everything was informal—or maybe secretive.

"I love how you corrected our description," she said, saving Annie from being labeled the one who actually said it. "The first free black nation in the history of the world."

"And how do you think, Miss Tanner, that description would make the people of Haiti feel? I know it's hard to project how someone else feels about something, but what do you think?" Dessi asked.

"It would make me feel good, so I guess it would make them feel good, too."

"An ice cream sundae can make you feel good. Please try to be more definitive in your description."

"Well, full of pride. Respected, I guess," Ashley said.

"Precisely."

That smile of hers burst into the room like a splash of sunshine. It was contagious. I noticed the whole room smiling.

"Help me understand," Ron Dean said. "You said

first free black nation. But African nations, predominately black, have always been free, right?"

"Yes, you are correct," Dessi replied. "Perhaps a better way to phrase it is that of the enslaved nations, Haiti became the first free black nation. Now, let's go over some house rules."

I thought I detected a slight smile from Mr. Dessi. One of the few I'd seen.

"Before you start, can I ask a question?" Ron Dean asked.

"You may."

"Is that all the breakfast we get? An almost rotten banana and hunk of bread? Doesn't seem like much. I could use a little protein."

Dessi stroked his beard. "When Mother Teresa served the poor, she often said that if they didn't have shoes, the nuns she served with took off their shoes. If the people they served had no food, the nuns did not eat."

Dean's expression, a quizzical scrunching of his entire countenance, told me he wasn't buying it. "We paid a lot of money to be here. If it isn't used to buy food for us, what's it going to?" He stared at Dessi.

"It is going to the process of teaching you how to be poor so that you may figure out if you want to serve the poor."

Dean looked like he wasn't buying that either.

"Very well," Dessi responded, pointing to Mirlande in the back of the room.

I hadn't noticed she was there. She wore the same clothes she'd had on last night—denim shorts down to the knee, a simple white sleeveless blouse, and worn sneakers.

"I took a very small portion of the money," Mirlande began, "and bought some food for the children at the school. For their lunch. Many days it will be the only meal they have."

There wasn't anything anybody could say to that, and I saw Ron Dean slump in his chair, his spirited stare fading as he nodded.

"Very well then," Dessi said. "Let's review the rules of your stay. We do our best to structure the next twenty-nine days for your benefit. And we rely on several rules to keep you safe and to make this experience come alive for you. The structure is flexible, to some extent, but the rules much less so. I suggest you write these down in your notebook. There will be a test. There is always a test. It's called life."

I expected him to crack a smile, but he didn't. I began to suspect I wouldn't be seeing many smiles from Lew Dessi.

"Rule number one: don't complain. You have nothing to complain about as you will quickly see. Make a mental note of how often you want to complain. You might be stunned at how often this is." He folded his arms, eyes roving over us as if to assess our understanding of the first announcement. "Number two: keep notes. You'll want to remember what you're learning, but at times you will be so overcome with emotion that you will lose focus and forget. Don't forget. Only through learning will new opportunities be opened for you."

I took notes, and so did everyone else, except Mrs. Dean who was dabbing her eyes with a tissue.

"Number three: let go of your wants and needs. It's not about you." Dessi's tone was brisk, businesslike. I was prepared to work hard but had anticipated some degree of appreciation for my donation of time and money. I wasn't sure how I felt about that lack of gratitude.

"This will be difficult for most of you because you have lived your entire lives trying to make yourselves happy. Your challenge is to be happy with what you have and where you are in this moment. As I said, difficult." Dessi paused for a second, maybe two, letting that sink in. "Keeping rule number four may be the most beneficial. Here it is: Let the process work. Don't try to rush it or control it. The thirty days in Haiti will work on you, and you must not come to conclusions too soon. Absorb it all and let it work. I have done this many times. When you don't understand the process, ask questions, but be patient."

Like everyone in the room, I found myself paying close attention, drawn in by this promise.

"Number five. Continually ask yourself: Is God present in this situation? And what is he trying to tell me? We will discuss these questions often in the evenings when you return to the *Acul Lakou.*"

Several people in the group mouthed the words and muttered, "The what?"' I hadn't heard that term before either.

From the back of the room, Mirlande said, "Lew, they don't know what that means."

His mouth pressed into a flat line, as if annoyed by Mirlande's interruption. Then it softened into a smile. "*Lakou* is a Creole word meaning courtyard and usually refers to a group of houses with a common courtyard in front. Since we have several buildings on this property, including the school, we have adopted the word." Dessi went on to explain that in Haitian history, the government tried to suppress the people by not allowing them to own property. This concept of *lakou* was an attempt to get around the government and establish local rule over ownership of land.

"A child's umbilical cord was buried in the courtyard and a fruit tree planted over it so that the people could claim ownership by birth to the land. *Acul* was the name of the province where the 1791 insurrection began.

"So, I named this place the *Acul Lakou*. That's your history lesson for today, but there is more to be discovered. You will learn much about the history of Haiti. You'll see how different it is from your American history —if you learned that.

"Finally," Dessi said, "rule number six: don't drink the water." At last, I saw a slight smile flicker and then disappear. "And that might be the hardest rule to follow of them all."

Dessi rose from his high-backed chair in the front of the room and began to pace. His sandals sounded like the flip-flop their name implied. I noticed his baggy shorts and the frayed cuffs on his long-sleeved shirt. He wore several bracelets on each wrist but no watch. I counted at least three rings on each hand. Like a musician or an aging hippie might wear.

He stopped near the back of the room as we turned in our seats to follow his movement.

"In a week, maybe less, you will all want a Burger King double cheeseburger, a fully loaded pizza, mass quantities of alcohol, and sugar-laden desserts. You will want to feed your face, fill your stomach and your ears and mind with all the things that give you comfort. When you are consumed with the pursuit of comfort, it is difficult to sense the word of God. To feel his presence, to understand what he is saying to you. Soon, very soon, you will find it impossible to be thankful for what you have right here, right now."

We all kept looking at him, waiting for what would come next.

"You must fight through that. If you do, you may connect with God. Only then can you be thankful for him. Then you will begin to learn. To feel. To understand your purpose. To get in touch with something bigger than your desires. That will be difficult for most of you and almost impossible for some. I am here to be your guide. Mirlande will assist. Andrelita will serve. But it is up to you—and God."

A somber mood settled over the room, each of us lost —well, I was—in thoughts of doubt. Could I let go of what I was, or thought I was, to see what God thought of me? Could I be someone different from the man who landed in Haiti only yesterday? I thought I could change, but my mouth was already watering for that pizza, and I could only wonder if I was strong enough to fight back against my urges, my comforts, to press on toward something that I couldn't really understand. At least I had an awareness that I really didn't know much. That was something, wasn't it? A first step in the journey maybe.

"You have so much to learn," Dessi said. "Now, let's review your assignments."

Finally. Annie, Ashley, and I were assigned to the school and the orphanage next door, a sister organization. We'd report to Mirlande.

Luke and Alan were to work on a building project that was adding an addition to a church and a school that also housed a daycare and a community center, and apparently many, many other things.

As for the Deans, they would be helping distribute and serve the food Dessi was given by several other organizations. They'd be assisting Andrelita.

"But remember," Dessi added, "the real project is you and your transformation. If you feel led to another path, to work in another way from the one where you begin, please confide in me. On the island, we have many needs. You must always listen to the voice of the spirit and be willing to serve. Do not be afraid of where it may lead or if you have the capacity. God will provide the power. You must only provide the willpower."

With that, I sensed nervous energy building in the room. The others packed their notebooks in their backpacks and sipped water from plastic bottles. We looked at each other with wide eyes and clenched teeth. I had a hundred questions and couldn't think of a single one to ask.

"Today we will begin with a tour of Port-au-Prince. It will be a grand introduction to the pulse, the epicenter of the country. Mirlande, is Sonson ready?"

She looked at her flip phone and grimaced. "Almost. He should be here in twenty minutes."

Dessi frowned and shook his head. "Your brother seems always to run on his schedule, not ours."

At first, Mirlande regarded him with a steely stare, but I noticed a hint of resignation as she dropped her eyes, quickly looking back at her phone.

Dessi told us that after the tour, we'd be dropped at our assignments and then reconvene in the evening to review. And, he said, answer our questions. "I fear if I open the floor now, we may be here all day. Better to jump into the ocean to see how cold the water is—and to see if you can survive the current."

I was already struggling to keep my head above the water. And I hadn't even felt the current yet.

That evening: Mirlande

THEY ALWAYS LOOKED LIKE THIS AT THE END OF Day 2. Sad, confused, hot, sweaty. We never had to prepare much of a meal on this night because they're sick to their stomachs from what they've seen. They can't imagine living like we do.

Lew had given them an hour after they returned to "freshen up," as he liked to say. When they straggled into the kitchen, they didn't look fresh to me. I noticed several had changed clothes, but some hadn't. They looked sleepy-eyed, like they'd laid down on their beds and fallen asleep. Typical reaction to a day in Haiti.

The two twin girlies, Ashley and Annie, looked stricken. The bigger one, Annie, looked to have had the righteousness slapped out of her. Like she was going to be sick to her stomach. I'd seen Andrelita clean that up more than once since Lew started this work. The pretty one with the fake smile and nice legs, Ashley, had no smile now. That had been ripped right out of her. Forty girls at an orphanage with little to eat, no running water, and no electricity will wipe those smiley cheeks clean and replace them with a grimace, somewhere between fright and hopelessness.

I wondered who would be the first one to start crying.

"The initial day in Port-au-Prince and at your assignments awakens you," Lew said, now sitting alongside the others at the big table. "Please do your best to avoid coming to any hard, fast conclusions. Or solutions. Give it time; it's a process."

The folks were sitting with the same people they'd served with earlier. The two twin girlies, Alan and Luke, the Dean couple. Only the *blan*, Whiteside, sat alone. He hadn't said much at the orphanage, but then again, the twin girlies were demanding. Always asking questions, trying to figure everything out, talking to the orphans. Not many of the forty girls spoke English, but they'd found a few. Whiteside, he just took notes and walked around the complex, checking everything out.

Despite myself, I was intrigued by his stillness, his intense scrutiny and careful deliberation of each scenario he'd encountered. He'd failed to hide his shock but seemed determined to heed Lew's instructions: Trust the process.

"Let's begin with observations. What did you see today?" Lew asked.

"Port-au-Prince looked like chaos to me," said Alan Waterman. "But then again, not unlike other cities in turmoil, such as Manila or Rome, or...well...New York City at times. Chaotic but not out of control. Maybe that's just the way I saw it, huh?"

"Yes, indeed, chaotic to us all, at times," Lew commented. "What else?"

"I saw so much sadness," the Dean woman said, her voice barely audible, even in the small room. "So much poverty, so much hardship. A lack of resources. So much...."

"There is poverty, of course, but how do you *see* sadness? How do you calculate that?" Lew asked. "Do you see it in the eyes of Haitian men and women? Do their shoulders slump? Do tears leak from their eyes? Sadness is an emotion better observed in one's self; it's hard to detect in others."

The room grew even more silent, if that was possible. I wanted to shout at them all. Yell. Scream. We are *not* sad. We are determined. We are fighting. With everything we have. Do not pity us. We don't want your pity. We are a proud people, and your pity disgusts us. If all you have is pity, go home. We'd be better off without you. Good riddance.

Then the Dean woman began to cry. I should have known it was going to be her, the first one crying, tissue in hand, dabbing her eyes. Then her hands dropped to the table, and she began to sob. Out loud, too loud for the small room. Gulping sobs, uncontrolled tears falling on the table, unobstructed, without restraint. I could see her shoulders hitch as she continued. Finally, the Dean man embraced her, put his arm around her and pulled her close. But she kept crying, and Lew did nothing to stop her.

I checked out the others. They stared down at their feet or their hands covered their faces. Maybe silently crying, too. Andrelita put several boxes of tissues on the table and looked to Lew for instruction. He just shook his head, his hands outstretched as if to say, what else can we do?

Finally, the Dean woman cried herself out. No more tears. At least not right now.

"It is good that the sadness overwhelms you, Mrs. Dean. Thank you for expressing the grief that all of us feel to some extent. Do not shy away from this feeling. All of you. Embrace it. Let it wash over you. A good cry can often cleanse you. And open new tenderness," Lew said. "Some of you do not know tenderness, real tenderness. You love your family or maybe a few close friends —you can show them tenderness. But can you show it— and use it—with people you do not know? Maybe. In due time. We will see."

I walked over and grabbed a banana. I needed something to take my mind off the crying and the pity party. I always took advantage of the food that Lew provided to the group. He encouraged me to help myself.

Finally, the Whiteside man asked an intelligent

question. "How many orphanages does Haiti have like the ones we visited today?"

"That is difficult to say," Lew answered. "Mirlande, do you have an estimate?"

I had no idea. I had my hands too full with one school and one orphanage. "Too many," I answered in a low voice.

"Mirlande knows more than she often admits," Lew countered, a sly smile almost spreading from his mouth to his eyes. Almost.

"Andrelita, please come here." Lew motioned for the young woman to move from the kitchen section of the room closer to the table. He stood as she moved toward him, his hand outstretched to clasp hers. It seemed he always to want to touch her. Others may not have noticed, but I always did.

"Andrelita is a product of the Haitian orphanage system, spending almost fifteen years in several on the island," Lew began. "Would you like to tell of your experiences, dear one?"

Dear one? I hated when he used that term for her.

She looked at her sandals and shook her head.

"Andrelita's mother died when she was very young. Her father traveled around the island looking for a job, finally ending up working in the DR, Dominican Republic. She went to live with her grandmama. But Grandmama had too many mouths to feed."

The shy young woman buried her face in the shoulder of the ever-sympathetic Lew. He rolled his arm up around her shoulder. I couldn't tell if she was crying or just play-acting. I shouldn't question it. She had a tough upbringing. But who didn't here?

Lew explained that food was the key reason so many children became orphans because, with too many mouths to feed, it was often hard for families to find enough. But the orphanages had connections with aid organizations that provided food. He emphasized that some of the orphans were not, in the true sense of the word, orphans. They had family on the island, but they got better care—and more food—if they lived in an orphanage.

"The problem," Lew said, "is we have too many hungry children and not enough orphanages."

Silence again in the room. This always happened on Day 2. Silence, like they had no words to express what they'd witnessed.

"So, technically, Mirlande was correct," Lew said. "We have too many orphanages. And too many orphans."

The Dean woman grabbed for the tissue box. Lew hugged Andrelita, now with both arms. I felt disgust rising in my stomach, but I couldn't tell its source. Was it how Lew was treating the "dear one"? Or how he made the case for helping the orphans while at the same time making the case that it felt hopeless? In Haiti, it was often a very fine line.

"We have a light meal prepared for tonight, if anyone is interested," Lew said, pointing to the kitchen. Nobody moved until they headed back to their rooms for the night.

DAY 3

Paul

AFTER BREAKFAST—A HARD-BOILED EGG AND A ROLL
—we walked over to the orphanage. I noticed that
Mirlande had braided her hair with small blue ribbons.
She brought extra ribbons in a plastic bag for some of
the girls. That seemed to be a great sense of pride for the
young girls both at the school and the orphanage. The
girls who attended the school and those residing in the
orphanage were separated by a concrete block wall—
and, I supposed, a dozen cultural and financial differences I had no idea about. The girls in the school wore
uniforms—dark-blue, smock-type dresses with a white
blouse underneath. The girls in the orphanage, well, no
two dressed alike. But both sets of girls spent time
making their hair look nice. Yesterday I'd noticed how
well-kept the kids in the school looked. Today the
orphans got hair care.

Since I didn't have a chance to speak much with Mirlande yesterday, I made a point of finding her and introducing myself. I felt I'd only been a fly on the wall yesterday and spent most of the day in overwhelm. I needed to burst through that today. I had to force myself to engage.

I approached her after she left a conversation with the woman who supervised the orphanage.

"We didn't get a chance to talk much yesterday," I began. "You probably know who I am, but I wanted to introduce myself. I'm Paul Whiteside."

Her eyes lit up, and she began to giggle, trying to suppress it with a hand to her mouth. "Sorry, sorry, I shouldn't laugh." She kept laughing, now out loud with no attempt to hide it.

"What? What's so funny," I asked, realizing I was smiling, too.

"When I read..." She took a deep breath to keep down the next laugh. "...your name on the roster, and then I saw you, I thought...I'm really sorry, but I thought, yes, you do have a white side." Now she giggled even louder.

"Well, I suppose that's true, huh?" I said, not knowing if the joke was on me. I tried to keep smiling, but it was forced. As she kept giggling, my smile faded.

"Listen, I didn't mean to offend you," Mirlande said. "I think it's funny, but I know you may not. It's just my way to poking a little fun your way. It's Haiti. We have to find fun where we can. Understand?"

"I think I'm beginning to," I lied. There wasn't much

I understood about Haiti, and I wondered if I ever would.

"You probably don't, but I'll keep at it. You see," she continued, lowering her voice a bit as some of the girls from the orphanage begin to drift toward us, "you are a *blan*. That's a Haitian word with a twice, how you say, a twice meaning?"

"A double meaning?"

"Yes, right, double meaning. *Blan* means white, but it also means foreigner. You are *blan*. Not a bad thing. Just who you are. In Haiti, a Whiteside is a foreigner. *Blan*. You see?"

I could see that, so I nodded.

"Maybe you do, maybe you don't. Part of my job is to teach you what that means. So you can understand our country better. As a Whiteside in Haiti, you have much to learn."

"That sounds like something Lew Dessi would say."

She cocked her head and lost most of her smile. "That's something Mirlande says."

Then she walked away toward two picnic tables under several palm trees. There wasn't much land-scaping in the quarter acre or so plot of land dedicated to the orphanage. Rocks scattered about mixed with gravel, but mostly just dirt and overgrown grass. The tables sat under a blue bedsheet strung between the trees to produce shade. The sun was intense this morn-ing, like every morning—at least the mornings I'd been there—and I found myself always looking for shade. I pulled an old Cincinnati Reds ballcap out of my back-pack to cover my head.

Mirlande sat at the table and opened her bag of hair ribbons. Several of the older girls drifted toward the table to look, but the younger girls watched from a distance.

Annie and Ashley appeared at the table and seated the girls on the picnic table benches and assembled a few hairbrushes and combs. Then Ashley began to comb out one girl's hair with long strokes. Annie started to braid the next one's hair with the blue ribbons Mirlande provided.

From a seat on a nearby bench, I observed the procession of care that the three women provided the young girls. It was easy to see this was a regular ritual. No rush, no pushing or shoving, no demanding. No commotion. Just waiting your turn. The orphans seemed to cherish this time when somebody cared for them. Paid attention, did their hair, and made them look pretty.

As I watched, a few of the younger girls still waiting their turn drifted over to the bench where I sat. Slowly they approached, as if they didn't know if I'd be okay with it. I smiled at them, and that seemed to be the sign they were looking for. In a matter of minutes, I found myself surrounded by five black girls, all preteens as best as I could tell. One sat on either side of me, two stood behind me, and one kneeled on the ground in front of me.

I felt a light stroke of fingers on my forearm. The young girl to my right was running her fingers through the light blond hair on my arm. This tickling—back and forth, back and forth—was completely unexpected. The two girls standing behind me then had their fingers in the back of my hair, lightly stroking my neck. I guess you'd say my hair was sandy-colored. Not really blond but much lighter than anyone I'd seen yet on the island. The girl to my left reached out and held my hand.

Surrounded, I did my best to let the moment take hold of me. I wanted to pull away my hand or brush away the fingers that seemed to need to touch me. Then I realized that was it. They wanted touch, feeling, contact. In the past, I'd had women grab my hand when walking together. Or brush my shoulder as they snuggled up close to me. But this was a new feeling for me. Young girls just wanting human contact.

Mirlande walked over to me. "You okay? You look even whiter than before."

"I've never...had this...happen before," I managed to say.

"Girls, listen up. I know you have chores to do, and Mr. Whiteside has things he wants to do, too. We'll see him again soon, but for now, let's all get going."

The girls slowly withdrew themselves from me. I squeezed the hand of the young girl to my left. She squeezed back and stood. They drifted away toward the hair grooming table to wait their turn.

Mirlande sat down at the far end of the bench and stared off into the warming morning. There was no breeze, only the faint smell of something burning, like a charcoal fire. In the distance, maybe a mile away, light plumes of smoke rose from the ground, drifted through the air. Maybe somebody was burning garbage in their yard. Or cooking breakfast over an open fire.

I picked at the peeling paint on the bench.

"They've probably never seen a white man like you before," Mirlande said in a soft voice. "At least not this close, where they could reach out and touch. They crave attention."

"They crave touch," I said. "Human touch."

She nodded. "Don't we all, at times."

We sat on the bench, me bouncing one leg in a nervous rhythm, her circling the toe of one tennis shoe in the dust.

As I reached into my backpack for sunscreen, Mirlande suddenly jerked her head toward the road at the sound of a trunk honking. I recognized Sonson, her brother, standing by his brightly painted taxi, a small pickup truck. She muttered a word, in French I think, but it didn't sound like a term of endearment.

As she stood and approached her brother, he pointed his finger at her accusingly. They were more than twenty yards from me, so I couldn't hear the conversation, but it was heated. Controlled but heated. Mirlande was shaking her head and turning away from him. But he kept circling around to get directly in her face to make his next point.

This went on for a good five minutes. Sonson pointing and gesturing, Mirlande countering. Finally, she put up her hands in surrender, shaking her head. He stormed off, walking in circles around her before jumping back in his truck. He didn't pull away immediately but sat there with his hands gripping the wheel, lowering his head and resting it on his hands. Mirlande approached and reached in to rub the back of his neck, but he pushed her hand away and started the engine.

She stood there as the truck drove off, then stared down at the red dirt of the Haitian road.

DAY 4

Mirlande

I NEVER SLEPT AT THE ORPHANAGE, AND I RARELY slept at the *lakou*, even though Lew reserved a room for me there. I had to get away, especially after a long day, and sleep in my own bed. To leave the girls. Not like I was escaping their problems. Their problems never left me. But just to create a little space. To try and live my own life, at least for a few hours in the evening each day.

I'd arrived early this morning. I hadn't been able to sleep most of the night. Sonson. Most of my sleeping troubles started with him. He wasn't the only problem I faced, but he was always the biggest one.

In some ways, I believed I'd failed him. He was my younger brother, and I should have kept a better eye on him when he was growing up. Momma tried, but he was too strong-willed for her. They always argued, seemed like every day and night. Papa hadn't been around much, and when he was, he was drunk. Then he left when we were both teens, and we never saw him again. Still don't know what happened to him or if he was even alive. Maybe he had a little money—he never had much money—and he got drunk and robbed, killed maybe, for what little he had. He wasn't good at hiding his money. I still thought of him, but I spent more time thinking about myself. And Sonson.

Andrelita wasn't even up yet when I arrived, so I made the coffee. I sat down at the kitchen table and sipped that first cup. The morning wasn't chilly at all, but the coffee warmed me and soothed me. That's one thing Haiti did right, coffee. Lew always bought his local to help a merchant nearby make a little money. He had it delivered every week.

My thoughts whirled back to my brother.

By the time my parents had saved enough money to put Sonson in school, when he was nine, he said he was too old for first grade. I'd made it through third grade by then, although it took me almost five years to do it. In school whenever we had enough money, and out of school when we didn't. Then Mama got a decent job cleaning at one of the newer hotels, and we finally had enough to put Sonson in, too. But he never took to school much. I'd taught him his letters and numbers, so when he got to first grade, he was beyond what they were offering. And he got bored, so he just stopped showing up.

"All those kids are too young for me," he'd say.

What did young boys do when they didn't go to school? He didn't get into too much trouble in the beginning. He just roamed the streets. Found a couple of other young boys and roamed together. They'd take a piece of fruit from the stand on the corner or coax a bean burrito from the nice man with the hibachi selling them in the market.

But eventually he got bolder. He'd steal goods from the open-air markets and resell them the next street over for a few *gourdes*. It wasn't much money but enough to eat on. And young boys needed food. At first, I thought that was all it was. Just a way to get a little something in his stomach. We had food at home but never enough for him. He was always hungry, but then again, he was a young, active boy.

Eventually, it became a challenge to him. Steal and resell. He got so good at it that others took notice. By the time he was twelve, he got recruited by a gang. That's when I stopped sleeping regularly.

"You're up early," Andrelita said, pulling me out of worry. "What time did you get here?"

"Around six."

She nodded as if she knew. "Sonson was here yesterday looking for Lew. Did you see him?"

"We talked."

"What are you going to do about it?" she asked, staring at me, demanding, so out of character for this sweet, demur little hospitality girl.

"Me? What can I do? I talk to him, but he doesn't listen. He can't listen. They've got him so strangled he can't even think straight."

"Well, it's up to you," Andrelita said. "Lew can't take this pressure anymore."

"Lew can take care of himself. If Lew doesn't pay, it's no skin off his back. Sonson will be the one...to get skinned."

"You never take Lew's side. You're always so against him. Why is that? He's given you a lot in life, hasn't he?" Andrelita asked as she came to stand over me, glaring.

It seemed she was itching for a fight. Again, not like her at all. I sipped my coffee and nodded, hoping she'd take it as agreement with what she'd said. Part of me wanted to tell her what she wanted to know. I think that flowed through the blood of many Haitians I knew. We couldn't always say exactly how it was because it was so bad much of the time. Not like we're in fantasyland, but that we're almost desperate to believe in something better. So, we just tell people what they want to hear.

"You didn't answer my question," she said.

"He has given me much, I agree. But Sonson is my brother. I have to look out for him. He's the only brother I have."

"And who is Lew to you?"

She knew exactly who Lew was to me, so I wasn't expected to answer the question. And I knew who he was to her, too. It was our mutual understanding, our little secret between this woman, child really, and me. A bond between us, and a wall both surrounding and dividing us.

She pulled a small wallet from the pocket of her simple shift dress. She opened it and showed me the photo I'd seen a hundred times. A serene looking black woman, not quite smiling at the camera. The photo was worn from being removed from the plastic covering protecting it many times.

I knew that photo well. I had the same one in my wallet.

That same day: Paul

I SPENT THE DAY AT THE ORPHANAGE, BUT IT DIDN'T seem like I accomplished anything. I wasn't any good with the girls, the orphans. At least Annie and Ashley knew a little French and tried their best to communicate with them. I knew no French.

The girls still wanted to be around me. I suppose I was a bit of a freak. A blond *blan*. A man with soft, silky hair. I was still uncomfortable when they touched me or huddled around me. I wasn't used to young girls—uh, young black girls—who didn't speak my language, who didn't understand what I was doing here. Did I even understand? From what I saw, they had very little to do during the day. Annie and Ashley were content to play games with the girls, do their hair, or walk around holding hands. I couldn't do any of those things.

I'd spotted a small plot of land at the back of the orphanage and put my energy into planning a garden. Then, realizing I knew nothing about growing things in the Haitian climate, I crumpled up the paper in frustration. Part of my exasperation was a result of Lew's refusal to give us specific tasks. I'd been assigned to the orphanage, but that was where the instructions ended. There was so much work needed that I didn't know where to start. With no supplies and no guidance and no solid understanding of what was even feasible, I was discouraged and annoyed. I'd come to Haiti looking for answers, enlightenment, personal growth, a deeper connection with God, and all I was getting was more confused.

As I wandered around the grounds, I was drawn to the orphanage building with its concrete block walls and corrugated metal roof. It was a big square building, maybe fifty feet by fifty feet, but without windows, at least on the front of the structure and the one side that I could see. The front door, slightly open, beckoned me. I desperately wanted to look inside, but then again, I was afraid of what I might see. I slowly walked toward the entrance and took one step up to the doorway.

I pushed the door fully open and looked inside. The entire building was a single room. I noticed ropes tied from one side of the building to the other with blankets slung over the ropes. It looked like a maze of dark grey blankets. I realized this was a way to divide the room into individual spaces. Some of the blankets drooped down, leaving the room open to my view. Small mattresses, clothes, a suitcase here and there, but not much else.

Several girls popped their heads out of their "rooms" to look at me. They seemed older than most of the girls outside. They stared at me for several seconds, then retreated back to whatever they were doing.

The air inside was stifling with a strong whiff of body odor, musty, offensive to my nose. But I didn't turn away and leave. I took a deep breath, and without moving, I looked around.

The floor appeared clean, but the wood was worn and had gaps that I figured opened to the dirt below. I saw no lights in the building, so it had only natural light from the door and from both sides of the building near the ceiling. Sections of the concrete blocks had been removed, or had never been there at all, providing a makeshift opening for light and air circulation. I counted nine blocks missing, three rows of three. You didn't have to worry much about cold in Haiti, but I suspected the frequent rainstorms blew into the room with regularity and caused havoc. I noticed that the blankets stopped about six feet from the wall to my right, probably a corridor to the back of the building and more blankets, ropes, and rooms. With forty-four girls, it would take many blankets to build an orphanage.

I wandered outside around the side of the building and saw four outhouses. For forty-four girls. Disheartened, I explored the other side of the building. Two girls were kneeling on the ground, pulling on a thick rope. One pulled and the other reached down into a hole and grabbed the rope, and then took her turn to pull. Back and forth they lugged. At the end of a rope, they finally reached a coffee can—a three-pound can—with water spilling over. Lord, it was a well. The two girls never looked at me but did their work and yanked up the water, which they dumped into a metal basin before disappearing around the back of the building. I knew better than to follow. I wasn't sure my legs were still working anyway.

———

LATER THAT EVENING, AFTER DINNER, LEW DESSI asked me to follow him to the porch. We eased our way into two old aluminum lawn chairs, the interspersed nylon slats in the seats fraying at both ends and sagging from overuse in the middle. Lew lit up a pipe, the tobacco smell reminding me of evenings with my grandpa, the last man I knew who smoked a pipe. I loved that smell.

We sat in silence, and for the first time in the four days I'd been in Haiti, a breeze moved the air.

Finally, Dessi spoke. "It's like a pilgrimage, this journey you're on. You travel long distances in search of something, but you don't know what. If you think you know what you're searching for then it's simply a quest. You travel, you get, you return. But a pilgrimage is different. You don't know exactly what you'll find. That's both the thrill of it and the fear of it. Oh, you have an idea. Maybe you'll find God, or peace, or passion, or your future. But it's uncertain. And it is not for me to say. You must observe and listen. Let the experience work on you. Don't jump to the first conclusion. The answers may come to you long after you leave."

"Well, I guess I'm in the right spot," I said, "because I still feel lost."

Lew blew out a thick, pungent puff of smoke. "You are not lost. You just don't know where you are. There's a difference."

I wasn't sure what that difference was, but I nodded anyway.

"How is the work at the orphanage going?" he asked.

"I have no earthly clue what I'm doing there."

He nodded and smiled at me. "You are a baker, right?"

"I am, yes."

"Good. Now I tweak the process and push you, ever so slightly, in a new direction."

DAY 5

Paul

I COULD TELL IN THE FEW DAYS THAT I'D KNOWN Luke Himes that he was a man who didn't mind getting his hands dirty. Today, after we all had returned to the *lakou*—we'd all begun using this phrase to refer to home base—I found him on his back with his head buried underneath the kitchen sink.

Andrelita stood nearby, drying the last of the dinner dishes and stacking them in a doorless cupboard to the right of the sink.

"Trouble?" I directed my question to no one in particular.

"No trouble, right, Mr. Luke?" Andrelita answered.

"Nah, just a clogged pipe. Food scraps," he replied. "I'm not sure they even have garbage disposals in Haiti. Almost done."

She smiled at me and shrugged.

"A man of many talents," I said.

The smile quickly faded, and she looked at me like I'd insulted her. What did I say? Did I insult her? Did the word "talents" mean something different in Haiti? I knew that talent, in the Bible, is a form of money. Maybe it was something like that here? I was always saying something stupid in this country. Sometimes words just came out of my mouth, and I didn't even know what they were conveying.

"*Merci*, Mr. Luke. Goodnight," she said as she headed toward the door.

"Andrelita?" I called. What had I said? That's what I wanted to know.

She turned toward me and bumped into Alan Waterman as he entered the kitchen.

"Sorry, my dear," he said in that polite way of his.

Her eyes widened, she backed up a step, then bowed her head and retreated out the doorway, saying, "*Merci, merci, merci.*"

Luke emerged from under the sink. "What in the world just happened there?"

I simply shook my head. "No clue. Probably something I said."

"Well, I heard everything you said, and you didn't say anything weird."

"I believe," Alan remarked, "that Andrelita does not quite understand our English language as much as she pretends. Especially when it comes to idioms, slang, and all the nuances of our words."

I couldn't remember what an idiom was, but I nodded in agreement. Every time I talked to Alan, he reminded me of the butler in the Batman movies. What was his name? Alfred, right? White haired, polite, ultra-observant, although Alan didn't speak with an English accent. English across the pond English I meant. Was that an idiom, I wondered?

As the three of us settled down at the kitchen table, I asked about the building project at the church.

Alan and Luke looked at each other. Alan extended his hand and dipped his head, gesturing, *You go first.* Luke removed his cap and scratched his head vigorously before putting it back on. He looked skyward, as if searching for something. Maybe how to answer the question.

"Man, it's just...a little weird. I've done some work in this country before and it's always hard, but I can't quite get my head around this project. They got some labor—mostly just guys from the neighborhood who I think wanna help out. They got some plans, rough-sketched, but pretty well done for Haiti, I suppose. And the addition's goin' up, but something's just off. Can't quite put my finger on it, you know? Yeah." He shrugged and looked to Alan.

"I'm really out of my element," Alan began, "both here in Haiti and at that construction site. Not really my sweet spot, but I suppose that's part of the process Mr. Dessi is always alluding to. There does seem to be a gentleman who looks like he's in charge, but the pace of the work is extremely slow. And from what I see, they're woefully short on supplies. Even with my limited knowledge of construction, I can figure that out. I wish I knew how better to help."

That did seem like the consensus among everyone who'd been sitting at this table for the past five days, wishing they knew how better to help. But I didn't say it. I wasn't one to verbalize what I thought was right, and it was also something everyone should hear.

"That's the nail bein' hit by the hammer, right there," Luke said.

Well, there you go. Luke said what I was thinking. We sat in silence, Luke moving his scratching to his unshaven chin and Alan searching for glasses to get us all water. We'd been told the tap water in the kitchen was filtered and didn't fall under the don't-drink-the-water rule. I had my doubts, wanting desperately to ask Luke if he'd found a filter under the sink.

"As I think about it more," Alan said, putting three plastic glasses of water down on the table, "maybe my first activity is to help find more supplies. I'd be willing to purchase whatever they need for the job. I know Mr. Dessi discourages us from throwing money at problems, but this situation cries out for contribution. And that is my sweet spot."

He turned back to Luke. They were tag-teaming the discussion, working off each other's words and making it up as they went along.

"Maybe that'll work. If we could find the supplies. And if we could find a way for them to use those supplies. Haitians are pretty proud people, and you can't walk all over 'em, telling them how to do things. Might offend them. As it might anybody. And that probably isn't our job."

"Well, of course," Alan continued, "we'd compose of

list of supplies with the supervisor's input and direction. What's his name? Jeffrey?"

"Jeffney," Luke said. "With an N."

"Do you know what they need?" I directed the question to Luke because I wanted to contribute to the discussion but wasn't sure how. I knew less about construction than I knew about orphanages.

"Most everything," he replied. "But that's not unusual for Haiti. Yeah, I suppose we could work with Jeffney. We could buy him a nice lunch one day. Get him off the property so he doesn't have to lose any face in front of his guys when we make some suggestions. I know they need some cement tools, like trowels and stuff. And other tools when they get to the roof. Yeah, we could make a list. And I know there's something like a Home Depot in Port-au-Prince. Depot something or other. Eco Depot, that's it. Yeah, that might work."

"What's the number one thing they need?" Alan asked. "The key to the whole project. The one thing that, if they had it, success would be more probable?"

Luke sat in his chair and took a long sip of water, squishing it around his mouth, moving his lips back and forth.

"Probably rebar," he finally said, "but it's pretty scarce around these parts. I saw a guy just yesterday, driving a little Moped-type scooter. He was dragging one single bar behind him, tied with a rope. Sparks flying off the end of that bike like the Fourth of July. What's one single piece of rebar gonna do? I suppose it's all he could afford." He shook his head and swirled his water in the glass.

If I wasn't willing to show my ignorance by asking a stupid question, Alan was. "Why rebar?"

Luke's smile was rueful. "Without it, you've got a house of cards. You know, you shake the table, and the cards fall down? It shakes a lot in Haiti."

DAY 6

Mirlande

"Why are we stopping here?" I asked Sonson as he pulled his truck to a stop in front of what looked like a tiny tent city. Earlier I had coaxed him into going to my place so I could cook him dinner. But this was an unscheduled stop.

"Gotta make a delivery. It won't take long. Whatever you do, stay in the truck," he said, looking me in the eye and squeezing my shoulder a little too hard. "Stay in the truck."

He got out and approached a makeshift gate, wide vertical boards held together by rope. I could see through the gaps in the mismatched boards and the large opening in the gate. A dozen or so young men milled around in front of the complex, and dirty white tents were visible beyond the place they stood. Three approached the gate when they saw my brother. After a brief exchange, they let him enter. One man stepped outside the gate, standing rigidly still and looking as mean as he could muster. I could see a large handgun stuck into the front of his jeans. He'd purposely opened his shirt to make sure I saw it.

The sentinel, who I guessed to be no more than a teenager, looked at me and sneered. I held his gaze and put my stern face on. I wasn't going to sneer back at him, which could provoke him, but I also wasn't going to cower away.

As I held his stare, in my peripheral vision I noticed a yellow bandana sticking out of the front pocket of his jeans. A symbol I knew. It marked the *Federasyon*, the Federation, one of Haiti's newer gangs.

The truck dipped, and I looked in the back to see several Haitian women getting into the truck bed. I rapped on the back window and waved them away.

"No service, no service," I shouted in Haitian.

Sonson often used the truck as a *tap-tap*, a taxi shuttling people between stops. Hop on, hop off. For a few gourdes, you could jump on and off wherever you were going. The women reluctantly hopped down and ambled down the road, looking for another ride.

When I turned back around to face the gate, I startled at the sight of the young sentinel two feet from the truck, just far enough away to look in my window.

"Who you?" he asked in a guttural, menacing voice.

I took a deep breath to quiet my increased heart rate, doing my best to not let him see me quiver. "Sonson's sister," I managed, hoping my voice was strong.

He took a step closer so that his waist was level with

the window. He patted the gun. Then he grabbed his crotch, moving his hand up and down. Bending down to face me, his expression turned from a sneer to a leer, showing crooked, yellowed teeth. His tongue moved side to side to emphasize his lewdness. I looked away, staring through the windshield but keeping my mean face on. I wasn't going to react or play his game. I had to show strength, but deep down I was hoping Sonson would quickly return.

Eventually, he backed away from the truck, walking slowly backward to his post, all the time grabbing his crotch. He pulled the makeshift gate open farther. Now I could see a row of rifles propped up against the first tent inside the gate. A large white bucket, one of those paint buckets we used for almost everything except paint, sat next to the guns. The sentinel took several steps inside the gate, his eyes never leaving me, and then thrust his hand into the bucket. He pulled out a handful of bullets and showed them to me before dropping them into his jeans pocket. Another display of force and intimidation that I tried not to react to. I wondered if my face was cooperating with my intent. I'd had many years to practice my mean face and could pull it off almost at will. I continued willing it now.

I stared straight ahead, forcing my right hand not to roll up the passenger side window. I wanted to give the sentinel no satisfaction. I was a strong Haitian woman, standing my ground. After several minutes of maintaining statue-like stillness, I saw Sonson walk in front of the truck. I shook my head to pull out of my self-induced rigidity.

As he slid into the driver's seat, I noticed his hands shaking. He gripped the wheel to steady them but quickly reached for his water bottle and took a long swig. Perspiration slid down the side of his temple, and I whiffed body odor. He was scared, and I hardly ever saw my brother display that.

"What happened?" I asked, almost in a whisper.

He just shook his head and started the truck. We rode the rest of the way to my place in silence.

He pulled the truck into the dirt patch beside my little home. It wasn't much, but it was mine. Our parents had lived here, and after my father left, my mother moved in with her sister. I stayed and made it my own. As far as my mother knew, my father had no land deed to this patch of property. Over the years as we got to know our neighbors, we found out that wasn't so unusual. But still, it was tough to swallow at times. Could somebody just show up—with a deed or a fake deed—and claim the shack as their own? I tried not to worry about it and installed many items of furniture and pictures of family into the place to prove it was mine. It was all I had. It was all I could do.

Several nights a week Sonson would show up late, usually after midnight, and fall asleep on the floor. I always laid out several blankets for him, hoping to hear his special knock on the door—two taps, pause, two taps —to let me know it was him.

Tonight, he sat in one of the two chairs I owned as I prepared the meal. Lew had given me a little chicken as he did several times a month. I had rice and beans cooking over a small coal fire in the back corner of the one-room house. I called it a home, but I knew it wasn't any more than a hut. Dirt floor, tin roof, two sides of concrete block, two sides of wood fencing. When it rained, I had to make sure the back wall was secured with sandbags, or the water would rush in and swamp the place. And it rained a lot in Haiti.

As we sat at the small table to eat, in my most sisterly voice I again asked, "You want to talk about it?"

"You know my life. There's no keeping secrets from you," Sonson replied as he shook his head.

He was eating my food, so he knew to keep the conversation civil. Many times in the past when we talked about his gang involvement, the volume escalated. I tried not to do that this time.

"You can stay here, you know, every night," I offered.

"With my sister? What kind of man stays with his sister?"

"A man who is loved by his sister."

His eyes soften slightly, but only for a moment.

"I have work to do out there," he said, grabbing his masculinity back.

Not sure I wanted to know, I asked, "What kind of work?"

"We are soldiers, keeping the ghetto safe from those who kill, rape, and rob." He thrust his chin higher in some misguided show of heroism.

He meant safe from other gangs, but I kept seeing that teenage sentinel grabbing his crotch and wondered who was keeping who safe. The lines were blurred.

"I thought that was the police's job," I meekly

offered, knowing how inept the police were, but not wanting to give any credence to gangs, who I believed had way overstepped their purpose. If they even had a purpose other than intimidation and chaos.

"The police are our friends. They tell us where the other gangs are and where they are headed, so we can cut them off...to keep...the streets safe." He forced that last part out without much conviction.

"You mean you bribe the police?" I was starting to lose my patience with where this conversation was headed.

Sonson shoveled the last of his meal into his mouth and wiped his lips with his sleeve. He gulped the rest of his water. Then he stood and paced in the tiny room.

"We don't bribe. We have no money. Our power is our currency." He stared at me with defiance.

I wanted to laugh in his face because I knew they had money. But I also wanted him to spend the night, curl up in my blankets, and share a cup of coffee in the morning. I didn't want him roaming the streets this night, so I backed off and cleared the table.

He settled back into the chair. "The gangs are not the people you see with guns. The gangs are the men in suits who rule and ruin this country with their corruption. We are not a gang. We are a political movement and want to change Haiti for the better. The only way we know how."

He didn't say how, but I thought only of the guns and bullets inside that tent.

"Maybe," I said. "I don't know."

"The *Federasyon* are my family." To emphasize his point, he shot to his feet with his fists clenched.

I walked the ten feet that separated us—it felt like a mile—and put my hand on his cheek. He flinched but let me keep it there.

"No," I whispered. "I am your family."

Finally, he pulled away and took several steps toward the door. "We will only get stronger. I will only get stronger."

I wanted to say, *if you live that long,* but didn't. I reached for him again, but he evaded my touch and disappeared through the door.

DAY 7

Mirlande

I HAD SOPPED UP MORE TEARS FROM THE TWIN little girlies at the *lakou* the past few days than I had from all the orphans in the six years I'd worked there. The orphans cried, I'm sure, probably at night in their beds when they thought about their mommas or papas. When they didn't know if their parents were alive or dead. Or when they couldn't quite remember exactly how their faces looked. That was probably the worst. When you'd been living apart from your real-life family —blood and bones—for so long that you couldn't remember what they looked like. Or how they smelled. Or what their touch felt like.

I still saw my momma once a week or so, and I didn't care what my pappa looked like. I'd been trying to forget his sorry face since he left us. So, who cares about him?

But Annie and Ashley? Lordy, it seemed those two

were always in tears. It was beginning to get on my nerves. I wanted to shake them, hard enough to make them understand tears wouldn't get anything done. Tears were just emotions leaking out, uncontrollable. They didn't have any place—at least not by the light of day—in my orphanage. We needed solutions. We needed help. A plan for the future. Some way out. Something. Not just tears.

I sat hunched at the picnic table, braiding little Josie's hair. She'd come to us two weeks back. Just showed up at our door with her cousin—at least he said he was her cousin. Could've been her papa for all I knew. Said if we didn't take her, he didn't know what was going to happen to her. I didn't want to take her. I couldn't take every poor child who showed up at our door looking for food or a handout. We had limited resources and if it got around that we were accepting every dirty little child that knocked on our door, we'd be swamped. Overrun. That wouldn't be fair to the kids who were already here. They had it bad enough. The more orphans we had, the less each got, whether it's food, water, or attention.

But that little Josie. Such a sweet little girl. About two years old, I reckoned, but of course, she didn't know how old she was, and the cousin never said. She clung to me whenever she got the chance, and every once in a while, I'd let her. I knew some of the older girls had taken her under their wing, caring for her, letting her sleep in their beds at night, carrying her around in their arms during the day.

The older girls were like that. They knew what it

was like to be tiny and lost. A few of the older girls had been here since before I got here. And several are now almost twenty years old. I could see it in their eyes, like they were lost all over again because we couldn't keep girls forever. We needed to make room for the little ones, and the older you got, the more we expected that soon you'd be leaving. Living on your own. But I knew what living on your own was like in Haiti. Tougher than most of these girls could take.

Josie had her little arms wrapped tightly around my calves as she sat facing away from me on the lower seat of the picnic table. As I combed her hair, she'd point to something in her view and stumble over the word to describe it. Her language skills—a mix of Haitian, Creole, and French—made little sense to me. I'd help her out when she couldn't get the word right—chicken, sky, sister, dirt. She'd eventually catch on.

Ashley sat down beside me, and I saw this forlorn look on her face. There I went again, wanting to shake it out of her.

"What's going to happen to her?" she asked, looking down at Josie.

"I'm not sure," I answered. "She'll be fine here. For a while. Then..."

"She's so cute, vulnerable. Maybe I could adopt her. Take her home with me," she said.

I noted sincerity in her question, but not much conviction. Pie in the sky.

"Show her a better life, huh?"

Ashley nodded, a slight smile spreading across her mouth but never making it to her eyes.

Enough, I thought. "You think we're gonna let white women come into our country and take our little black girls away? Just like that?" There was a little more venom in my voice than I intended—but only a little. "Take them to a place where they know nobody. Have no family. No cousins, no mommas, no friends. Take them away from their history, their heritage, their country."

Ashely looked stricken. But she needed to hear this. I saw her eyes moisten.

"Save them from all the horrors of Haiti, huh?" I continued, even louder. "Waltz right in and snatch them away. Whatcha gonna do with the other ten thousand? Save one and let the others just rot here in this filthy land?"

She made a movement to leave, but I grabbed her wrist and held her down.

"Sit. Stay," I said, softening my tone.

"It was just an idea," she offered softly. "I don't know what else to do."

"You been here six days. You don't have to know what to do just yet. Like Lew says, it's a process."

I continued with Josie, now adding pretty red ribbons to both sides, a double high ponytail, even though her hair almost wasn't long enough.

Annie joined us, sitting on my other side. "What are you two talking about?"

"Adoption," I said.

I saw a look of not-quite-horror spread across Annie's face. I couldn't help but smile.

"Kidding. We didn't like that idea too much, did we, Ashley?"

Both little girlies seemed to relax as Ashley shook her head slowly. Annie let out a deep breath.

"We could raise money," Ashley offered after a minute of enjoying a rare December breeze.

"Money is good," I said, not wanted to squash every idea that popped into those two sheltered brains sitting on either side of me.

"How much would we need?" Annie asked.

Not sure she was directing the question to me, I didn't answer. I wasn't sure there was a right answer anyway.

The two women batted that question and several ideas back and forth. Leaning their heads together in front of me with one idea, talking over the top of my head with another. I felt like a net in a tennis match. I just kept working on Josie's hair as the ideas flew. But I sensed desperation settling into them. Every idea had a stumbling block. A *how do we do this?* A *how would that even work?* Good questions—tough answers.

Every few minutes, they'd stop batting the tennis ball over my head and look to me with these quizzical looks on their faces. I supposed they wanted me to give them...something. Feedback? Attagirls? Not really my style. Let Lew be the harbinger of bad news. They had no clue. But at least they were looking for one.

My head swiveled right and then left. "All good questions," I offered. "Letting the process work. Good for you."

Both little girlies nodded their heads and slipped out

of conversation. I had no idea where their naïve little brains were taking them, but somehow, I believed we'd made progress this morning. A little. I kept squeezing Josie between my knees, not wanting her to leave me. Annie and Ashley kept quiet. Then the breeze died.

That same evening: Paul

I LAY ON MY COT IN MY LITTLE ROOM, READING A Paul Farmer book about Haiti. I needed all the history of the country I could get. A quiet knock at the door brought me out of a discussion about the lack of medical care on the island.

"Come in, it's open." I didn't need to say that last part. These doors had no locks.

Dessi entered, and he looked even paler and skinnier than he had the day before. He wore the same pair of baggie shorts and sandals as every other day. A different faded Hawaiian shirt hung loosely from his shoulders. He sat at the end of the cot as I scooted up to a sitting position and leaned against the wall.

He stared at me with those piercing green eyes just long enough that I began to feel uncomfortable.

"It is not fitting," he said, "when one is in God's service, to have a gloomy face or a chilling look. Francis of Assisi."

"S-sorry," I stuttered, "I'm not gloomy, it's just..."

"Just what? And you do look gloomy."

I nodded. I was a little gloomy. "I'm having trouble figuring out how I can help at the orphanage. It's like I don't fit in or...I don't relate. I mean, I feel for those kids, but I can't seem to focus on any possible ideas that could move the needle forward."

Lew smiled. "Move the needle forward. Did you know that's a reference to LP vinyl records? You know what those are, right? You had to manually pick up the needle and move it forward to play the next song. Seems archaic now, doesn't it?"

"I didn't know," I admitted.

"Typical of our society. When we don't like something, like a song, we want to skip to the next one without ever hearing the ending. Like that old Righteous Brothers' song, *Unchained Melody*."

Then in an almost perfect falsetto, he began to sing the lyrics.

Oh, my love, my darling,
I've hungered for your touch, alone.
Lonely time.

I made a mental note to YouTube that song because I only vaguely remembered it.

"If you got bored with the beginning of that song, you'd have missed the crescendo—the meaning, the feeling, the utter heartbreak—of the ending. But I understand, boredom is frustrating. Nobody wants to be bored these days."

"I'm not bored," I offered, a little too defensively.

"I get it. But boredom I lump into the category of stillness, quiet, contemplation, thinking, struggling. Sometimes you need to stew in the stillness of not knowing in order to hear the gentle whisper of God. You cannot force it—or quickly skip to the next song. See what I mean?"

I let out a deep breath and shrugged.

Lew smiled again. Huh? Two smiles in one day. I almost smiled back.

"Perhaps you have been sitting in that stew long enough. And you're cooked."

Now I smiled. This man did have a sense of humor after all.

He rose from the end of the bed and ran his fingers through his salt and pepper hair. Mostly salt. I wondered how old he was. Fifty? Sixty? It was hard to tell. Maybe he looked older than he was.

"You are a baker, correct?" he finally asked.

"I am," I answered, but he knew that already. It was on my application.

"I have a friend who owns a bakery not far from here. It is small. Just a few employees. But he struggles."

I sat up straighter on the bed. He had my attention.

"Perhaps you could help. But he is a proud Haitian man. He would not like you to tell him how to run his bakery."

"Hmm. Maybe I can start out," I began, "by just working there for a while."

"I will talk to him tomorrow. You can accompany me."

"Sure."

He turned to leave, but I needed to ask the question that had started floating around in my head. It wasn't like me to confront him, or anyone for that matter. I took a deep breath.

"Lew?"

He turned toward me, but his smile was gone. It was the first time I used his first name, but I felt I had earned that right by now, even though he hadn't given me permission.

"Why did you have me work at the orphanage all this time if there was this opportunity at the bakery?"

"You had to see the poverty. You might not see it at the bakery. You had to break out of your comfort zone. You are much too comfortable in life. And it is killing you."

He nodded once, emphatically.

Before he left the room, he said, "Yes, you may now call me Lew, in case you were wondering."

I plopped back down on the bed. That hurt. Not the calling him Lew part, the comfortable part. Wasn't I supposed to be comfortable? What was wrong with comfort? Everyone wants to be comfortable, to some degree, don't they? I'd studied, I'd worked hard, started a business, made it work mostly on my own, sweat equity. I deserved a little comfort. And I came to Haiti. No comfort here, that's for sure, as I punched the lumpy mattress. It's a process, I heard Lew saying in my head. I decided to let that thought—that comfort was killing me —stew a little since I was in a stewing mood.

Then the image of those two girls at the orphanage —pulling water from the well with a rope and a coffee can—popped onto the adjacent wall like a movie playing on an old reel-to-reel projector. A short five-second clip that kept looping over again and again. Hand over hand, one girl pulls, then the next. The coffee can almost emerges from the well. But not quite.

I slumped over and rested my head in my hands, trying not to look at the wall.

DAY 8

Paul

BEFORE DAWN, LEW AND I ROSE, LEFT THE REST OF
the household sleeping, and quietly made our way down
to the kitchen. We each grabbed a cold biscuit and a
banana. I started to make coffee, but Lew shook me off.

"Doval will have coffee. Come, let's go," he said.

"Who's Doval?"

"The baker. I talked to him about you again, and he
knows we're coming this morning. He seems more interested in your help than I let on last night when you and
I spoke. It's a short walk. It won't take us long."

I wondered when he'd had time to talk to Doval
between last night and this morning.

As we walked the quiet street in the pre-dawn
hours, Lew shone a flashlight at the road to guide our
way. Several women trekked in the opposite direction,
large baskets balanced on top of their heads, likely

heading to the markets. Every few minutes, a *tap tap* would putter along, but at this hour they were mostly empty. Their colorful graphics, hand-painted in rainbow hues, Haitian sayings, and talking head caricatures were muted in the dim light, barely visible in shades of grey.

"Doval has what you might say in the States is a commercial bakery," Lew said as I tried to keep up with his fast-paced gait. "No walk-in daily trade. He sells mostly to hotels and grocery stores. But business has been slow lately. He wants to get contracts with some of the bigger hotels and stores, but he's confessed that they are hesitant to give him big orders because the consistency of his product is lacking."

"Uh-huh. Go on," I said.

"He may not tell you that. He is a prideful man. But I know he is desperate to fix his problems."

"I understand. I've run into that scenario before myself."

"The lack of consistency in the bread?" he asked.

"It's pretty common in a bakery."

"You have some ideas already? Without even seeing his operation?" he asked, a look of surprise spreading across his face.

Even in the darkness, I could see his hopeful expression.

I nodded. "It usually comes down to one of four things: ingredients, time, temperature, or technique. Baking, it's a...process." I couldn't help myself.

Lew burst out laughing. "Good one! Touché, my man." He reached over for a high five. We smacked palms up top, and it added a little bounce to our steps.

We arrived at Doval's bakery before sunrise. It was located in what I guessed was something like an industrial park. I didn't see any homes—or any people for that matter. To my untrained eye it appeared deserted. The bakery occupied a corner of a larger building. Several other buildings surrounded this one, all connected by an uneven gravel road, pockmarked by long, jagged ruts carved by rain.

A large open garage door revealed a small operation with all the necessities of a bakery—big oven and refrigerator, industrial-type sink, long rectangular metal tables for prepping baked goods, and racks for storing finished products. All compacted tight with no room to spare, which wasn't different from most bakeries. An efficient space with no wasted steps for the bakers as they worked. I breathed deep the smells of freshly baked bread.

Lew made the introductions. Doval spoke passable English that I could mostly understand, but I doubted the other two workers did. They simply nodded to me as I was introduced.

Doval wasn't what you would call heavyset, but he carried a few extra pounds. Probably from sampling his baked goods. I glanced at my own waistline, and although I knew I'd lost a few pounds since I'd been in Haiti, the same description fit me, too. He wore a white tee shirt, white pants, and a smudged white apron that draped below his knees. His face and hands displayed a smattering of flour.

Lew and Doval spent the next ten minutes discussing my role at the bakery. I caught most of the conversation, but occasionally they switched to Creole. I didn't know if they were hiding something from me or whether they just needed to use their native language to get a point across and they couldn't find the right words in English.

Lew spoke to me first. "I think we're all set. Your job is to help where you can—an extra pair of hands, so to speak. And Doval will accept any ideas you may have." Lew looked at Doval, who nodded his approval. "Remembering, of course, our conversation from the walk over this morning."

The one about Doval being a proud man. I got it and flashed a thumbs up.

"I'll do whatever I can. I'm ready to work for you, Doval. What can I do first?"

He looked sheepish and stared at his feet. I sensed he was embarrassed to ask me to do something.

"Anything," I said, smiling slightly.

"If you would be so kind. We got far behind in clean-up this morning," Doval said, pointing to the large sink, overflowing with baking pots and pans.

"My specialty," I replied.

Lew patted me on the shoulder and slipped out the open door. As he left, I noticed a small group of men loitering outside of the bakery. Maybe waiting for a handout. Or work. There was a need for both in Haiti.

I spent the day in the bakery, mostly observing as I made headway on the pots and pans in the sink. I also worked alongside Doval and his two helpers. A light breeze blew through occasionally, offsetting the heat generated by the large oven.

I noted a few telltale signs of inconsistent products when, disgusted, Doval threw out a small batch, maybe twenty loaves of bread, because the bread was too "heavy," meaning it hadn't risen enough.

The bakery didn't produce much bread that day. I had kept an eye on the large sack of flour they were working from, and they didn't use even half of the bag. In my own bakery I could go through two similar-sized sacks a day, sometimes more. I saw no product other than loaves of bread.

As Lew had said, the business side of the bakery was struggling. They needed another product, one they could make a profit on quickly and consistently, which meant they'd need to sell it every day.

I glanced out the door and saw that same group of men loitering. I didn't quite have a light bulb flashing in my brain with an obvious solution, but an idea started to flicker.

DAY 9

Paul

DOVAL CLOSED THE BAKERY EARLY ON MY SECOND
day, so I had some extra time in the afternoon. I decided
to be bold—for me, at least—and explore the area
between the bakery and Lew Dessi's compound. Port-
au-Prince was about five miles away, but I wasn't quite
ready to jump on a *tap tap*. I wanted to stay closer than a
trek into the capital city.

Before I started, I texted Abby.

*Just got a new assignment. I'm now working in a
BAKERY! Go figure, huh? Duh. It's still a little daunting,
being Haiti and all, but I know my way around a bakery.*

*Sounds perfect for you! You sound up about it. Excited?!?
Yeah, I am. I know I'll be comfortable there. Maybe I can
make a difference after all.*

I know you will. What are you doing for Christmas?

Almost forgot about that. I haven't heard. Probably something though. Although nothing major, I'm sure.
Whatever you do, have fun, okay? And call me if you have a chance.

I will, for sure. Take care. Bye for now.

Bye back!

As I put my phone away, I realized this was the first time I'd been on my own in Haiti. I still felt intimidated by the country—the culture, the people, the language— everything. I hadn't traveled internationally much and only ventured into the third world for that Mexico trip. I wasn't an adventurous type who saw everything as a challenge. More often, I saw hurdles or walls. Deep down, I wanted to bust through those walls and jump over those hurdles, but I had no experience in how to do that.

I had a handful of gourdes in my pocket, but I hadn't mastered the exchange rate yet. I suppose I could have put a few in my hand, boarded a *tap tap*, and let the driver take out what was appropriate. Who cared if he took more than a normal fee? Not me. Money wasn't the issue. I just didn't feel comfortable. And I wondered if I ever would.

I knew the route back to the *lakou*, and I headed in that direction. I had Lew's mobile phone number plugged into mine, so if I got lost, as a last resort I could call him for directions, although I rarely had a good signal. If I headed straight back, I'd arrive in ten minutes or so. Since I wanted to explore, I mentally mapped out a more circuitous route.

As I walked down the road, I made a point of observing all I could. I wanted to get to know this country better, and even if I couldn't speak the language and engage with people, I could see how they lived their days.

The first thing I noticed was the road, paved, but probably not in the past twenty years. No painted lines to denote lanes, bumpy pavement, and entire sections gone so that the underlying dirt and ground-up blacktop presented a pitfall for vehicles. Not that it seemed to slow down traffic. I wondered how vehicle suspensions held up. Maybe you could make money running a car repair shop. Then again, maybe nobody had enough money to repair cars. I kept looking for a sidewalk but quickly realized those must be a first-world luxury because I never saw one. Just roads or dirt paths.

The streets were crowded with people and commerce. I passed small marketplaces with outside booths selling produce or cheap clothing, lots of tee shirts, and a few Christmas decorations. I'd forgotten how close Christmas was. Each marketplace had one tiny section where a man or woman had a small hibachi going, cooking something that smelled good and was offered to passersby. Small business buildings, those selling groceries or cell phones or, well, I couldn't really tell what else, were followed by homes, vacant lots, or abandoned buildings. I passed gas stations with small convenience stores attached. Seemed like the ones in the States until I noticed an armed guard at the door. Gasoline was a scarce and valuable commodity in Haiti, and after observing the station for several minutes, I deduced the guard was making sure drivers paid for what they pumped.

The early afternoon had turned warm and sunny, so I decided to stop someplace for a cold drink. I had seen young men on the street selling water in small containers that resembled balloons. But I wanted something in a sealed bottle, so when I passed a business called a Café Internet, I chanced it and went inside.

Behind the counter, a young woman scrolling on a cell phone raised her eyebrows at me as I approached. Then she looked back at her phone.

"Do you speak English?" I asked.

She held her thumb and forefinger a quarter inch apart.

"Cold Pepsi?" I asked.

She scrunched her face, not knowing what I meant. Then she pointed to a standup cooler to her left behind the counter. I walked over and pointed to a blue and red can that looked like it might be close to a Pepsi.

She grabbed it, placed it on the counter, and tilted her head to one side. I figured she wanted to know if I wanted anything else. I pointed at the can. *That's it.*

I dug into my pocket, pulled out a handful of coins, and extended my hand to her. She eyed the coins, took several, and nodded. I took another coin and laid it on the counter as a tip. She shook her head and pushed the coin back to me. No tipping in Haiti, I guess.

Although the room didn't seem air-conditioned, it was cooler than outside, so I sat and sipped the drink. Much more syrupy and less carbonated than I expected. Half of the dozen or so tables were occupied with a few patrons clicking away on laptops. The place was bare bones. Besides the cooler with cold drinks, a hand-written menu of hot drinks was on a white board behind the counter. Four shelves at one end of the café held food items to purchase, but most of the shelves were empty. The others held wrapped sandwiches, packaged sweets, and candy bars. The floor was off-white linoleum, and the walls were painted the same color. A bit antiseptic looking, not warm, inviting colors. A pounding reggae beat pulsed at a decibel level just beyond "cranked up."

I quickly finished my drink, buzzed from the caffeine, sugar, and reggae. When I reached the street, a Haitian man about thirty years old stepped in front of me and blocked my path. He started talking, but I couldn't understand a word he was saying, all quick language and big gestures. He put his hand out, palm up, and pointed to my front jeans pocket. He pointed at me, then at himself, then to my pocket. I got it. He wanted me to pull out my coins like I'd done in the café. He wanted money. I shook my head and said, "No, no."

He kept pointing back and forth and moving closer to me as I backed up several steps. I looked around for help, panic welling up inside. No one saw what was happening. I kept backing up and finally shoved his hand away as his pointing finger began hitting me in the chest.

I turned to walk away. He grabbed my arm and swung me around. Now I saw the menace in his eyes. I tried to match his stare, failing miserably, I'm sure. A stalemate. Finally, I reached into my other pocket, pulled out a few paper bills—I'm not even sure how much—and shoved them into his chest. He grabbed my hand and extracted the bills. The look of triumph on his face humiliated me. I wanted to punch him. But I turned and walked sullenly toward the *lakou*, defeated.

As I got my bearings and found the street I was looking for, I rehashed what had just happened. What could I have done differently, I asked myself. I didn't want to fight the man. I hadn't been in a fistfight since grade school. Maybe he had a knife or a gun and all I had were soft, puffy baker's hands to punch him. Not happening. I could have turned tail and ran. I hadn't run much since grade school either, so that didn't seem like a great option.

Maybe he'd seen my incompetence with Haitian money inside the café as I let the woman behind the counter take my money. Maybe he saw me as an easy target—and face it, I was.

Right there, on that dusty road full of potholes, I resolved to step up my game. Learn the money system, be aware of the culture. I had to take steps to protect myself—and stand up for myself. Could I actually do all that? I'd find out soon enough. I still had three more weeks on the island, and I could make the most of each day. At least I could try. I took a deep breath, gritted my teeth, and kept walking.

That same evening: Mirlande

EACH EVENING BEFORE DINNER AT SIX P.M.—OR AS
Lew liked to say in military jargon, 1800 hours—we all
gathered in the kitchen to debrief the day. It was mostly
a bitch session, but now after a week in Haiti, some
began to feel the pain of the people of the island more
than the pain in their bellies or their bowels.

When I walked in, Ron Dean held court. He was
talking and gesturing, like he often did, but tonight he
had more shout in his bluster.

As soon as he saw me, he asked, "Where's Dessi?" a
little too loud for my taste.

"I don't know. What's wrong?"

"What's wrong? I'll tell you what's wrong. I've been
robbed! Go find Dessi, will ya?'"

I didn't like his tone or him telling me what to do.
Andrelita got my attention and let me know that she'd
find Lew, so I settled down a bit.

I let Dean rant and rave, and I kept my ear on the
conversation without joining. Finally, Lew arrived and,
in his fashion, got everyone to take a seat and quiet
down.

"Let's start from the beginning, Mr. Dean. What
happened?" Lew asked.

"I was robbed, that's what happened!"

"From the beginning, please. Where were you?"
Lew asked in a calm voice.

Dean rubbed his thighs with his hands and then
rubbed his hands together, prepping himself for the big
speech.

Here it comes.

"Gloria and I had finished the work at the orphanage, preparing the dinner meal and inventorying the incoming supplies. I needed a walk, so I left the compound, figuring I'd get in five or six thousand steps. You know, to blow off a little steam."

He looked around the room, hoping for agreement, I supposed.

"Anyway," he continued, "I got a ways away, five minutes maybe, and I stopped, just looking at this small gathering of people arguing outside...what do you call it, a market, a store? This mean-looking dude walks up to me and asks me if I have a problem. I say no, just minding my own business. I start to walk away, but he cuts me off and gets right in my face. This close." Dean stuck his hand in front of his face, about a foot away.

"Then he flashes this blade at me. I didn't even see where it came from, but suddenly, it's right under my chin like the dude's gonna cut me or something. I'm just staying cool and tell him I'm minding my own business, but I sure don't like this huge knife in my face, you know. But there isn't much I can do, can't even look around for help cuz now it's touching my chin and I can feel how sharp it is. Then he says, 'How about some cash?' but I know it's not a question, it's a demand. And what am I gonna do, say no? Now I'm mad and I want to smack this dude, but I don't dare cuz he's crazy or something. I reach into my pocket and pull out a few coins and hand them over. And he laughs at me! 'That all you got, man?' he asks, but again, it's not like a question. Now I'm sweating bullets, but I try not to show it, and I say, 'Put down the knife and I'll find a little more'. He grins and lowers the blade enough that I think I can make a run for it, but I still don't know if he's crazy, so I reach into my other pocket and pull a few bills out and give them to him. He grabs them and starts to walk back to the crowd, and as I look over, they're all looking at me and some are smiling like they just screwed me. And now I'm madder than ever, but I stay under control and just walk away. And keep walking."

"How much did you give him?" Lew asked, again in his typical, low, controlled voice.

"Twenty bucks, American. A Jackson. I hadn't changed some of my bills."

Lew nodded. "So, not a lot of money then."

"Well, I mean, no, I guess it's not much money, but that's not the point," Dean countered. "Where were the police? This was happening in broad daylight! Should we report it or something?"

Lew rose and walked over to the sink. He poured himself a glass of water and slowly drank.

I noticed Paul, the *blan*, pacing behind the table, looking like he wanted to say something. So, I blurted, "Paul Whiteside, do you have something to add?"

Lew shot me a look.

"I was accosted, too," the *blan* replied.

Lew looked straight at me and shot me an even harder look. "What do you mean, accosted, Paul?"

"A guy approached me on the street, not far from the bakery, and asked me for money. Kind of mean-like, demanding."

"Did you give him money?" Lew again.

Paul nodded and looked down at his shoes.

"How much did you give him?"

"Not much. I don't think it was much at all."

"Did he have a knife?" Dean wanted to know.

"No, but he was forceful," Paul said. "What was I going to do?"

"Well, something. But you weren't robbed," Dean said with a disgusted look on his face.

Again, Lew returned to the sink for more water. He was stalling. Or thinking. The whole room was buzzing now. Lots of energy, but not the kind Lew liked. He returned to the table and took his normal position of power at the far end in his high-backed chair.

Lew began, "I don't want this to sound like a lecture or a sermon. You both," and here he looked directly at Dean and the *blan*, "must feel terrible, violated even. I do not want to make excuses for my countrymen. There is no excuse for robbery. And Paul, yours must have felt like a robbery, even though technically, it was not."

He let that sentiment settle over the group, and the nervous energy level drop.

"In reality, what you both experienced today is a significant part of understanding the poor. Those two men, if either had a job, probably make about two American dollars a day. Statistics tell us that one of those men didn't have a job. Unemployment in Haiti is above fifty percent, probably higher. It's difficult to accurately gauge. I don't condone robbery, but I also don't condemn the one man for asking for money. If your family didn't have enough food to eat, you might do the same."

The Dean man was now silent, staring at the floor. His wife sat beside him, tissue box at the ready.

"I do not want to quote Bible verses," Lew continued, "such as love thy enemy, turn the other cheek, or give them your coat and tunic, too, because they trivialize your experience and the situation in Haiti. But there is wisdom in the words of Jesus. How do we love these people? How do we understand their situation? How do we participate to make it better? How do we experience being so poor that we could put a knife to another man's throat for twenty dollars?"

Preach it, Lew, I said to myself. These people had no idea how hard it was living here.

"You are correct, Mr. Dean, when you say it's not about the money. We could all give twenty times that twenty-dollar bill, and it wouldn't make a difference. Not really. Here at the *lakou*, we are determined to find the bigger issue. And the bigger solution."

Andrelita began shuffling plates in the kitchen area. Maybe to break the tension, maybe to give Lew an out.

He took it. "Let's have Andrelita serve the meal, and perhaps we can discuss the issue in greater depth."

Ron Dean nodded. But he still had a menacing, disgusted look on his face.

DAY 10

Mirlande

Lᴇᴡ ʜᴀᴅ ᴀsᴋᴇᴅ ᴍᴇ ᴛᴏ ᴋᴇᴇᴘ ᴀɴ ᴇʏᴇ ᴏɴ Rᴏɴ Dᴇᴀɴ the following day when he and his wife were working at the school, so I came up with a reason to be on school grounds instead of the adjacent orphanage. I had reason to be at the school often, so it wasn't anything out of the ordinary.

Gloria Dean always worked with the children. Whatever she was doing—helping in the classroom, reading, English language assistance—children surrounded her. She was an attraction to the kids. They loved being around her. She laughed almost constantly, hugged often, and would burst into song whenever the spirit moved her, which happened frequently. She didn't pull off that demeanor around the *lakou*, but somehow, she transformed herself around those kids.

Like night and day. Sad and weepy, then happy and singsong.

Ron worked almost exclusively where the kids weren't. He transformed the outside of the school in the first few days, cleaning up what little landscaping existed. He helped in the kitchen, hauling food supplies, dishing out lunches, and cleaning up afterward. As much as he moaned about conditions when he was around the adults under Lew's roof, I never heard him complain at the school. Sure, he had ideas and wasn't afraid to voice them, but they didn't come off as demands. A hard worker, who surprised me and most everyone else. I always thought he'd be a slacker.

During the afternoon when the younger kids were watching a movie in French and the older kids were prepping for math exams, I saw the Dean couple settle under a shade tree at a picnic table in the playground yard. The same table that Ron had painted the week before. Where he got the paint, I didn't know, but he was resourceful, I had to give him that.

I'd been keeping busy in the yard and trying not to eavesdrop on what looked like one of their typical deep conversations. Ron had been making a point, usually emphasizing it with a pointed finger, and Gloria either shrugged or raised her hands, palms up, which to me meant 'who cares?'. I observed this give and take for several minutes when I heard my name.

"Mirlande?" Ron shouted at me. "Can you come over here for a minute?"

"Please," Gloria added.

Ron looked at her, and I noticed a small head shake.

I thought to myself, this could be interesting, and after all, it was what Lew told me to do. So, I walked over and sat down beside Gloria.

Ron immediately began. "Let me ask you a question. We've been here ten days or so, and I've noticed a big discrepancy between the food that the school gets and what the orphanage gets. Why is that? Shouldn't it be equal? I mean they're all kids, orphans or not, so I'm thinking it isn't fair—"

"Ron," Gloria interrupted, "let her answer the question."

"Not much is fair in Haiti," I said. I let that sink in before I continued. "The school has income from tuition. Kids' families pay to send them to school unlike schools in the States. So, there is money to buy food. The orphanage mostly depends on donations. Simple."

"What you mean to say is that the kids in the orphanage go hungry," Ron said.

"Do not tell me what I mean to say." I didn't like this man. "Hunger is a persistent problem in Haiti. You may see hungry kids at the orphanage, but the school kids may only eat once a day, too. You don't know if they eat anything else besides the lunch we feed them. Many kids go hungry." I rose to leave, but Gloria patiently placed her hand on my arm and gestured for me to sit. Her smile swayed me to put up with her husband—at least temporarily.

"If you have more questions," I said, "perhaps you should talk to Lew."

"I've talked to Lew," Ron countered, "and he answers questions with more questions. I get that he's trying to teach me something, to figure it out on my own, but sometimes you just need answers. Without some answers, it's hard to figure anything out. Know what I mean?"

"What do you need to figure out?" I asked.

"Now there you go answering a question with a question," he replied, and I saw a small smile on his face.

I smiled back at him and said, "Been around Lew a long time." Maybe this Dean fellow wasn't so bad after all. At least he had a sense of humor. Hadn't seen that before.

"I'm trying to figure out how to get more food here. At this rate, these kids will grow up malnourished. They might not even grow at all."

"Ron, maybe these kids need love more than food," Gloria said, almost in a whisper.

"Love is great, but it doesn't fill your stomach."

"It can fill your soul."

"You fill their souls, Gloria, I'll fill their stomachs."

They both looked at me as if asking me to settle the argument about which was more important. Food or love? How could I possibly answer that question? I sat motionless, hoping they'd keep talking. They did.

"Personally, I think the orphanage is getting the short stick," Ron said. "These kids in the school—their families have at least some money. Look at the uniforms they're wearing. Those cost money. The kids next door wear rags most of the time."

"Actually, they're hand-me-downs," Gloria corrected.

Ron looked skeptical.

"She's right, for the most part," I said.

"Whatever. I still think the orphanage needs more help."

"All kids in Haiti need help, Ron. Haven't we discovered that in the time that we've been here?" Gloria asked.

"Gloria never met a hair she couldn't split," he said, glancing at me. But I noticed no meanness in his voice.

"Mr. Dean," I said, "you seem to want to solve every problem you see. That is commendable. And Mrs. Dean, you want to understand every situation. Again, admirable."

"What are you trying to say?" Ron asked.

I wasn't sure myself. "You asked what is more important, food or love. There are many days I am hungry. And many days that I feel unloved. Or at the very least, lonely."

I'd stopped looking at them. I didn't want them to see the pain in my eyes.

"Some days I just want to stuff my stomach with as much food as I can get my hands on. Gorge myself. Be full—at least for a day. That would feel so good, so satisfying. But on other days..." I stopped for a second to gather myself and to understand my own feelings without being too vulnerable in front of these strangers. "Other days I feel so alone that I would do anything for love. For companionship. To hug my parents. Well, my mother for sure. Or my brother. It's hard, living only to work and feed your body. I know I can't live without food, but I think you could actually die without love."

That shut them up for sure. I noticed Ron grab

Gloria's hand. Then he withdrew the hand and rose to walk away.

"Thank you for being so honest with us," Gloria said.

"I don't know what came over me. That's not me," I managed to reply.

"Like you said, you've been around Lew a long time."

"Yeah, well, maybe. Anyway, I hope you figure things out for yourselves."

"We've been trying to do that for thirty years," Gloria said.

She smiled, but it never spread across her face. For some reason I couldn't pinpoint, I knew exactly how this woman felt. She had everything I could only imagine wanting—a husband, fancy clothes, food, love. Yet there was an emptiness in her eyes. What else did she need?

I had none of what she had. But I could relate to the emptiness. I could make a long, long a list of the things I needed. But now, seeing her, I began to wonder if those things would really fill me up.

Later that evening: Mirlande

I DESCRIBED MY CONVERSATION WITH THE DEANS to Lew, and we withdrew to the kitchen, where his troops were assembled for their dinner. Andrelita had done her best with a simple meal of rice and beans, adding as much flavor as she could with her limited supply of spices. I suspected by this time—ten days into their journey—their expectations had been lowered considerably as far as food was concerned. Just another day in the jungle without much to eat. Welcome to Haiti.

"Could I have your attention, please?" Lew asked.

The crowd grew silent. He didn't even have to shout but used his regular preacher voice.

"Tomorrow is, as I'm sure you're aware, Christmas Eve," he continued. "Some of you have asked me if all Haitians celebrate Christmas and the answer is yes, of course we do. Many of us worship the same God. And his son. Much of Haiti celebrates Christmas on the Eve, so tomorrow I suggest we go to our respective places of service for half a day, if they are in operation. If not, you're welcome to return here. If they are in operation and celebrating in some manner, please join them. You're not expected to bring presents. Your service is your gift to them. Then let's meet here for a light lunch, and we'll have extra time to talk and relax, tell stories of Christmases past, and do our best to connect with the spirit of the holiday for the remainder of the day."

The group's energy definitely rose with that.

"What about Christmas Day itself?" Ron Dean—who else—asked.

"A day of Sabbath and rest. Here or wherever you like," Lew answered. "We will prepare sack lunches if you want to get away, go to the beach, or plan a picnic. Your choice."

Smiles increased, and you could sense the feeling of relief spread throughout the kitchen. Nobody complained that night about rice and beans.

DAY 11

Paul

I WOKE EARLY. MY NEW HABIT. I SEEMED TO NEED less sleep in Haiti. I drifted out to the porch and the warm morning, I listened to and observed what was around me. Birds chattering in the trees and the wind blowing the fronds of the palms. Not much else. In the darkness before dawn, Haiti seemed like any other place. Quiet, asleep, resting for the day to come. I used the time to settle my mind, or rather, emptying it. I didn't need to plan anything, not like typical days back home running my business. There, it seemed my brain never stopped racing. Here, I sensed I needed to erase much of what my mind rushed toward, but old habits die hard.

I was uneasy when my brain wasn't cranking a mile a minute. It took less effort to stay focused on however many thoughts filled my life than to shut down the thinking and try to allow new ideas to flow in. A void could be filled with good things—and bad. Like surfing channels on TV and finding a trashy sitcom. Just because I cleared my mind to find peace and inspiration didn't mean bad mojo couldn't slip in when the door was cracked open.

I made a mental note to call Abigail tomorrow on Christmas. We hadn't talked since I'd left, only exchanging several text conversations.

I sent another text.

Happy Christmas Eve Eve. I just found out we WILL be celebrating Christmas! But no gifts under the tree, that's for sure. Let me know if you have time for a call tomorrow. And what time works for you. I'm open all day.

Then I waited for a quick text back. Finally realizing that no way Abigail was awake at this time of the morning, I let my mind drift again.

The last ten days had been eye-opening for me. I still felt tense most of the time—a little afraid sometimes, too. But I'd learned not to let that fear stop me. I got up every morning and went to the bakery. I worked alongside Doval and the other two men—Emil and Henri—from dawn to mid-afternoon. I didn't mind the heat anymore, and I'd gotten used to the food, or lack of it. I'd been able to push those luxuries of comfort to the back burner. I'd made new friends easily at the *lakou*. We'd come to spend almost every evening talking about our experiences, our lives, our hopes and dreams—and our fears.

I didn't know what I feared, outside of what everybody fears. Illness, death, neglect, being alone. When my mind drifted to new places of understanding, more things came to me that I probably feared, but I couldn't understand or articulate them. I'd been so busy in life making money to realize that kind of fulfillment left me empty. Maybe that was closer to what I feared. Being unfulfilled.

Huh.

I left the porch and walked to the bakery. I arrived before Emil and Henri, which was unusual. Those two always beat me to work.

"Merry Christmas Eve," Doval said, greeting me as I approached the open garage door. He was beaming, hands on hips, looking down at four small cakes, each decorated with bright yellow and white frosting, each about seven inches in diameter.

"Merry Christmas, Doval." I bent down to inhale the aroma of the cakes. "Coconut?"

"Yes, coconut and vanilla," he replied.

"Excellent, they're beautiful. I bet they taste wonderful."

"We shall see in a moment once Henri and Emil arrive. I told them to sleep a little later today."

And I thought I'd finally beaten them to work.

He poured a cup of coffee and handed it to me. "Thank you for all your help. I want you to know how much I appreciate it."

"I haven't made much of a difference, I'm sure," I replied, sipping the coffee.

"More than you know. In only a few short days."

Just as I began to ask him to elaborate, Emil and Henri came through the door, all smiles. So much for sleeping in. When you've been in the bakery business for a while, you tend to wake up before the sun, no matter what you tell your body. That internal alarm clock just goes off. A nice sense of kinship warmed my heart as I imagined bakers rising before the sun in small villages like this one all around the world.

Doval poured more coffee and cut one of the cakes, giving each of us a generous slice. Rave all you want about bacon and eggs for breakfast, there's nothing better than a slice of cake for the first meal of the day. A blast of sugar and sweetness burst in my mouth as I savored the first bite.

We praised Doval for the flavors, the textures, and the fluffiness of "CocoVan" as he called his creation. I knew Emil and Henri were calculating in their heads, as I was, how early Doval must have arrived at the bakery to have these cakes ready for our arrival and how he'd splurged for the extra ingredients.

As we ate and sipped, the men spoke of their families. Emil had two daughters, Henri a son. Doval talked about his three children and his wife's mother, who lived with his family. Each of the men bragged about their wives—how blessed they were to have women like them in their lives. I mostly kept silent, leaning in to hear their stories and enjoying their company and comradery.

After twenty minutes or so, Doval reached under the counter and produced three pink boxes. He slipped a cake in each, presented a box to the three of us with a Christmas greeting, and gave us the rest of the day off. I wanted to linger, but Emil and Henri—after handshakes all around—quickly disappeared into the brightening morning.

With a low bow, I thanked Doval for his delicious Christmas present. I also rubbed my stomach and smacked my lips.

"Goodbye, my new friend. Have a wonderful Christmas in Haiti," he said as I waved at him on my way out.

It was still early, I was carrying a cake that would quickly melt with the heat of the day, but I wasn't in a hurry to return to the *lakou*. I walked the now familiar route between the bakery and the *lakou*, taking my time and letting my mind wander. Hoping it would empty out and refresh, like hitting restart on my desktop computer.

The village seemed to be slowly coming alive this morning. Maybe more slowly than other mornings. I suspected not many were working today.

Each day as I walked home from the bakery, I passed the same house. Painted a bright blue from top to bottom, it begged to be noticed. The small plot of land it occupied always showed the care of its owner. This morning, I noticed a small, dark-skinned woman sweeping the porch. Her hair was wrapped with a bright red bandana, and she wore a blue top and a long, yellow skirt to her ankles. No jewelry, makeup, or shoes that I could see. She meticulously moved the three worn chairs and a welcome mat, cleaning in all corners and under all coverings. But she didn't just sweep the dust and dirt onto the porch stairs or off the sides. She swept into little piles, grabbed a dustpan, and deposited what she captured into a pail.

As she looked up, catching my stare, I waved to her, a small left to right hand gesture. She stopped and cocked her head, a look of confusion spreading over her countenance. She didn't wave back but nodded once.

I took a few steps toward the house and said, "Merry Christmas!"

Finally, a bright smile lit her face as she shuffled to the edge of the porch. "Merci," she beamed, lowering her head slightly.

I turned to walk away but stopped suddenly. I didn't know why.

Impulsively, I rushed up to the porch and offered her the box containing the cake.

At first, she didn't take it, even taking a step back.

I put one foot on the bottom step of the porch and reached the cake out to her. "Merry Christmas to your family. For you and your family." I opened the top so that she could see the delicacy within.

She looked in, her eyes opened wide, and she leaned the broom against the house.

I rubbed my stomach, hummed "ummm," and extended the cake closer to her.

She took it. I retreated, walking quickly back toward the street. I waved again.

This time, she waved back.

My mind was now empty, I thought of nothing, but my heart overflowed.

That afternoon: Mirlande

LEW ASKED ME TO STAY AT THE *LAKOU* THAT afternoon to help Andrelita prepare what he called a Christmas feast for his guests. He liked to think of himself as a converted Scrooge from that Dickens book he read once a year. Benevolent, kind, and giving—completely different from the character he'd portrayed so far in the lives of these American guests. I knew he'd been to the market and spent a little money to find food items he rarely served—*plantains, marinad,* and *pen patat.* Andrelita could cook the bananas to an adequate level of satisfaction, but Lew had purchased the chicken fritters and sweet potato pudding at the local outdoor marketplace. Those were far beyond her limited culinary capabilities.

There wasn't all that much to prepare, so Lew wanted me to experience the day with his guests. I think he suspected I could always throw a little reality on their delusions of being these white saviors to our bleak land, but it was also his way of trying to soften me up. He believed me to be too harsh, too hard-edged, too in-your-face—a skeptic of his effort to teach people to love Haiti and better understand the poor. But I thought that even spending a month pretending to be poor never amounted to much if, at the end, you just returned to your life of privilege. Thank you for coming, now goodbye.

Earlier, the men had helped us move the kitchen table and chairs to the back porch, shaded now from the midafternoon sun. We brought out the not-so-new tablecloth and a few bright colored napkins to add to the festive atmosphere. Alongside the table sat a big, squat bucket full of Red Stripe beer, a few soft drinks, and what had once been ice, now mostly melted. It almost looked like a party.

Nice try, Lew.

This was going to be a long afternoon. I knew Lew, and he liked to drag these meals on for hours, squeezing out every story he could from his guests. Limbering them up with beer (never wine or hard liquor) and good food so they'd dig deep into their backgrounds and traditions to appreciate how much they didn't understand about the poor. I planned to meet my mother later that day, but we didn't set an exact time. She knew Lew, too.

Today I sat at the table with everyone else. I hardly ever did that, preferring to eat with Andrelita, usually in the kitchen. After all, I was hired help and I knew my place, which was not at the banquet table with the other guests. No matter how hard Lew tried to make me fit in, I didn't. Not really.

"Merry Christmas Eve," Lew began when most all had finished eating. "Rather than discussing your experiences these past few days in Haiti. I'd like to spend a few minutes talking about your individual Christmas traditions. That will give us time to get to know one another better. Who would like to begin?"

The room fell silent. I guessed the others, like me, were calculating how much they wanted to share. In my experience, Christmas wasn't always a happy time. Most of mine were dismal. My mom had done her best to give us presents she couldn't afford and tell stories of the Christ child I wanted so much to believe.

Gloria Dean raised her hand. Waiting for Lew to call on her? This wasn't school. Whatever. I resented having to play along with Lew's contrived intimacy. Hearing about the wealth and gluttony of American celebrations only reminded me of what I'd never had. And probably never would.

He nodded and she began, "We always let the kids —we have a boy and a girl, three years apart—open one gift on Christmas Eve. They got to pick which one they opened. It heightened the excitement of Christmas morning for them."

"Yeah, we were never the kind of parents," Ron Dean said, "that would stay up late at night assembling and wrapping gifts. We had it dialed in way before that."

"I suppose in hindsight there were too many presents," Gloria added, not looking at anyone in particular and concentrating on her not-so-pretty-anymore fingernails. "It seemed right at the time, and I don't think the kids were too spoiled, but then again... Christmas was always about...gifts." Her voice dropped off, and she searched for the tissue box again.

"We lived in the mountains of North Carolina," Luke, the construction guy said, "and our biggest tradition was the tree. We'd always head out a couple of weeks before the holiday and chop down a big old pine. We'd drag it—well, Pa would drag it and me and my brothers would try to stay out of trouble as he did—back to the road. Most times we could heft it on the back of the pickup and drive it to the house. Pa always let me and my brothers sit in the bed and hold the tree. Once it even fell out, but luckily, nobody fell out with it. When we got it home, it took us a whole day to decorate it. But Pa never let us put it inside the house. He always said, 'God meant for trees to be outside, even chopped down ones.' It's hard for me not seeing many trees in Haiti."

I knew why nobody saw trees in Haiti—most of them had been used for firewood. The Christmas tree tradition had always seemed wasteful to me, like a lot of things Americans did. Must be nice to spend time and maybe even money on things you just threw away two weeks later. I was lost in those thoughts of head-shaking envy when Annie placed a plate of plantains in front of me. I shook my head, but she bumped my shoulder with the plate again, indicating that I should pass it on to the next person. I wasn't used to sitting at this type of table full of fond memories and extra food.

"I was a preacher's kid," Ashley, the tall pretty girlie said, "so Christmas ranked right up there with Easter. The celebration of Jesus lasted all week, but my dad always emphasized the sacrifice Christ made, not the other traditions, like lots of presents and huge meals. We never received many gifts, usually one per kid. I have five siblings so I suppose one per kid was all my folks could afford. Or maybe just teaching us that sacrifice idea. Sometimes I felt left out, envious of other kids who got tons of presents, but once I grew up, the gift envy sort of faded away. Besides, we were always working pretty hard at all the church services to get too wrapped up in much else. But good memories, not bad, for sure."

"Sounds like a lovely tradition, Ashley," Alan Waterman said. "It includes all the right ideas."

"How about you, Mr. Waterman?" Ashley asked.

"All the traditions...and many more I suppose," he replied.

Mr. Waterman wasn't the type to reveal much about himself. I wondered what he was hiding. Maybe nothing, but then again, in my opinion, rich men had much to conceal. Especially that they were rich.

"My folks got divorced when I was young," the other girlie Annie said in a tight voice. "I had to spend half of Christmas at each of their houses. Christmas always seemed split in two. But I got twice as many gifts because of it." She shrugged, as if to imply the bounty of presents made up for being caught between her parents' animosity. She never made eye contact and swirled the leftovers on her plate like she wanted to hurl them at the wall.

I could relate to this tradition of a broken family.

"How about you, Paul?" Lew asked the *blan*. The conversation had hit a lull, thanks to the downer that Annie dropped on the group. She had a knack for doing that.

"Oh, Christmas was fun. We had all the traditions," the *blan* said without an ounce of conviction in his voice. "I was an only child, but we did Christmas breakfast, opening of presents, a trip to the grandparents.

Living in Cincinnati—in southern Ohio—we always wished for a white Christmas, but it never snowed much. It just got cold, but never much snow. Yeah, that's about it."

I didn't buy a single thing he said.

Now it was Lew's time to share. I'd heard these stories before. I tuned him out for the most part and thought about the people at this table. Which one wouldn't make it the whole thirty days? Which one would actually get something significant accomplished while they were here or when they returned home?

"...always served at soup kitchens during Christmastime," Lew droned on. "My parents were hippies in every way you might expect..."

Would those two little girlies grow up and put their obvious love of kids—I could see that every day at the orphanage—into something more than just working in childcare? I didn't know what the answer was for all the orphans in Haiti, but maybe they did. Forget it—that might be way too much to ask of two young, naïve women from America.

"...spend the entire Christmas day afternoon with friends and neighbors." Lew was on a roll. "...thanking everyone for all that they'd done for us that year."

The expressions of the guests were pure envy, like they wished they could be half the man as reverential Lew. Don't get me wrong. Lew probably did live that way. He just poured it on a little thick this time of year.

What about the rich guy, Waterman? He was like a ghost most of the time. Usually, I got to know all of the guests well by now, but he was elusive, spending only a few hours at dinnertime with the group and then retiring to his little room to do...well, I'd checked, and nobody seemed to know what he did the rest of the evening. Lord knew there wasn't much to do in that tiny room except read and he had no books that I knew about. But he was rich, and in my experience, most men didn't get rich without being smart and resourceful. Maybe he was both.

"...that night, Mother would cook a simple meal to signify that we didn't need a huge feast to make us happy."

I swear the crowd was now completely humbled by Lew's upbringing. Even Ron Dean couldn't look anybody in the eye and that seemed to be his specialty, looking people in the eye, trying to intimidate them.

In all the years I'd known Lew, I'd never asked him if those Christmas stories of his were real. Maybe I really didn't want to know. Better to believe in something than not.

As Lew held court, my thoughts drifted to Sonson. I hadn't heard from him since that night he left my home. We always got together around Christmas, but something told me this year would be different.

That scared me.

That afternoon: Paul

WHEN LEW CALLED ON ME, I'D BEEN READY. NOT with the truth but a lie. I'd practiced it so much over the years, it came out naturally. I didn't want to tell all those people the truth. I hadn't figured out what the truth meant yet. And it was too painful.

I couldn't say I was a PK—a pastor's kid—like Ashley. My dad seemed nothing like hers. My dad was a soldier for Jesus. A hard charger, a saver of souls, all fire and brimstone.

He traveled much of the time, even at Christmas. He didn't have a church of his own when I was growing up but was a guest preacher and an interim pastor at lots of churches. He was always pushing me to follow in his footsteps. He liked to say, "Follow my footprints in the sand. I'll lead the way," but I wasn't the smooth talker he was.

I had a heart for Jesus, but I'd heard so much about pleasing Jesus and doing things for Jesus and living up to Jesus' expectations that it was overwhelming, and my heart hardened. Like nothing I did could ever live up to what *he* wanted—Jesus or my father. In my sight, they were both tough role models. Too tough.

Was Christ so demanding that I had to spend my life pleasing him? No matter what I wanted? How could you live that way? Wouldn't that be overwhelming? For me, it was.

I remembered traveling with my dad on the weekends when I was a young boy. He would often speak in churches, raising money for this cause or that—all in the name of Jesus. He'd get a speaking fee, of course, but he'd also raise funds for a local crisis pregnancy center or homeless shelter. I had my black suit and tie on, hair slicked down, shoes shined. If it was a small enough church, he'd finish his talk and have the entire congrega-

tion—this was after the offering plate had been passed—
dig down deeper in their pockets for his cause and come
forward to make another offering. To me. I'd be standing
there in front of all those people, holding a big basket,
trying not to look into the eyes of people who wore a bit
of anger as they were coerced to contribute a second
time the same morning.

With bigger churches, he worked out in advance
what percentage of the offering would go to his selected
charity. Or maybe those churches couldn't bring themselves to pass the plate twice. It was way beyond my
little boy understanding, but too many times I saw
resentment in those eyes as they trundled up to me, like
they resented me, not my father.

The weekends I wasn't traveling with my father, I
liked to spend time in the kitchen with my mother, a
loving soul who softened all the hard edges of her
husband. She taught me a different way to view life and
faith during long afternoons baking or preparing a meal,
often translating one of my dad's hell fire and brimstone
sermons for a young, soft-hearted boy. I was much more
like my mom than my dad, and she was the reason I had
a relationship with Christ at all. Because of the God my
mom taught me about, I continued to worship and
attend church and tithe and pray. To seek answers and
meaning. Even braving my fears to take that quest to
Haiti.

"Son," my dad had said every time we traveled, "I
want you to be a soldier for Jesus."

It must have been quite disturbing for him, but I
discovered I liked to bake. I wanted to be a baker. A

baker man. I couldn't imagine how disappointed he must have been, but I did see it in his eyes, always that same look, a combination of disappointment, disgust, and sadness. He likely believed I was disappointing not only him, but Jesus, too.

That scared me.

DAY 12

Paul

"Hi, Abby, Merry Christmas!" I said a little too loudly into my phone. The reception was always bad in Haiti.

"Paul, you don't have to shout. I can hear you," Abigail countered.

"Oh, I'm sorry, but it's good to hear your voice. How are you?"

"I'm well, but the better question is, how are you? What are you doing? It seems like ages since we talked."

It did seem like ages.

"I'm working in a bakery. I texted you that, remember?"

"Yes, at first you were working in...an orphanage or something. That didn't seem much like you. Certainly, the bakery is right up your alley," she said. "And what are you doing at this bakery?"

"Now, just helping. But I've got this idea, still in the formative stages, of how we might be able to turn it around."

"I'm sure you will," she said, "I have faith in you."

I quickly changed the subject. "How's your Christmas Day been going?"

"Oh, quiet and contained. I stayed at Mom and Dad's house last night, and we spent a leisurely morning sipping coffee and opening presents. You?" I could hear the contentment in her voice.

"Well, no presents but plenty of coffee. I have the day off, and I'll probably just hang around the *lakou*, rest up, visit with the other guests."

"The what? Hang around the what?"

"The *lakou*. L-A-K-O-U," I spelled it out for her. "In Haitian, it means something like a bunch of homes all connected together."

"Oh."

"How about that decade dinner thing you've been planning? Has that happened yet?" I was trying to steer the conversation back to her.

"Next week, before New Year's Eve. But it won't be the same without you, Paul."

I liked hearing that. It made Abigail feel less far away.

We exchanged a few questions about her family and mine, the weather, and the food in Haiti.

Finally, in a voice filled with question and concern, almost a whisper, she asked, "Paul, do you think about me as much as I think about you?"

"I'm not sure," I said as honestly as I could.

"I guess you wouldn't if you didn't know how much I like you." Her voice sounded cheerful almost.

"Maybe we can figure that out together as we go," I offered.

"I'd like that. I really would."

"Me, too."

After a few more minutes of talking about Haiti, we made plans to get together after I returned.

But my thoughts quickly returned to what I wanted to accomplish in Haiti—to the point that they completely overshadowed my longings for a new romance at home.

DAY 13

Mirlande

LIFE SLOWED DOWN ON SATURDAYS AT THE orphanage. It never moved real fast, but Saturdays were a day of leisure. No school, no classes. No cooking. We ate leftovers if we ate anything at all. The girls prepared their outfits for church the next day. Of course, there wasn't much to choose from. Each had a suitcase—and everything they owned fit inside. So, they exchanged clothes with each other and tried different combinations of tops and skirts and dresses. They spent hours just styling each other's hair—ribbons, bows, cornrows.

I wasn't required to be at the orphanage on Saturdays, but when Lew had his American troops in for his *Experience of Becoming Poor,* he asked me to be available. I wasn't accomplishing much today, mostly helping the girls with their hair, telling stories, being a friend.

Through the steel gate, I saw Sonson's dilapidated

tap tap pull up in front of the school. That seemed strange to me, so I went to investigate. What business did he have here, and why wasn't he coming to me for that business?

I stopped at the corner of the security wall as I glimpsed my brother and Lew in a heated discussion. I held back.

"You know we have no money to pay you," Lew said in a controlled voice. "I've told you that many, many times."

"But now you have Americans here. Now you have a new source of money," Sonson countered.

"I couldn't ask them to do that. I wouldn't ask them. No. No." He pounded a fist into his palm for emphasis.

"You want the food to keep coming, don't you?"

"What do you mean?" Lew asked, his eyes squinting.

"We could block the shipments. It would be easy. We can be very, very persuasive, you know?"

Lew looked a little stunned. He took a few steps to his left, away from Sonson, then did a small, complete circle until he was facing him again. His usual look, steely determination in his eyes, was back.

"You'd do that to these young women? Girls, babies? You'd stoop that low? I always thought better of you, Sonson."

"You never thought of me. Only Mirlande. You think of her too much, you lecherous old man."

Lew balled up his right fist like he wanted to punch Sonson. But instead, he growled, "Get out."

"I can leave now, but that doesn't finish our business. Think about what I said. I'll come back for the payment. Maybe tomorrow."

"Don't come back—for anything."

Sonson reached out and pushed Lew hard, knocking him off balance, but not to the ground. He drew back his shirt and exposed a gun strapped to his hip. He patted the gun, gently, but the intention was obvious. I'd never seen my brother with a gun, but it didn't shock me.

"Tomorrow, old man." Sonson strutted to the *tap tap* and drove away.

As Lew's eyes followed my brother, they found me, still concealed by the wall. He stared at me, but I wouldn't look away. I approached him.

"What was that all about?" I asked.

Lew rubbed his whiskers and looked at the ground, like he was searching for the answer. Or one that he was willing to tell me.

"Your brother is being a punk. A dangerous punk."

I listened for more.

"He's demanding money. Or else he will stop the food shipments."

"It's not him. It's the *Federasyon*."

"At the moment, I don't see the distinction."

I wanted to defend Sonson, but I couldn't. "Now they are strong-arming orphanages? He was shaking you down for money? They must be desperate."

"Or he is desperate," Lew said.

"What do you mean?"

"I don't know how long he's been with them," Lew said, "but I do know they demand that their young recruits meet an extortion quota."

"A what?"

"They're required to bring in so much money a month," Lew explained. "A rite of passage."

I hadn't known that about the gang. I guess I'd heard so much of Sonson's drivel about being soldiers defending the people that I was beginning to believe it. Extortion? Of orphanages?

"It's protection money," Lew continued. "I've talked to other businesses in the area. Most pay to keep their supplies coming or to protect their property from damage. It's never much money, but it adds up month to month. They don't want to drain you of your money—kill the golden goose—just trickle it away a little at a time." Lew shrugged helplessly. "Some folks consider it the cost of doing business; others refuse. It's a constant battle. The *Federasyon* has more power than you think—and it's growing all the time."

"Are you going to pay?" I asked, lowering my voice.

"If I pay, he will just keep coming back for more. It'll never be a one-time deal."

"And if you don't?"

Lew shook his head. "I don't know. It's bad for us. They can stop the food."

"But if you don't pay, then he doesn't reach his quota."

"Then it's bad for him."

Lew's heavy hand on my shoulder was nothing compared to the weight of worry for my brother.

That evening: Paul

"I REMEMBER A FEW YEARS AGO," ALAN WATERMAN said, "when I was giving a seminar to a gathering of American businessmen on successfully conducting business in South Korea. I'd done quite a bit of work in that country. I made an off the cuff remark about corruption and how it was a fact of doing business there. One Korean man raised his hand and was righteously offended that I had disparaged his country so badly. I backed away from my comment and made apologies, but most in the room knew it was true. I suppose today it's fading but not completely."

We'd finished the evening meal—rice and beans again, spiced up with a little too much curry. We remained at the kitchen table, which was our custom. There wasn't really anywhere else to go for these discussions. Waterman's comment was a result of Ron Dean asking Lew to explain how corruption worked in Haiti. We'd all heard the stories. Alan's remarks followed.

"What does that have to do with the price of tea in China? Or South Korea?" Dean asked in his ever-present snarky tone.

"Corruption comes in many forms. It can be different in most every country on the planet," Alan responded. "In South Korea, it was subtle and never spoken of. Hence, that man's response. But it still existed. I often had to grease the palms of a purchasing agent to get my product in the door. America isn't much different."

"What does that mean?" Now Dean was indignant.

"Is it really any different than American lobbyists buying influence in the halls of Congress to pass laws that help their clients?"

"I don't know much about that," Dean answered, "but I still want to know what that has to do with Haiti."

"You must play the cards that are dealt in the game that is being played," Alan said. "That's all I'm saying."

"Well, that certainly clears everything up." Dean turned to Lew. "Hey, help me out here."

Lew's amused expression showed how much he enjoyed the give and take between the two men. At the end of our second week on the island, he'd become more congenial, smiling a good bit of the time, not so instructional. Letting us figure out the process. "In my experience, corruption—bribery, dishonesty, extortion even, whatever you want to call it—can be produced from either poverty or greed. The corruption you speak about in Haiti stems from poverty, not greed."

Ron Dean rolled his index finger in a circle, meaning go on. I sensed his impatience.

"Many Haitians struggle to feed their families. They're not afraid to ask for money. I don't consider that a completely dishonest way to do business. If it helps feed their families."

"That seems like an oversimplification," Dean said. "Not everyone is poor in Haiti."

"That's true. But only a very small number of people hoard the wealth in Haiti. Most struggle to find jobs, put food on the table, and send their children to school. I do not hold it against my countrymen to ask for money to help do that."

"Can you get around that? Do you have to play the game with the cards you're dealt?" Dean asked Lew but looked at Alan. "Does honesty still work?"

"In many cases, I'd answer yes," Lew said. "Honesty can still work in Haiti."

"Good to hear."

Lew wasn't finished. "Of course, honesty doesn't always work. Being moral and upstanding, righteous, is commendable. But it can be dangerous, too. There are limits to the effectiveness of honesty."

"Like what?"

Dean again. He dominated the conversation, and even though several at the table seemed uncomfortable with the direction it was headed, they stayed engaged.

Lew look directly at Mirlande, who was standing in the kitchen. He held the stare so long that many of us in the room turned to look at her. "When the corrupt will not take no for an answer and it turns to violence," he said.

Andrelita dropped a dish, and the sound reverberated throughout the room. Mirlande, usually unreadable, was clearly distraught, eyes wide and jaw clenched. She turned and fled out the door, prompting me to wonder what message had passed between her and Lew Dessi and why it alarmed her so badly.

DAY 14

Paul

THIS SUNDAY MORNING LEW ARRANGED FOR US TO attend a church service. It really wasn't an invitation but rather a part of the itinerary. I didn't get the feeling that I could opt out and just spend time alone at the *lakou*. Not that I wanted to. I'd heard a little about worship in Haiti and was eager to attend. He'd briefed us the night before and when we gathered early this morning, we were dressed up and ready to go.

Gloria wore a nice pair of beige slacks and a colorful, silk top. Although the facilities here and the heat and humidity didn't make it easy to maintain even the simplest woman's hairstyle, hers looked as if she'd just stepped out of beauty salon. Ron sported a long-sleeve shirt and tie as did Alan. Annie and Ashley wore khakis and conservative tops, and a touch of makeup, a change from the day we arrived. In comparison, Luke and I were dressed way down. Luke wore shorts and a tee shirt, me in jeans and a collared shirt. Nothing fancy. Lew assured us it didn't matter, but I still felt a little self-conscious, something I'm not sure Luke shared. At least, he didn't let on—his smile always seemed to deflect bothersome emotions.

As we began the walk to a nearby church, I realized Andrelita and Mirlande were missing from the group. Everybody deserved a day off, but I still wondered about the stare down between Lew and Mirlande last night. After she walked out, I didn't see her again that evening. I'd felt drawn to her lately, probably because she provided a contrast to Lew. He always expressed his view of Haiti in a positive way. He looked at the country not necessarily with rose-colored glasses but rather in possibilities. He often redirected conversations from all that was wrong in Haiti to what was able to be changed for the better.

Mirlande didn't talk like that. She lacked pretense and chose callous honesty. Not always negative, but barebones reality about things Lew often glossed over. Lew could wax eloquent on the future of Haiti. Mirlande dwelled in the day-to-day brutality of life on the edge. I began to see the distinctions between their views—and the combination of both painted a more real version of what I'd had little vision of before.

A question from Ashley to Lew drew me out of my thoughts. "Will there be an aspect of voodoo in this service?" she asked.

"No, absolutely not," he replied. "This is a Christian church. The two rarely mix. *Vodou* in Haiti is mostly practiced by backward spiritualists that hold onto misguided and misplaced sentiments. But it's a stubborn tradition on the island, so your question does not surprise me."

"What percentage of the population is Christian?" Alan asked, joining the conversation.

"Hard to determine," Lew said. "Ask ten Haitians the same question, and eight times you'll get the standard answer: forty percent. It's almost like they put it in the country's tourism brochure. I suspect it's close to correct, but as I mentioned, the grip of *vodou* is tenacious. It keeps the country shackled to a terrible past. A shame, really."

We'd arrived at the front of a nicely kept but unremarkable building. It didn't look much like a church, except for the small wooden cross on the white-washed wall adjacent to the wooden doors. I couldn't read the Haitian name of the church below the cross. Flowers bloomed on the ground right in front of the steps leading to the church doors, and they were a harbinger of the splash of color we'd see as we entered. About thirty people gathered inside, talking with enthusiasm. Although I couldn't understand the words, I saw the smiles all around. More flowers adorned the pulpit area, and most of the people wore colorful outfits, splashing the interior with reds, yellows, greens, and blues. I got a mixed whiff of perfumes, splashed abundantly this Sunday morning. Several homemade religious accoutrements—Jesus on the cross, two hands praying—hung on the walls.

As we entered, most eyes turned to us, but the smiles only grew larger as several people came up to Lew and shook his hand or gave him a hug. We settled in a low backless bench halfway to the front. The church had eight to ten pews, divided down the middle by a center aisle. The warped boards of the worn wooden floor revealed the dirt ground a foot below.

Quickly, a group gathered on the slightly raised wooden platform in front of the pews. And the music began. It didn't stop for forty-five minutes.

I counted twelve people on the stage, equally divided between men and women, including two playing the guitar and two on drums. Each man wore black slacks with shiny black shoes and different colored shirts and ties. The women wore brightly colored dresses, and several were in high heels. These were the best dressed of any of the people I'd seen in the two weeks I'd been on the island.

The exuberance of all engulfed the crowd, and halfway through the first song, the congregation was on their feet, swaying to the music, hands outstretched or clapping to the beat. I couldn't sing along like most were doing because they sang in Creole, but I clapped with everyone else. Eventually, they sang a song in English, *Hard Fighting Soldier*, and it must have lasted ten minutes or more. But nobody seemed to care, and the enthusiasm only grew the longer everyone sang.

Eventually, the music subsided, and a stately

gentleman dressed in a light gray suit with a red shirt and black tie walked onto the stage. The preacher welcomed everyone in both Creole and English and began his talk. He mostly spoke in Creole, only occasionally translating a phrase or idea into English, pointing to our group of Americans and mentioning Lew Dessi by name several times. He displayed great passion and emotion, but my mind drifted to other days in starkly dissimilar churches.

Before my father began his traveling preacher days, he ran an evangelical church. We spent all day Sunday in the church—arriving early for set-up and rehearsal, three services, a break for mid-afternoon lunch, and then back again for a Sunday prayer session.

All my friends played baseball or soccer on Sundays.

We sang hymns—lots of hymns—in those services, and we generated enthusiasm for Jesus for sure. But my adolescent brain often thought it was self-manufactured. Not quite fake, but I wondered if people really got so amped up for God. These Haitian singers seemed to love the musical high, the worship of song. But I often saw the onstage manipulations that my father employed to inject the crowd with the power of God—that's the part that seemed more Broadway than Sunday to me.

I remember sitting in those services, thinking that I didn't know enough about Jesus to push his worldview on people who didn't know him. That was always the emphasis in that church—tell people about Jesus, lead people to Jesus, in every way possible, and here are three ways, or five ways, or the top ten ways you can do that. But I was a kid. I mostly wanted to know why Jesus would love a kid like me. I'd never done anything for him. I never preached a sermon or led anyone to the altar to dedicate a life to him. Oh sure, I'd served in soup kitchens, passed out clean socks to the homeless, cleaned up the disabled neighbor's yard, handed out devotionals at the mall entrance. But that was my duty as a pastor's kid, not my love of Christ.

Even as an adult I never pushed my love of Jesus—and I had learned to love him—on anyone else. I always wondered if my dad held that against me. Deep down, I wondered if Jesus did, too.

Huh? Maybe that was one of the keys to unlock the mystery of why I was in Haiti.

That evening: Paul

AFTER THE CHURCH SERVICE, LEW LED US TO AN open-air market to pick up whatever we wanted to eat for the day since Andrelita did not prepare meals on Sundays. I followed Luke around the market because I knew he often ate "off the street", as he called it, and it never seemed to bother him. Most of the time when I'd ventured to a marketplace, I couldn't tell what was being offered. We settled on what looked like Haitian tacos with what we believed—or maybe hoped—was chicken inside. The vendor put the tacos in paper bags that were soaked with juices before we got back to the *lakou*.

After we ate and spent a few free hours with nothing scheduled, we reconvened on the front porch for a regular Sunday bull session. No topic off was limits. We could ask whatever we wanted, express whatever we were feeling. The group enjoyed these sessions. The mood had lightened when we all got together, lighter than the first few days on the island, and that meant the conversation flowed more freely. Of course, we weren't talking about ourselves as we had when we first met. Our differences had become muted as we settled into the routine of life in *The Experience of Becoming Poor*.

"Why is Haiti so poor when other countries in the Caribbean, while not rich by any means, seem far better off?" Gloria asked the question that was always in the front of my mind.

"That is a long and complicated answer," Lew said, "but I will do my best to give a rather concise answer. It's a question I hear in chat rooms online. When somebody asks why America is so rich and yet still has so many problems with race or poverty or inequality, I think about the need to look at the history of a country to understand. You can't look only at the present."

I swatted a pesky gnat—at least I thought it was a gnat—that had been bombardiering my eyes ever since I sat down. I only managed to divert it to my ears.

Lew continued by talking about the Dominican Republic, Haiti's neighbor to the east. "Same island, Hispaniola, similar terrain, and at one time in history, the same people," Lew said, "but they took a different route to traverse through civilization. One thing, and perhaps a major impact, was that the DR embraced Catholicism. Haiti never did. *Vodou* dominated here."

There it was again, I thought. Religion. Lew

acknowledged the damaged history of the Catholic church in many parts of the world and its current struggles. But the church was an effective way to tame the heinous tendencies of the uncivilized culture in Hispaniola.

"The second difference is more economic," Lew said, going on to describe the Dominicans' economy based on ranching and livestock, first dominated by a few land barons that employed and paid ranch hands.

"For some reason that has been lost to history, Haiti used slave labor to cultivate an agricultural society. Even low-paying ranch work is better than living a hopeless life of slavery, and those slaves eventually revolted," Lew explained. "That sent the whole system topsy-turvy, and yet, here we are two hundred years later, and it seems many Haitians are enslaved to the system."

"Why is that?" Ashley asked.

"The third reason, politics," Lew said. "Democracy eventually came to the DR but never to Haiti. Not really. The elitists have always put their interests above the masses in this country and placed disreputable men of power in seats of government. Shameful. And so destructive. Even the early freedom fighters couldn't quite bring themselves to turn over the government to the people."

I listened to Lew recount the history that I'd read about while I was still swatting bugs away from my arms and legs, although I wasn't sure there were really bugs on me. Maybe just a sensation that my body was reacting to what it thought might be bugs. I never got used to that. In the distance, I heard a donkey honking an intermittent cranky protest against something. Maybe bugs.

"Even in America," Ron Dean said, "we have a history of corrupt politicians. And it seems the more we dig, the dirtier they become."

"Like Clinton?" Lew asked.

"He wasn't the first to come to mind, but now that you mention it, why did you name him?"

"Because of his duplicitous role in Haiti," Lew replied without hesitating. "In 1994, as president, he put an embargo on our country. Earlier this year he came as a special UN envoy and spoke like he's a savior. What are we to believe about U.S. presidents? It's very confusing for most Haitians."

"Not much of what presidents do makes much sense to us either," Alan said.

A few nodded, but the conversation had veered off course.

"Perhaps our president now, Preval, will change the pattern," Lew said. "Some here have hope that he will. Me, not so much."

"It always sounds so depressing," Annie said with her usual sad countenance. "Do you ever think, Mr. Dessi, that God has forsaken Haiti?" Her expression was earnest, and there was a hopelessness in her eyes— and a little bit of fear there, too.

"Do you think that, Annie?" Lew asked.

"I don't know."

"You'd hate to think God is holding out from Haiti," I added, "just because Haiti hasn't fully embraced God. Although in the Old Testament, God was awfully harsh on the Israelites who didn't fully embrace God's way."

"You are more of a Biblical scholar, Paul, than I," Lew said. "I'm more of a New Testament guy, the Jesus part. Love rules." He gestured with hands upturned, in front of him.

"I get that we're supposed to love everyone," I said. "That's probably why many of us are here. It's just hard sometimes to believe that God loves everyone."

"You think God doesn't love Haiti, Paul?" Lew asked me.

"I'm with Annie. I'm not sure."

Annie gave me a faint head nod in acknowledgment.

Lew nodded. "I don't think of God that way. A harsh God of retribution. My way or the highway. Tow the line or I'll cut the line—and punish you. To me, God is love. You remember what the brochure says? God didn't neglect this place. You did. I did. We all did."

I nodded. I had that brochure almost memorized.

"I'm not waiting around to witness one of the great miracles of the Bible, Old Testament or New, for Haiti," Lew continued as he paced around the room. "Oh, it could happen, but I'm trying to make a difference on my own, with God's guidance and help. I'm trying to do God's work here. And teaching you how to do it, too."

I glanced around the group gathered and noted everyone on the porch had contemplative looks on their faces. We'd been here two weeks, and we knew what we were up against. We'd seen the poverty. We'd been taught the history in discussions like this and many others. We'd learned to live without—good food, comfort, necessities. All of us were working alongside Haitians to experience the people and their poverty. We saw their plight, but each one of us had an escape hatch. A way back to our former lives. These Haitians had no quick escape. Some seemed to be looking for one; others were content—at least as far as I could determine—to work hard to better their situation.

It was hard to figure out which were which.

DAY 15

Paul

I'D BEEN OBSERVING DOVAL'S BAKERY OPERATION for several days, and I was ready to put my ideas to work. I'd treaded lightly so far, asking questions of Doval, reviewing past successes and failures, and talking about my experiences in the trade. I believed I'd gained his trust. I'd made several small suggestions, mostly on how to keep the workplace clean, a top priority for any bakery.

Doval, Emil, and Henry were experienced, efficient, and patient bakers. They didn't rush the process. You can't hurry kneading the dough, for instance. It might take eight to ten minutes with a large batch. The three always tested their kneading, poking the dough to make sure it sprang back to form. If it didn't spring back quickly, it needed more kneading. Their operation wasn't big enough to automate that part of the baking process, so it had to done by hand.

After the first rise, when the bulk of fermentation happened and before the bread was shaped into loaves, they always tested to make sure the first rise was good. They'd meticulously snip off a small bit of the dough and drop it in water to make sure it floated. They never skimped on the shaping process, folding the dough over on itself constantly to make sure it rose tall in the final loaf. And most times, they put the dough into the fridge after shaping, which increased the flavor of the final product.

On this particular morning, I relayed my observations to Doval to reassure him about how well he ran the bakery. I didn't want to come off as a know-it-all or a critic, just a helper, a partner. He wanted to make his business a success, keep his employees working, and expand. And we'd formed a nice working relationship. I was ready to test out one of my ideas and hopeful Doval would be excited about it.

Once he got Emil and Henri working on their tasks for the morning, we huddled up in one corner and discussed the art of baking.

"Ingredients, timing, and temperature are everything in baking," I began. "Every baker knows that, and you do a really good job in the exact process."

Doval nodded, his way of saying thanks.

"You let the dough rest for very consistent times," I said. "You're meticulous about that, and you've trained Emil and Henri well. Your mixing times are precise, too. Remarkably, that oven keeps the temperature at the right level all the time." I smiled. We'd talked often about his ancient oven. "And your baking times seem to be perfect."

"Then why is my product inconsistent?" Doval wondered.

"Must be the ingredients," I answered.

"Like what? Where do we start?"

"The yeast. Do you proof your yeast?"

"I did when I first started but not lately. It has always been good yeast." Doval frowned, as if he questioned my reasoning.

"Yeast is a fungus. You know that word?"

"Yes."

"So, that means it's alive, a living thing. If it's old yeast, it might be hard to wake up. And if it is, that affects the finished product, the bread."

Again, he nodded because that was basic knowledge for bakers.

"Then let's proof it. Okay?"

He looked skeptical but shrugged.

I heated the liquid he used in his bread recipe to 110 degrees Fahrenheit. Doval took a small amount of yeast and dropped it into the liquid. Next, he scooped about a half teaspoon of sugar and dribbled it into the concoction. Sugar wakes up the yeast, but it takes time.

"How long to we have to wait?" he asked.

"Five, ten minutes at the most," I replied.

We both knew that over time, the mixture of these ingredients will produce carbon dioxide. We'd see it begin to bubble on top like carbonation if the yeast was fresh. No bubbles, not fresh.

Most bakers don't wear watches because their hands are always working in flour, but Doval had a clock on the wall with a second hand. We glanced at it as the proofing process began. At five minutes, no bubbles. By eight minutes, we saw only slight bubbling at the top of the concoction. At ten minutes, nothing much had changed.

"I think it's the yeast. It's old," I said in a low voice. "Not dead, but it could be fresher, and that would make a big difference in the finished bread. Maybe all the difference in the world."

Doval agreed. "I will contact my supplier and tell him I am very unhappy."

"Perfect. Now, are you ready for another idea? A way to increase sales?"

His eyes lit up.

"Okay, here goes. Every day I see several men hanging around the bakery, sometimes all day. I assume they don't have jobs, right?"

Doval said yes as he glanced outside.

"Are they from the neighborhoods around here?"

"Yes, probably."

"And it would be good if they had jobs, yes?"

"Every man needs a job."

"What if we made a product, say a very small loaf of bread that would fit in the palm of your hand—the size of a small croissant—and we hired those men to sell them?"

"Sell them to who?"

"People in the neighborhood."

He looked out the door at two men standing across

the street. I could almost see his brain working. I left him to his thoughts and inhaled the aroma of fresh bread in the oven. It acted like an aphrodisiac for my creativity.

"One big question," I continued. "Would people in the neighborhood, or on the street, or maybe even at the marketplace, buy them? Is there a need for this?"

"I believe so. We would have to price it so they could afford it. And we already know we can make it delicious," he said as a smile burst across his face. He quickly got serious again. "How would we make money?"

"Well, we'd have to figure the cost of the product. Say it costs us two cents to produce this mini-loaf. What's that in *gourdes*?"

"I know American money. You can talk in cents. Then I can figure the exchange. Go ahead."

"Great. If it costs us two cents to make and we sell it for, say, eight cents, then for every piece they sold, the men keep two cents—and we make four cents. Could somebody afford eight cents for this mini load of bread? Fresh-baked, tasty, delivered fresh every day?"

Doval bobbed his head back and forth as he considered the question. "Maybe. Maybe not. But if we sold it for six or seven cents, we could still make a few cents each, right?"

"Yep." I liked his thinking. He'd caught on.

"How do we begin?" he asked.

"I think we should start slow. Like a test run. We make fifty the first day and see if we can sell them. Do you know one or two men that you trust that could make this work?"

He looked down at a piece of paper he'd grabbed and started to take notes on. I saw him scribble a few names that came to mind.

"Perhaps," he answered, "or Emil or Henri might."

"We'd need to provide something for them to carry the mini-loaves in, a bread carrier. I don't think they'd need to be individually wrapped, do you?"

"Not in Haiti, no. But we could provide something to put on their hands, like paper or a towel so they wouldn't touch the bread. And maybe a covering for the carrier, to keep them fresh. We'd have to bake them fresh every morning and have them ready at a certain time, say seven o'clock, ready for sale."

He continued to jot down ideas on his note paper. He walked over to Emil and Henri, who were kneading large batches of dough, and began a lively conversation in Creole. I could see the give and take and the enthusiasm on Doval's face. After several minutes of this, he walked back over to me.

"Let's start to build the recipe and calculate the costs. I want to make sure this will work on the bakery side before we begin. Emil says he has two brothers who would be perfect for the job. I've met them. They might work."

"Could Emil and Henri absorb the extra workload every day?" I asked.

"Yes, I'm sure."

We talked for another twenty minutes and worked out the details. It was a good idea, but I wasn't certain it would work. I didn't know the market at all, with its many variables that had to come together. It might have been a long shot, but a shot worth taking. At least it was an idea that got the whole bakery excited. I could see it on Doval's face, and even Emil and Henri grabbed a slice of enthusiasm, evidenced by their lively banter throughout the morning.

Finally, Doval laid down his pen, looked me right in the eye, and smiled. He put out his right hand and vigorously shook mine.

"I like this idea, Paul. Thank you so much. It will help the bakery, it will help the men or women selling the loaves, and it will help the people eating the loaves. Everybody will win. Now, let's make it work!"

Even a long shot pays off every once in a while. Maybe this one would.

DAY 16

Paul

EVER SINCE THE SUNDAY DISCUSSION ABOUT GOD neglecting Haiti, I couldn't shake the idea that I had a bigger part to play. I didn't know if that was in Haiti, through Doval's bakery, or something else. I felt good knowing I'd contributed something to the bakery, whether the mini-loaves idea worked or not. If not that idea, Doval would come up with something to boost his business—and maybe even help the surrounding community. Someway, somehow, he could launch an idea that could spread across the country. It wasn't out of the question. Small, local ideas could catch fire and spread nationally very quickly. America had seen service organizations, like Kiwanis and the Salvation Army, blossom at the turn of the twentieth century and spread like wildfire. Just because it wasn't happening now in my home country didn't mean Haiti wasn't ripe for something similar.

By this third week on the island, I'd figured out that Lew Dessi wasn't the harsh, in-your-face taskmaster that he'd portrayed in the first few days. He probably used that brutally honest persona to weed out the people who weren't committed to finishing the thirty-day experience. If he could scare them or intimidate them enough early on, he wouldn't have to waste his time later. But by now he'd turned into more of a cheerleader. Nobody in our group had left Haiti early, and now that Lew saw them working and contributing, his role had shifted.

But I was getting this feeling that his lack of brutal—or maybe direct—honesty wasn't helping me much right now. Lew never sugar-coated anything, and he was usually practical. But it was in his best interest to keep us all engaged and productive. He needed us to review his experience positively for future attendees to help his livelihood prosper. If he came down too hard and any one of us came away discouraged or resentful, it could hurt his future business prospects. So, he'd softened his approach. It made for a friendlier atmosphere at the *lakou*, but now, I needed more.

I never came across as aggressive or pushy but was more likely labeled as "methodical" or "contemplative." I knew my own strengths and had developed them over the years as I ran my successful business for a decade. Okay, I was a baker man. But I thought of myself as a successful baker man.

If I was going to commit to Haiti—in some way, form, or fashion, and I had no idea what that meant —I needed to ask tough questions that Lew seemed hesitant to answer. I needed the honest, down-to-earth truth.

I needed to talk to Mirlande.

Or maybe I just wanted to.

That evening: Mirlande

I HAD NO IDEA WHAT THE *BLAN* HAD IN MIND WHEN he said he needed to talk to me tonight after dinner. My days weren't long enough? Now I had to extend them into the evenings? But I didn't have any reason to retreat to my little home shack, so I reluctantly agreed.

This Paul Whiteside had surprised me. I thought he was a quiet, weak man who would never make it in Haiti. The island would crush him. Eat him up, spit him out. Thirty days—if he made it that long—and then bye-bye. We'd never see him again.

But from all reports Lew gave me about Paul's job at the bakery, he worked hard, he enjoyed working alongside Haitians, and even contributed good ideas to the business. Quietly, he had gained the trust and admiration of his fellow peers at the *lakou*. He wasn't pompous and loud-mouthed like the Dean dude or weepy like his wife.

Maybe this evening could be interesting. But I had some questions for him, too.

"Thanks for coming," Paul said, as we settled into wicker chairs in the secluded front porch of the *lakou*.

I nodded and tried not to display my mean face, which I did too often. Instead, I smiled, but only a little.

"Okay, *blan*, would can I do for you?" I asked.

"You still think of me as a *blan*?"

"It will take more than two weeks to change that."

Disappointment showed on his face.

"Although, the Haitian sun has made you a little less white. Looks good on you," I added. Made him smile.

"How is the bakery doing?" I asked, needing to make a little small talk. "Doval has good things to say about you."

"You know Doval?"

"Yes. Haiti is a small island. He says you are a hard worker and funny. I never see you funny."

He got this sly smile on his face and took a deep breath.

"How do you entertain squirrels?" he asked.

"What?"

"It's a joke. How do you entertain squirrels?"

I shrugged.

"Act like a nut."

I had to think about it for a second.

"Get it? Squirrels like..."

"I get it, I get it." Trying not to smile, I rolled my eyes, shook my head, and then let a smile escape. "Oh boy. I think Doval was wrong."

He laughed out loud. I'd never seen him laugh so

freely before. Maybe there was more to this *blan* than I knew. That was hard for me to admit.

This little porch was one of my favorite spots. You had a glimpse of the nearby mountains, the tips now hidden by clouds mixed with sunlight, giving off an eerie, swirling mix of black, white, and yellow. It looked like a witch's caldron brewing on the other side. Maybe it was just a storm coming over the mountain. We were isolated here from the sounds of the city, and a slight breeze blew through. Even though the flowered vines had a pleasant fragrance, every so often, I caught a whiff of smoke, acrid. Probably some homie burning garbage.

"You like working with Doval?" I asked.

"I do. It's right up my alley."

I didn't know that expression, and I'm sure it showed on my face.

"It means it's exactly what I like to do." He said it in a way that didn't make me feel stupid for not knowing.

"And you will make a difference in the business, feel good about yourself, then leave in two weeks?" I asked. Might as well drive down that alley and get to the point.

He looked away and rubbed his hands on his shorts, nervous like.

"I don't know."

"Which part don't you know?"

He didn't answer right away. Then he told me about the mini-loaves and sharing the profits with the neighborhood locals. He went into detail about the size and shape of the loaf, how much it might cost, and how it would be sold.

"That, *blan*...excuse me, Paul Whiteside...is brilliant. That's one idea that will work and change lives in the neighborhood."

He smiled, a little sheepishly, and looked down. Huh, this man is humble, too?

"It won't be enough. It will help only a few people," he said.

"How many people do you want to help?"

"The whole country, I think."

"That may take an act of God."

He looked away from me and massaged both eyebrows with his fingers. "I know. That's who I've been praying to."

Since neither of us kept talking, I guess that confession made us both think.

"Who is this God you pray to? Has he answered your prayers before?" I finally asked.

"Yes, many times."

"Has he answered this one?"

"I don't know yet."

"What exactly are you praying for?"

"I don't know that either. I guess I'm waiting for him to tell me what to do."

Curious, I wanted him to tell me more. "And you often hear him speak to you this way, Paul?"

"No, not often."

I got up and walked over to the edge of the patio to get another look at the mountains. The gravel crunched beneath my feet. Still brewing up there. I noticed a man with a small stick switch herding three cows down the street.

"This is confusing to me," I said. "You don't know

what to pray for, you don't know if this God hears you or answers you, and yet you continue. Why?"

"It's what I do."

"Right down your alley, huh?"

"Up. Up your alley."

I smiled at him to break the tension and let him know I understood the phrase. "Up, down, sideways. Makes no difference."

"That's how I feel. Up, down, and sideways," he said.

"Haiti will do that to you. That's Haiti. That's just Haiti."

He joined me at the edge of the patio and stood a distance away.

"Can a guy like me make a difference here?" he asked.

"Maybe, but I'm not sure I know you well enough. Sometimes you seem strong, other times very hesitant. Sometimes very serious, sometimes almost funny."

"Almost?"

"Tell me another joke, then we'll see."

He smiled again. He had a good smile, working his whole face.

"What do sea monsters eat?" he asked.

I shrugged.

"Fish and...ships."

We both faked being serious. Then we laughed.

We sat back down, enjoying the silence of the evening.

"Maybe you know what God is saying," I offered, "but you do not want to obey."

He looked at me without moving his head, only his eyes. Then he looked away.

"Now I'm the one who's confused," he said in a soft, low tone.

"Haiti will do that to you, too, Paul."

"That's three times you've called me Paul tonight."

I looked him in the eye and squinted. "That's your name, Whiteside, but don't get cocky. You're still a *blan* to me."

But I said it with a smile and a flash of my perfect, white teeth.

DAY 17

Paul

I SAW THE MISSED CALL ON MY CELL PHONE AND the voicemail notification. I was sitting with the others in the kitchen after dinner, talking about the day. I stepped outside to listen to the message.

Paul, it's Abigail. Please call me as soon as you get this message. It's very important.

Her voice sounded a little shaky, emotional. I immediately got a sense that something was wrong.

"Sorry," I said to the group as I stuck my head back in the kitchen. "I have to return this phone call."

"From the look on your face, it sounds important," Lew said. "Anything wrong?"

"It's my...friend...and... I hope not."

I stepped outside again. Abby picked up on the first ring. "Paul, thanks for calling back so quickly."

"Sure, Abby, what's wrong?"

"What? Oh, nothing's wrong. I just haven't talked to you in such a long time."

"It's only been a few days. From the sound of your voice, I thought something terrible had happened."

"No, no sorry. I'm just feeling a little lonely over the holidays."

That didn't sound like her. She'd never come across to me as being lonely. Or clingy or needy. In the short time that I'd known her, she was always strong and independent.

"Paul, you still there?" she asked.

"Yeah, yeah. I'm here. I'm sorry you feel like that, Abby."

"I really miss you. I wanted you to know that."

I wanted to say the same thing to her, but I also didn't want to say something that wasn't true. I hadn't miss her lately—I was too busy.

"Oh, jeez, now I've gone too far. I don't want to sound needy. But it's the holidays, and I'm lonely for you, and I'm off work this week. It'd be so, so much fun to be with you, you know. Don't you think so?"

I detected a slight allurement in her voice.

"Well, sure it'd be fun, Abby, but I made a commitment. Thirty days, remember?"

"Oh, I know. I know. I guess I just needed to hear your voice."

I didn't know what to say, so I stayed silent.

"I didn't know if you'd actually stay the entire thirty days," she said, the tone of her voice noticeably different, cynical, a little mean.

That felt like a voodoo needle stabbing me in the

heart. I kept quiet, not wanting to say anything to hurt her back. But I was tempted.

"Again, I'm sorry," I said, becoming angry with myself. What was I apologizing for?

Ten seconds of complete silence. The caw of a nearby bird, likely calling to a mate, sounded harsh.

"Well, can't blame a girl for trying. Take care. Talk soon." And she hung up.

I plopped down in the chair, put my head in my hands, and tried to figure out what had just happened.

When I finally returned to the kitchen, I noticed the door wasn't entirely closed. As I entered, Mirlande stood at the cabinet next to the door, stacking dishes.

I realized she could have heard my side of the conversation. We locked eyes for a millisecond, but she turned quickly away, looking guilty.

DAY 18

Paul

TODAY, THE LAST DAY OF 2009, DOVAL TOLD US WE could leave the bakery a few hours earlier than usual. I didn't know if Lew was planning festivities for New Year's Eve, but I knew that Doval liked to give Emil and Henri time to spend with their families whenever he could, especially on a holiday.

"I'd be happy to do the cleanup today and the prep for tomorrow," I said to Doval, "if you want to let Emil and Henri leave even earlier. I don't have any place I need to be, and I suspect the celebration at Lew's tonight will be low key."

His eyes lit up when he let out a throaty sing-song chuckle. "Lew might surprise you. You never know."

"Well, I suppose he could really break out and throw a wingding of a party," I said, "but somehow, that doesn't seem like Lew."

"I don't know what a wingding is, but it sounds a little dirty, no?" Doval's eyes gleamed as he asked the question.

"No, no, it just means...well, to tell the truth, I don't know what it means either," I said. Maybe it was an idiom.

Now Doval laughed so loud that both Emil and Henri looked at us, wondering what was so funny. He had me laughing, too, so that neither of us could catch our breath long enough to explain it. Both workers shook their heads in mock exasperation, smiling broadly, and returned to the task of packaging the loaves of bread just coming out of the oven.

I had only spent two weeks with these three men, but I now considered them my friends. Doval and I had formed a good, solid working relationship. We shared our ideas and received genuine feedback. I liked his honesty and his outlook.

"Thank you for your offer," Doval said to me, his face still smiling from the wingding thing. "The cleanup won't take us long."

"You seem very happy today," I said. "Any special reason?"

"Do I need a special reason to be happy?" Doval asked.

I shook my head.

"We must all find our own happiness in life. I choose to be happy every day. Almost every day. Some days, I groan, but most days I'm happy." He paused, as if gathering his thoughts. "It's easy to be unhappy, especially in a place like Haiti. Many, many things in Haiti are hard. You've seen only a bit of that. But I cannot live in that way, feeling that everything is hard. I believe God has blessed me in many ways, and I am thankful."

How come everyone was beginning to sound like Lew to me?

"Tomorrow begins a new year," Doval said, speaking slowly, as if carefully considering each word. "So, there's much to be hopeful about. Hope, I believe, is one of the keys to happiness. You must be hopeful for the future. I am. This next year could open many possibilities for me as a business owner, as a man. Those are important to me. Of course, I want to be a good husband and father, and I'm not saying those come in second. But I must provide for my family first. And in that regard, there is hope."

I always knew happiness was a choice, but I hadn't tied it so closely with hope.

Emil and Henri finished their work and wished us a Happy New Year. Doval and I cleaned up, then I left him at the bakery to close down the equipment and lock up. He gave me a hug when I left—the first time that had happened. It caught me off guard, but I returned it with gusto.

Hope can do that to you.

I had a few free hours this afternoon and found myself wandering toward to orphanage where I knew Mirlande was working.

That afternoon: Mirlande

Paul Whiteside slipped through the gate from the *lakou* and waved to me. I checked my watch and realized Doval must have given his crew the rest of the day off. We didn't have many days or hours off at the orphanage.

"Doval gave us the rest of the day off," he said, "so I thought I'd drop by here and see if there is anything I can help you with."

This man had changed in the two plus weeks he'd been in Haiti. At first, I couldn't explain exactly what it was. Now that I looked at him, I realized he wasn't so white anymore. He had color on his face and arms. Sometimes he looked only red, but now I saw that he'd tanned a little. Maybe he'd lost weight, too. And he seemed to be smiling more today than I'd ever seen him. He usually seemed so lost in his thoughts. Not today.

"Mirlande? Is there?" he asked.

"Is there what?"

"Anything I can help you with?"

I nodded absently. "I'll think of something."

We walked over to the kitchen pit—it wasn't anything that resembled a kitchen, only a fire pit where we cooked the meals. Two cement block walls, blackened by a thousand fires, and a tin roof comprised our kitchen. Annie and Ashely were preparing the lunch meal over an open fire. They handled a huge pan with a long handle, propping it on the metal grate, inches from the fire. If we served it a little later in the day, midafternoon, it would be the big meal of the day and might keep the girls satisfied. At least I let myself think that way. I knew they wouldn't really be satisfied. Hunger never got satisfied.

"Whatcha cooking, ladies?" Paul asked.

Annie ignored him, but Ashley spoke up, "We got a shipment of Kids Against Hunger meals yesterday, so we're cooking it up."

"What's that?"

"Mostly rice," Annie said.

"But with lots more, too. Like a protein powder and soy, so the kids get lots of nutrition. It's good for them," Ashley said, aiming the comment more toward Annie than Paul.

She was right. It was a treat for the girls, and the meal stayed with them longer than just plain rice. We got a shipment from a nonprofit somewhere in the United States, but not regularly, and we never knew when it was coming. Ron Dean said he was working on that, but he said a lot of things.

I slipped onto the nearby picnic table to make sure the two little girlies followed the directions to prepare the meal. Paul sat down next to me but not close. I could smell the meal with its faint odor of curry and fried rice. I'd sampled the meals before. It tasted fine, and the girls were already gathering around in anticipation. I shooed them away, although two of the younger girls cuddled beside me at the table. I never shooed them away, not the younger ones. They needed as much affection and human touch as they could get.

We sat in silence as I stroked the backs of the two girls at each side of me. Paul was anxious, unable to keep still. Fussing with his backpack, shifting positions, and rubbing his hands together. He was squirming.

I let him squirm for a time before I spoke. "Did you have a fight with your girlfriend last night?"

His eyes opened wide, but the question didn't seem to rattle him like I hoped it would.

"I don't know what that was...last night," he replied, shaking his head.

I figured he'd go silent, closing down like most men I'd known. I didn't have much experience with men, never married, but I'd had boyfriends.

Then he said, "She's not really my girlfriend. We've only gone out a few times. She's fun, but yesterday she turned weird, like she was trying to manipulate me. Or something."

He surprised me with that. That confusion. Maybe that was what I'd been seeing in him. Not lost in his thoughts but trying to figure something out.

"What was she trying to get you to do?"

"Not sure," he answered. "Maybe to go home. Give up this trip."

"Aren't you doing what you're supposed to be doing? Working at the bakery."

"Like I told Abby, there seems to be more."

"Abby, that's her name?"

"Short for Abigail," he said, nodding.

"I like Abigail better. Abby sounds like flabby. Is she flabby, this girlfriend of yours?" Why that escaped from my mouth I had no idea.

He chuckled but didn't answer the question, thank goodness.

One of the girls at the picnic table pointed toward the dark storm clouds gathering above us. Paul looked up, too, and the sky seemed to mesmerize us all.

"You must be careful of the *Gede* with this Abigail of yours," I said to him.

"The what?"

"The *Gede*. *Vodou* gods," I replied. Then looking at him, making eye contact, "Gods of fertility."

That rattled him. He scratched his head and looked away.

"They are very mischievous. They rule fertility—and the dead. Very hard to explain to a Westerner. The people of Haiti, they love the *Gede*. They are both crude and caring at the same time. The Gede drink and cuss and smoke and cause havoc, but they are not evil. More fun than evil. And sometimes in Haiti, you need fun. You need entertainment."

He looked at me, and I thought for sure he was going to ask me if I really believed in *vodou* gods. But he didn't.

"Fertility, huh?" was all he said. I couldn't read his face. Was he amused?

"Yes. Do you need to be worried about that with this Abigail?"

"Not now, no. But then again, I don't know how powerful the *Gede* really are."

"Nobody does."

The storm clouds were moving fast now. I suspected the rain would hit any minute, but there wasn't much I needed to do. It rained often in Haiti and didn't disrupt much. Unless it turned into something dangerous.

"Do you love her?" I asked for no other reason than I wanted to know.

He thought for a moment or two before answering. "It's way too soon to think about love."

"When will you start to think about it?"

He stared at me, and I noticed the wind from the oncoming storm blowing his hair around. "It's complicated," he said.

"That usually means you don't want to say. I know that phrase."

"Or...that I don't know. It could mean that."

"Hmm. Maybe," I said, "but maybe you only love the thought of her. What she offers. What she demands. What she controls in you. You are a *maroon*."

He looked confused. "Maroon? Like the color?"

"No. *Maroon* is a Haitian word for runaway slave. You are a slave to her. But you have run away. She will probably drag you back. The slave is always recaptured by the master."

I first felt the rain on my face. Then I noticed droplets on Paul's shirt. The two girls sitting with us stood up and ran to the orphanage building. Now the rain came quickly and strong. Paul never moved from the picnic table. He lifted his face to the sky and let the rain pummel him. He rubbed it into his face and tilted his face back to the heavens, pushing his sandy hair away. He laughed out loud.

"First the *Gede*, now the *maroon*," he shouted above the pounding of the rain. "I have much to learn, don't I?"

It wasn't a question I was supposed to answer.

172

. . .

That evening: Mirlande

LEW ASKED ME IF I'D LIKE TO STAY FOR A LITTLE
New Year's Eve party he was planning with the guests,
and since I had nothing better to do, I said yes. After an
evening meal of chicken and rice—the usual—he gave
the guests a few hours off and asked them to return to
the kitchen at eight thirty.

That gave me some extra time, so I walked home to
clean up and change clothes. I mostly wore cutoff jeans
and a tee shirt during my days at the orphanage—no
reason to get any more dressed up than that around my
girls. I knew they looked up to me, so I always made sure
I was clean and I didn't smell. I often wore flip-flops, but
I kept my feet washed and manicured as best as I could.
I washed my body every day, either at the orphanage so
the girls could see me or at home in the evening. I took
care of my fingernails, and although I didn't splurge on
polish, the girls never saw dirt under the nails. We did
each other's hair, and I taught the girls hair hygiene and
new styles to try. I had to teach them to take responsibility for their bodies, keeping them clean and cared for.
At least I could do that for them.

But I wouldn't be seeing the girls tonight, so I
thought I would dress up a little. I didn't have much to
work with as far as clothes went, and I never wore my
better things in front of my girls who had so little, but
tonight I primped.

I scrubbed my important body parts with a fresh bar

of soap in the water basin. I'd picked it up when a church was giving away free soap last year and added it to my collection of small bars that I stacked in a drawer of my dresser. It smelled like coconut.

I put on a nice, reasonably new, fluffy, frilly white blouse—a peasant shirt you'd call it, and what would be more appropriate for me? It matched perfectly with a flowered print skirt in vibrant colors I'd recently picked up in the marketplace. It hit just below my knees. I didn't own many pairs of shoes, four in total, but I had some black flats that were comfortable and not too awfully shabby. I slipped on an inexpensive fake gold necklace, the only piece of jewelry I ever wore.

I was included tonight with the people of the *lakou*, and it would be nice to spend time with others. I got lonely in my little home, especially at night.

I walked back to the *lakou* in my flip-flops, carrying the flats so they wouldn't get dusty and dirty. Before I entered, I changed shoes and stored the sandals on the porch.

When I entered the kitchen, all the guests had already gathered around the table. The boisterous chatter stopped suddenly, and all eyes turned toward me. If that Ron Dean whistled at me, I swore I would slap him. I held my chin up and strolled toward the back of the room. Still, no one spoke, and it seemed like heads swiveled slowly, following me as I walked.

Finally, I said in a tone that I struggled to keep light and civil, "Whatcha all looking at?" That eased the tension I was feeling. Lew broke out in a big smile, and the rest of the guests mimicked him.

"Okay, now that we all finally see how beautiful Mirlande is beneath that mean girl exterior she often exhibits," Lew said, still smiling, "let's get on with the festivities." He motioned to Andrelita.

She had the fancy glasses, not the plastic ones, on a tray, and she ceremoniously placed a glass in front of each guest as she walked slowly around the table. Then she passed out chilled bottles of Red Stripe beer. Geez, Lew, couldn't you spring for a bottle of champagne for New Year's Eve? Does it always have to be beer?

In the background, I heard music and recognized the staccato beat of Twenty Cherry, a Haitian rapper.

"Let's make a toast," Lew said, raising his glass. "To the new year! May it be immeasurably more than we could ask for or imagine, according to the power than is within us all, to the glory of God, and for the betterment of Haiti. Here's to 2010!"

We raised our glasses and sipped the bitter beer. All except Gloria Dean, who I'm sure just pretended to take a drink. As I looked around the table, I saw a different group of people than those who'd arrived less than three weeks ago. Gone were the looks of despair and disgust. No more fear seeping out of their pores so you could almost smell it. During the first two weeks, most looked tired and worn by the trials of living in Haiti. Now, there was determination in their eyes. Even exuberance. Like the change I'd seen in Paul the *blan* earlier in the day when he just howled at the rain.

These people showed strength. I could see it not only in their eyes, but their postures, their smiles, their willingness to let Lew lead them into unknown territory without the hesitation I'd seen when they first arrived. Didn't mean nothing to me that they might accomplish great things. But finally, they weren't this scared group of privileged white folks from the States entering what they thought might be the closest country to hell.

"I want to take a few minutes to go around the table and talk about hopes and visions for the future," Lew said. "I gave up New Year's resolutions a long time ago. That's simply a pagan ritual for fun. I always considered Lent the time of year when we resolve to get closer to the people God made us to be by ridding ourselves of all things unwanted. But the new year can offer us hope for the future and it's a perfect setting to express how we envision our lives playing out in the near term."

"I know," he continued, "that some of you have a clear path plotted for yourselves, and others are still in the planning stages, so I don't expect long, drawn out speeches of how you're going to change the world or Haiti. Please express something simple and plain that you're beginning to verbalize to yourselves about a vision—or a hope—for your future. Who'd like to begin?"

"I'll start," Gloria Dean offered. "I'd like to find a way that I can continue to love on those girls at the orphanage longer than another week or so. Maybe for a much longer time. Or permanently. That's my hope."

I looked at Ron Dean, and his face didn't hide his utter shock at what his wife had just confessed.

Lew nodded. I knew this technique he was using, having seen it many times before. Now wasn't the time for correction or clarification. Just dreaming. He'd get to reality with each guest individually, as he'd been doing since they'd arrived.

Alan Waterman raised a finger and nodded to Luke. "Luke and I have been talking, and we'd like to find a way to help Haitians build stronger, sturdier structures. We've seen the way things are constructed here, and we know there's a better way. We're kicking around some ideas to make that happen. That's a vision we share. It's not real clear right now, but we're working on it."

Luke gave him a high five. "Yeah. What he said." That brought a laugh from everyone, even Andrelita.

"I feel exactly what Gloria feels," Ashley said. "Those girls need so much. I don't see how I can help right now, but I'm determined to find out. I'm smart and talented, and I know people will want to help when they hear the stories I'm gonna bring back. I'll figure it out."

I could see a fortitude in that little girly I'd never noticed before. Maybe she would figure it out.

"It just seems so overwhelming to me right now," Annie said in her typical low, sad voice. "Some days I think I'll just move here and work in this orphanage...or another orphanage that really needs me." Here she gave me a look like she was disgusted with me.

What did I do? Yeah, I was a little tired of her wallowing in pity, but I liked her. She worked hard. Why blame me?

"And other days," she continued, "I have no idea of how I can actually make one iota of difference."

I wanted to shout the words HOPE and VISION to

her, but I didn't think Lew would appreciate me snapping her out of her funk.

"Well, I can make a difference," Ron Dean declared, "and I'm starting with the food supply to this island. The world can do a lot more, and I'm going to do what I can to make it happen. Whether I have to go to the U.S. government or USAID, the Red Cross, the UN, whoever, it's gotta happen. And soon. Mark my words." He banged the table hard with his fist, making most of the group jump in their seats.

Lew ignored the robust rebel yell of Ron Dean, like he usually did, and looked at Paul.

"Mr. Whiteside, you are often the last to speak. Are we saving the best for last?" Lew asked.

"Probably not," Paul said, shaking his head. "You all know I've been working at the bakery and we're putting some ideas together that we think can help a lot of people. But there's so much more I could do. I just can't nail down what that is. I think I will, but it hasn't come to me yet." He spiked his grit to find the answer with one sharp nod of his head.

"And my hope is," Lew said, "that in the next ten days you'll all get a much clearer vision of where God is leading you." He raised his beer glass again, followed by everyone in the room, and we drank a toast to the future.

With all this talk of hope and vision of the future, I felt a little depressed. Maybe it was high time I started to think more about my future. And I was staring at the *blan maroon* that might have the answer.

DAY 19

Paul

SINCE TODAY WAS SUNDAY, THE BAKERY WAS CLOSED, so I spent the day at the orphanage. I was looking for reasons to spend more time there, but I didn't want to admit to myself that Mirlande was the motivation. I wasn't ready to acknowledge that I wanted to get to know her better. Spend time with her. Understand her. I kept telling myself that since she knew Haiti so well, if I wanted to learn more about the country, I should spend more time with her.

I didn't understand my feelings for her. I'd been awake last night thinking about the talk we had about the *Gede* and Abby. I didn't believe in little gods that controlled life and death, at least not the way she described them. Sounded more like leprechauns than gods. I did believe in a God of life and death, so I supposed the Haitian version of the *Gede* wasn't that far away from my version. They twisted it to match what they needed—entertainment, Mirlande had said, and what served their purpose. I'd been guilty, too, of shaping my interpretation of God to serve my needs. If I needed to be lifted up, he was a God of love and grace. If I'd pushed the limits and craved correction, he became a God of instruction and wisdom—or even judgement.

Luckily, Lew arrived at the orphanage to break me out of my self-assessment.

"Paul, I thought you had the day off today. What are you doing here?" he asked.

"Only a few days left, so I wanted to immerse myself in anything I could in the time I have left," I mumbled, not believing it myself.

"I see. I think."

Annie and Ashley ambled over to join our conversation. Then I realized Lew had invited them to talk, since they both had their notebooks with them.

"I'll make myself scarce," I said.

"No, no, join us," Lew said. "These talks are good for all of us. You might get a nugget out of it, and I'm sure the ladies won't mind, will you?"

Ashley shook her head, but Annie just squinted at me.

"So, ladies, you've been here two-thirds of your thirty days. What are you feeling right now?" Lew asked.

"Inspired," Ashley replied. "It breaks my heart to see all these children. I want to help, but I don't know how."

Lew shifted his gaze from her to Annie.

She stared at the ground beneath the picnic table where we sat. "Sometimes I feel inspired. Sometimes..." her voice trailed off.

"Uninspired?" Lew asked.

"No, more like hopeless, I guess."

"That's normal, Annie. A lack of hope is simply a lack of vision." Lew let out an almost imperceptible sigh. "I didn't expect you would have developed a vision for solving the orphan situation in Haiti after a couple of weeks. Many have come before you, and nobody has solved the problem yet. But please don't let a lack of hope be a barrier. You just need more experience."

"You both are very young," Lew continued. "Your experience in Haiti is fresh and vivid. But I often notice that the emotion of seeing so much poverty can be overwhelming. The sorrow can block the vision. But you must begin with the sorrow. I have seen how you care for these girls, and I have seen the sorrow in your eyes. That's a good thing. Begin there. But as Oswald Chambers says, 'Experience is the doorway, not the final goal.'"

Both young women let that sink in. So did I.

"But aren't we supposed to have a plan before we leave here? A plan to contribute? A plan to participate?" Ashley asked.

"Not necessarily. Some come to this experience and leave with a plan. Some don't. Many just return home and contribute how they can. Like the sign says, 'Once you see what breaks God's heart, you can't ignore it.' But not everybody is equipped to solve every human condition in the world. Sometimes you contribute. That's all you can do. Nothing wrong with that. We need contribution in many forms."

"But the situation seems so complex," Annie offered, shaking her head.

"Like I said, you both are not yet even twenty-five-years old. You may not yet have the skill to improvise and develop. Take Paul here. He runs his own business. He could probably tell you stories of every time he had to improvise, re-invent, backtrack, and try a new path forward. That's what experience gives you."

I acknowledged Lew's wisdom by nodding and saying, "My folks wanted me to be a pastor. And I tried that path for a while. But it wasn't me. Once I started my bakery, I was mostly alone and made more mistakes than the average guy. But eventually I figured it out. Lew's right, there's no substitute for experience."

"I don't think I'll have a vision before the thirty days is up," Ashley said. "Then how do I stay engaged and gain more experience?"

Even Annie perked up at this question and looked eager to hear some advice. She leaned forward and clasped her hands together.

"Great question," Lew said. "Let's brainstorm. Paul chime in here, too."

"There could be over one hundred orphanages in Haiti," Lew continued. "It's hard to get an accurate count."

Lew tried to clarify the complex orphanage situation, unlike what most of us from the U.S. had heard about. Many operated with absentee owners, people who lived the U.S., in places like Miami. They raised the money, secured the food, and visited regularly, but the orphanage was run by a paid caretaker. Some facilities incorporated a school, like the one Lew ran, but others were supported by local or foreign organizations and didn't include schools. If Ashley and Annie were looking for answers, they had to first understand the many models for orphanages, and all of them needed help.

"Besides caregivers and food, what other help do they need?" I asked. I opened my ever-present notebook to take notes.

"Great question. What do you think, ladies?"

"Adoption options?" Ashley offered.

"Sure, absolutely. What else?"

Both young women looked up, searching for an answer, maybe from the sky. Ashley stroked her chin.

"What about training?" I asked.

"Bingo. Most orphanages don't have the ability to offer a path forward for their wards. Job training and acquiring the skills to find jobs," Lew pointed out. "What happens to these young adults when they time out of the orphanage at eighteen, nineteen, or twenty? It's a real-world dilemma. Many end up on the streets. That'll break your heart more than the conditions in the orphanages."

Annie moaned. "And makes the problems even bigger."

"Reality stinks, for sure," Lew said. "Okay, here are some options. I'm not saying any of them will work for you. Just ideas. Go home, raise money, adopt an orphanage, stay focused to help a single facility. Then grow the model once you see what works. Or stay here, live here, be the hands and feet of Jesus to every child you can serve. Maybe that's the experience you need. Stay a year or two, then go home, start a non-profit company, work with existing aid organizations, dedicate your life to the mission. Or build a model where donors adopt an orphan with money and aid. Not literally adopt, just support, on a monthly basis. This model works all over the world."

Lew lowered his voice, and we had strain to hear him. "Whatever you do, don't give up. Never forget what you saw and felt here. Find a way to continue to tap into that sorrow—then tell others about it."

I noticed that both Annie and Ashley were writing in their notebooks, stopping for a moment or two, then writing again. It seemed like the ideas were flowing. The brainstorm had opened their thinking. Smiles hadn't yet returned to their faces, but their creativity seemed to be flowing onto the paper.

Lew looked at me and winked. Smooth operator.

Later that evening: Paul

As we were finishing dinner, Lew got up to speak. "I'd like to report that Ron Dean has abruptly left the *Acul Lakou*. He's flown home to Houston. We had a short conversation earlier today, and he believed he could contribute more to his experience of becoming poor by not being here. He'd seen enough. Now he had to get to work. His exact words."

Lew let that sober the group, which had been boisterous and especially enthusiastic after enjoying the delicacy of fresh fruit with the evening meal. Where Andrelita got fresh peaches, nobody knew.

"Gloria, could you shed light on this situation?" Lew asked.

She put her clenched fist in front of her mouth like she was suppressing something before she spoke. "Ron is a motivated individual... And sometimes impatient."

Lew waited for more, his eyebrows raised. "That's not much light shedding."

"At times he thought progress was too slow here," she continued. "We didn't always agree on that. We... don't always agree."

Lew stood, hands folded together, fingers tapping. Waiting for more.

"Ron finds it hard sometimes to be in the moment. He's always rushing forward, planning the next thing," Gloria said. "It was hard for him to see those kids in the orphanage and not do something."

"He was doing something," Lew countered. "He was helping them by understanding their situation."

She slowly nodded, like she agreed but not completely.

"He likes to say he's a man of action. But I know his actions can get him into trouble. I've seen that in our marriage. At times"

I didn't know what she meant by that, and as I looked at Lew, he seemed to be deep in thought. Maybe he was contemplating whether he wanted to pursue that issue. Without blinking, he kept his gaze on Gloria.

"I tried to talk to him," she continued. "For the last several nights we talked and talked. But he wasn't listening to me. When he gets an idea in his head, he's laser focused. Like he doesn't hear me at all. Well, I suppose he does. Maybe he just...I don't know." She looked down, studying her nails.

Maybe he doesn't care—that's how I finished her sentence in my head.

We'd lost one of our team. I hadn't particularly liked Ron Dean, but with only seven of us in the program, when one left, we felt the loss. He was aggressive, sure, but he was also a hard worker. As I looked around at the rest of the group, I saw a mixture of worry and fear in their eyes. Knowing how most of us felt about Ron, maybe they were unsure how this could affect the program. Or maybe they felt the same way Ron did. I had similar frustrations.

"Why didn't he talk to me more?" Lew asked her.

"He thought you'd try to talk him out of leaving. And when he gets his mind made up..." She lifted one shoulder in a helpless shrug.

I got the impression Gloria was defending her husband but without much conviction. She left all these questions unanswered and expected us to fill in the blanks.

Now Lew paced around the kitchen, rubbing his hands together. I could tell he was upset, but I didn't know what part of the situation most bothered him. Ron Dean had been a thorn in Lew's side since we'd arrived, questioning everything. But he wasn't happy now that Ron had left.

Finally, Lew stopped. "People have left the experience early before," he said, "and it rarely turns out for the best. I designed this program for thirty days for a reason. The experience grows into you, it deepens into your soul. It changes you to the extent that you're a different person at the end. You have new perspective, yes, but you are fundamentally and forever changed. You will not look at the world, or Haiti, the same way ever again."

He stopped, but I doubted he was done and waited for what would come next. He took several deep breaths and let the last one out slowly.

"Ron didn't change. At least not that I could tell. He may do wonderful things for Haiti, but I'm afraid it didn't touch his soul. His heart."

"I think maybe it did," Gloria countered, barely above a whisper.

Lew looked at her. "Maybe. We'll see."

DAY 20

Mirlande

I woke up and saw Sonson asleep on my floor. I knew he had a key to my home, but I hadn't heard him come in last night. I'd been dreaming about green grass and tall pine trees like ones I'd seen in books. I remember something about a cool stream running through a valley but not much else. Since I'd never been outside of Haiti, and even though there are pretty spots up in the mountains of my country, this hadn't looked like anything I'd seen before. So, I must have seen it in a book somewhere. There was someone with me in the dream, a man I think, but I couldn't see his face. He didn't look familiar, but he seemed familiar in a way I couldn't pinpoint. When I awoke, I tried to remember more about the dream, but then I saw Sonson.

Even asleep he had a worried look on his face. His brow furrowed, and his lips pursed. Through that all, I saw the turmoil his life had become. With our father gone at such an early age, somehow Sonson had decided he needed to become a man much earlier than he was ready for. Our mother worked, but it was always a struggle to live on her salary alone. As a young boy trying so hard to be a man, life was harder on him than me. I had my mother to talk to, but Sonson gradually drew away from us. I suppose it was hard to confide in your mother or sister when the pull to be your own man was so strong. Haiti toughens you up quickly.

As an older teen, he'd worked several decent paying jobs, but jobs often didn't last long in Haiti. He'd worked at the port hauling for a freight company and with his strong back and sheer determination, he lasted longer than most. But the company failed when it couldn't pay its bills and the job disappeared. A warehouse job assembling a simple backpack for a clothing line didn't last much longer. Many manufacturers came to Haiti looking for cheap labor, but they offered poor working conditions, no benefits, and low pay. Many fizzled out.

Now, as a young man of twenty-three, his life had run off course, if he'd ever had a course. He didn't have a high school education—only two percent of Haitians have one of those—and he had no job history of success. His lack of achievement in life, even at such an early age, gnawed at him. I knew it did. He didn't need to explain it to me. I'd had that same feeling, too, many times in my early life before Lew took me in. But to a man, surrounded by a culture of failure at many levels, it could be devastating. To feel you were powerless to create success, that the entire system—education, economics, opportunity-- worked against you. It had driven him to a life on the fringe.

Forget his cock and bull story about power, or revolution, or policing—this gang he embraced was just a tribe of young men without a future. Grasping at any handhold to get something out of life. Anything. Bonding over guns, bravado, and violence. For many, it was the only way. For my brother, it was the worst way. He wasn't built for this. He had people who loved him and wanted to help. But he turned us away. Too macho for his own good. It broke my heart.

He stirred, opened his eyes, and saw me staring at him.

"When did you get here?" I asked, feeling warm toward him and offering a smile.

"Late."

"You look beat."

"Rough night."

"You okay?"

When he looked at me, I saw fear in his eyes. He turned away without answering. He didn't have to. I knew he wasn't okay.

"Want some breakfast?" I asked.

"I probably shouldn't stay. They might..." He didn't finish the thought.

"What?"

"Nothing." He sat up, rubbed his rough hands hard against his face, stretched his neck, then laid his head in his hands.

I noticed the gun on the blanket. He reached over to

pat it, like a man does when he pats his back pocket to make sure he has his wallet. Reassurance.

At a random clanging noise outside, he turned sharply toward the sound and grabbed the gun. It was a cool morning, but his forehead was covered with beads of sweat. His gaze darted from the door to the window and back.

"I should go. I shouldn't have come here," he said.

"What about breakfast? When did you eat last?"

"No time."

He quickly laced up his shoes and stood. He glanced at me, his eyes turning so sad I thought he might cry. The macho man disappeared, replaced by a lost boy.

"Love you, sis." Then he was gone.

Later that evening: Paul

WHEN THE WALL CREAKED AND THE BUILDING shook, everyone stopped talking at once.

"What was that?" Luke said, too loud for the kitchen at the *lakou*.

We all waited for something else to creak or to move. Nothing happened. I started breathing again, not realizing I'd stopped.

"I thought you lived in California," Lew said with a grin. "Haven't you felt earthquakes before? Just a little shaking. Pretty common for Haiti."

"I don't care how many of those you feel, it still freaks me out. I hate those things. Sends willies down to my willy," Luke said, immediately turning beet red. "Oh, sorry, ladies. Sorry."

Alan Waterman rose from the table and walked toward the wall that creaked. He got within six inches of it and ran his hand over the painted surface. He peered up into the corner, along the expanse of the room, then did the same with the far corner. He examined the wall joints in the four corners. The folks in the room followed his eyes, craning their necks to see what Alan was doing, like a game of Simon Says. Now Simon says look at the corners of the wall.

"What are you doing, Alan?" Lew asked, but as if he already knew the answer.

Alan smiled back at Lew. "Cracks, damage. That was a pretty big jolt."

"So now you're an inspector?" Lew asked, again with no accusation.

"Young Luke has taught me much."

I glanced at Luke, still red from his faux pas.

"Not to worry," Lew said. "I had the building reinforced with rebar about six years ago. We've had some serious shakers since then, and except for a few cracks in the stucco outside, it's none the worse for the wear."

"We've noticed at the building site," Alan continued, "that rebar is a scarce commodity. I offered to supply some, no charge, but they said no."

"They probably didn't want to appear to be accepting charity," Lew said.

"Nonetheless, Luke has assured me the building needs rebar," Alan said.

"Then have it delivered, if you can find it, and don't

say who it's from," Lew offered. "I'm sure they'd use it if they had it."

"A mystery delivery." Alan beamed. "I like it."

"I'd say this one was under a 4.0," Luke said. "How big have the others been?"

"I don't really keep track," Lew answered.

Luke nodded slowly, still looking at the walls and pensively staring off into a space only he could see.

"These third world countries, they don't build like they should," Luke said. "Oh, sorry, foot in mouth again. I didn't mean third world like..."

"That's okay, Luke. Haiti is third world, no denying that," Lew said.

Suddenly, I caught Mirlande staring at me. She chopped one hand on the other, indicating I should change the subject.

"I've seen reports published about California," I said. "You know, the ones where they map out each little earthquake that happens every day in the entire state. Has anyone seen those before?"

No takers.

"Well, they show concentric circles, and each circle represents a quake," I said, making circles with my hands. "The bigger the circle, the bigger the quake. It looks like the whole state is filled with circles everywhere."

I glanced back at Mirlande. She rolled her eyes.

"So, like, nothing much happens from all the earthquakes," I said, trying to back out of this topic. "Very little damage. That's what I meant to say."

Another look to Mirlande. Another eye roll.

"This isn't California. How much rebar did you use on this place?" Luke asked.

"I'm not exactly sure," Lew answered. "But a few thousand dollars' worth, as I remember."

Luke nodded. "Better than none at all."

I saw concern on the faces of most everyone in the room, except Lew. Most were staring up into the corners of the room.

"Should I be concerned, young Mr. Himes" Lew asked Luke.

"Oh, no," Luke replied, "I'm sure you'll be fine."

He wasn't convincing. Had he meant what he said?

We all kept looking up at the corners of the walls.

DAY 21

Paul

EVEN THOUGH TODAY WAS SUNDAY AND THE BAKERY was closed, I got up early. I'd asked Doval for access earlier in the week for a special project and he'd given me the key. I had a wild hair idea to bake a pie—for Mirlande.

I don't know why I thought this might be a cool idea. I didn't know how she'd take the gesture. I wasn't even sure what the gesture meant to me. It was a gift, a nice gift, I supposed, but it wasn't over the top or anything. Just a lemon meringue pie. I made a delicious lemon meringue pie, a specialty of my bakery back home.

We didn't have desserts on most evenings at the *lakou.* They were a rarity in a society that had little time or inclination to spend money for luxuries. When you're trying to put basic food on the table, desserts weren't necessary. That's what made me want to bake a pie for Mirlande.

I bought the best lemons I could find at the marketplace the day before and stored them under my bed in my room. I knew Doval's bakery had the other ingredients—and I didn't need anything other than what a typical bakery keeps on hand—fresh eggs, sugar, corn starch, flour, butter. I had a simple recipe, but the combination of zesty lemons and the sweetness of the meringue made for a sumptuous clash of sweet and tart.

I hoped Mirlande liked pie.

Yesterday, I'd made a lame excuse to stop by her place later this morning, saying I needed to ask her some delicate questions about Annie and Ashley outside of earshot of the *lakou*. She reluctantly—or maybe suspiciously was more accurate—gave me directions to her house. She asked me if we couldn't meet at the *lakou*, but I said that was out of the question, that this meeting had to be secret. Then she suggested we meet at a coffee shop, and I told her I wanted to talk with her alone. To say I wanted to meet in secret wasn't a good way to put it, and that probably made her even more suspicious. I said I'd stop by around ten o'clock.

The crust was the most delicate undertaking, but I'd made so many crusts in my day that I relished taking the time to do it correctly. I made the crust myself, knowing that no baker man would ever make a pie with a premade crust. Even if such a thing existed in Haiti. The lemon filling took no time at all, and after sampling the zing of the lemons, I was satisfied the pie would be tasty. The meringue was just a question of beating the egg whites to foamy perfection, forming the peaks, and making sure once it was added to the top of the pie, that I baked it to a golden brown. The whole thing took under two hours.

I mean, it was just a pie.

I did add a little shaved coconut to the top. I'd found coconut chunks at the marketplace, too. A special ingredient, but nothing over the top—just on the top.

I slipped the pie into one of the white boxes Doval used to deliver baked goods to grocery stores and dug out the hand-written directions to Mirlande's home from the front pocket of my jeans. She told me there weren't many street signs in her neighborhood, but her home had a number. I'd made sure I understood the directions when she gave them to me, asking her to explain the map several times.

I arrived without the slightest hiccup and approached her house. That's when I saw Mirlande standing at the front door with her arms folded across her chest, eyeing me. She didn't have her usual stern expression, but something closer to curiosity, with her mouth scrunched to one side, and one eye squinting. She wore a flowered top, a skirt, and sandals—not her normal attire.

"Good morning," I bellowed, maybe a little too loud, from ten yards away.

She nodded with a slight smile. *"Bonjour."*

There was an awkward silence when I came closer.

Finally, she said, "Whatcha got in the box, *blan?*"

"I thought I was Paul from now on."

"You'll always be a *blan* to me," she said, but then added, "Paul Whiteside."

"Thank you, Mirlande..." I froze. I'd never asked her last name. What an idiot.

"Baptiste," she said, her voice soft, almost demure. "Now that the more formal introductions are complete, are you going to tell me what's in the box?"

I laughed, "Of course. It's a treat. For you. As a thank-you. Shall we go inside so I can show you?"

She hesitated. "It is not much to see." The smile had faded.

"I understand, but I didn't want to do this at the *lakou*."

She opened the door and stopped at the threshold. She turned back to meet my eyes, and I thought I detected sorrow there. Or maybe shame. She continued in.

Her home was small, tiny even. I tried my best not to stare as I delicately placed the box on the table covered with a yellow and oranges plastic tablecloth.

"It's a pie, that's all," I said. "I thought you might like it. It's only a pie." I didn't want to keep rambling on but was at a loss for words.

"What kind of pie?"

"Oh, right," I said, opening the box. "Lemon meringue."

She peeked inside, leaning over the box and exaggerating her sniffing. "It smells delicious."

"Shall we have a bite?"

She vigorously nodded and smiled at me. "I'll get a couple of plates." She retrieved two mismatched plates and forks from an open cupboard next to her sink. She grabbed a long knife and handed it to me.

When she bit into the first bite, her eyes opened wide, and for the first time I saw her smile with her whole face.

"It's sweet and sour all at the same time," she said, giggling.

"In the business, we call that...tart," I replied, trying not to sound too businesslike.

"Tart," she repeated. "It's delicious. Thank you."

"It's just a pie."

We sat staring at each other across the small table. I couldn't hold eye contact and shifted my gaze. But I didn't want to come off as scrutinizing her home, so I again focused on her.

"Why did you make me a pie, Paul?"

"To be nice, that's all."

"Can I have another piece?"

"Sure." I dished up another piece for both of us.

After we finished, she said, "I wish I had some milk or coffee to offer you, but I didn't expect..." her voice trailed off.

I continued to stare at her. It was the closest I'd been to her, and I noticed that her skin was smooth, without a blemish. She didn't have a deep black skin tone, but more like chocolate brown. She wore a little makeup around the eyes. And her teeth were perfect, straight, and white. Of course, I'd noticed that before, whenever she smiled. Which she was doing more often in recent days.

"What are you staring at?" she asked, breaking me out of a spell I'd fallen into.

"Uh, nothing," I stammered.

"Do you find me attractive, Paul?"

"What?" I'd heard her, but I didn't know how to answer. She'd caught me off guard. The heat on my forehead and neck told me I was blushing.

She had a mischievous smile now. "I see the way you look at me, you know."

"I...I...was trying to be friendly. It's only a pie."

"Maybe in your country, that's true, but in Haiti, it's much, much more."

"What?"

She broke into a deep-throated laugh and slapped the table. "Got you, didn't I?"

I took a deep breath, exhaled, and laughed a little myself. I blushed even more, and my hands were clammy.

She rose from the chair and glanced down at me. "But you do find me attractive, don't you?"

"Yes," I admitted. Not only to her, but for the first time to myself. Again, I couldn't hold her stare.

"But you're not sure. I can see it in your eyes. I'm pretty. But I'm black. Have you ever been attracted to a black woman before, Paul?"

I wasn't sure I liked her calling me Paul. It sounded serious, too much so. I wanted to go back to being a *blan*. Or a *maroon*. I didn't know how to answer her question.

"Sure," I finally said, not sure it was true.

"I have a nice figure, too, right?"

Where was this all going? Maybe I should have made muffins instead. An odd thought.

"Oh, it's not your typical American figure. Like women with well-toned legs and butt. But I have no time for the machines American women use. Those machines that work out the legs and butt. My legs are a little skinny."

I couldn't stop my eyes from fixing on her legs.

"And my tummy has a little pouch."

Why did I look at her stomach? I couldn't help myself.

She laughed again.

"Why are you saying these things, asking these questions?" I mumbled.

"I'm making you wrestle with what's going on inside. To examine yourself."

"Now you sound like the lieutenant."

She looked away. "He has taught me much. About many things. Like things between two people."

"What do you mean?"

"That is not for you to know right now. You still have not answered my question."

"I did answer. I said I found you attractive."

"Not in as many words."

We seemed to be at an impasse. I didn't know where to take the conversation, and I didn't know what I felt.

"You're examining me. Being nice to see how I will react. To see if I will tell you if I find you attractive. And you don't seem happy with yourself for acting this way. You're confused. Aren't you, Paul?"

Call me *blan*, please. Let's go back there.

I kept silent, scraping some of the lemon meringue pie off the plate with my fork. But deep down I knew she was right.

That same morning: Mirlande

I'D SPENT MOST OF THE EARLY MORNING MAKING MY little home as clean as I could. I tidied up everything in the house, as little as there was. I scrubbed and scrubbed, trying to erase years of wear and tear and poverty from tables and chairs and rugs and dishes. I even cleaned both windows. With no success. I burned a scented candle to wash away the stink of the stagnant air.

Paul approached the house with a goofy grin and his loud greeting came from way down the street. He held a fancy white box in his hand. Was he bringing me a gift? What was he up to now? He'd first been so quiet around me, but lately he'd started opening up about why he was in Haiti and how he believed he could do so much more. We all wanted to help Haiti, but most of us just needed to help ourselves. I was too busy worrying about my future and Sonson and my mother to wonder about where my country was headed. Why was he here now?

"Bonjour," I said to him, trying to keep my look not too threatening. Lew often told me I wasn't approachable. So, I put a little smile on my face.

He said nothing, but that goofy grin stayed put.

"Whatcha got in the box, *blan?*" I asked, knowing that would throw him off a bit.

"It's a pie," he answered, and then he yammered about it being just a pie and nothing else, like he was apologizing that he made me a pie and making me feel less worthy of a gift. I wanted to feel special enough that he'd spent time making me something with his own hands.

When he asked to come inside, my breath went shallow. I bit my tongue hard to keep from blurting that there was no way I was going to let him see the inside of my home. But I opened the door and he followed.

"Lemon meringue," he answered when I asked him what kind of pie he'd brought. When I smelled it, I couldn't help the smile that burst across my face.

After our second piece, I thought maybe this wasn't so bad. But then he kept staring. His eyes would leave me but come right back, leaving me self-conscious and defensive under his scrutiny of me or my home—or both. It was time to take back control of the morning.

"What are you staring at?" I asked, flustering Paul. Good, that's what I was aiming for. I enjoyed his blushing. I wasn't trying to be mean or anything but needed to shake him up a bit and keep the conversation rolling. He brought me a pie. Now we could get down to why he brought it.

"Do you find me attractive, Paul?" I asked. Might as well ratchet up the tension, huh? He blushed more. I told him I'd noticed how he looked at me. Then he really lost it, stammering about the pie and how it didn't mean anything. Maybe I'd pushed him too far because it seemed like he might get up and leave and I didn't want that. He'd made me this wonderful pie after all.

I made the point that in Haiti his gift was much more than a pie. Okay, so I pushed a tiny bit more, pushed him over the edge.

Then I couldn't help myself from giggling all girly like—and that finally broke the tension. I rather liked playing with this man. Sure, he had a hard time admitting his attraction to me, even to himself. He liked to laugh at himself, though. Men in Haiti can be hard SOBs, and even though I sometimes struggle with finding humor in situations, I've also learned that sometimes you have to laugh. It tends to burn away the fear. The fear most of us live with every day.

Let's see if he was willing to play a little more.

"I have a nice figure, too, right?" I said as I stood. His eyes were all over me. I'd seen that before. I didn't mind. I liked the way he stared.

Then, almost too easily, I made him look at my legs, then my stomach. His eyes betrayed him, and he kept looking at me, then away. Maybe he was used to women —like that Abby he kept sneaking phone calls with—that weren't so direct. A strong, Haitian woman like me would treat him with more dignity. I almost felt sorry for him, making his squirm, but keeping the pressure on him. I wasn't trying to be mean. Well, maybe a little. For his own good.

I couldn't help but laugh. This was so much fun. The man brought me a wonderful gift, and I tried to make him admit that it, that maybe he found me attractive. But then he went all yammering, stammering fool on me. Men can be so funny, right?

"Why are you asking me these things?" he mumbled.

"I'm making you wrestle with what's going on inside of you. To examine yourself," I replied.

To say it was a special gift. To admit that you find me attractive. To give a little of yourself to me. Just for this moment. I had no other expectation. None. I just wanted somebody to tell me that they cared. I mean, the pie said so much, but I wanted him to say it out loud. That wouldn't be so much to ask.

"I said I found you attractive," he said finally.

I hadn't heard that before. Maybe I was too busy twirling him around like a piñata that I never heard it. Had he really said that once before and I missed it?

Now what do I say?

"You're examining me. You're being nice to see how I will react," I said. So, how would I react? By pushing him into a corner? By forcing him to come to terms with his feelings?

"To see if I'll tell you if I find you attractive." Did I? Was I willing to admit to myself that I did? To even, for a minute, see him as something more than a ticket out of Haiti. There, I said it. "And you don't seem happy with yourself for acting this way. You are confused, aren't you, Paul?" Oh, sweet Jesus, what was I doing? Why was I treating this nice man this way?

He made me this wonderful, delicious lemon meringue pie—and I felt I was shoving it right in his face.

What was he feeling now as he scraped the pie off his plate?

DAY 22

Paul

WHEN I ARRIVED AT THE BAKERY MONDAY morning, Doval beamed at me. Emil and Henri also flashed big grins. I hoped they hadn't found out about the lemon meringue pie. I'd cleaned up the bakery the day before, leaving no trace of what I'd done.

I almost said it was only a pie when Doval rushed over and said: "Emil's brother sold all the mini-loaves in two days!"

"What? No way."

"Yes way, Jose," Doval laughed. "The first day was slow, he said. But you were right to give him some samples so people could try them before they bought. The second day word got around, and he sold everything we'd made on Friday." He shook his head like he didn't believe it.

"It worked, Paul, it worked." He spoke in a low but firm voice, looking me right in the eye.

"Excellent. But it wouldn't have worked if the bread wasn't so delicious. It's your bread that made it work."

"Thank you, but it was your idea. You deserve most of the credit."

We each put our hands on the others' shoulders and basked in the mutual admiration of the work we'd done.

Later that afternoon, after Emil and Henri had left for the day, Doval and I huddled around his small, wooden office desk to strategize the next phase of our plan.

"We've made it over the first big hurdle," I began. "We had a really good idea that the market would buy this product. That's our market research, and although it wasn't extensive, I think we can predict that if we can deliver, the market will buy. Do you agree?"

"Yes, definitely. What's next?"

"We need to come up with a schedule to ramp up production. Ingredients, costs, delivery, everything. But we need to do it gradually." I held up one finger. "One, so we can keep the quality topnotch." I held up a second finger. "And two, so we know how much our two salesmen can sell."

I began to sketch out a rough draft of a spreadsheet on paper. I'd learned that Haiti was a country where people often felt comfortable with plans drawn up with paper and pencil. And I was that kind of guy, too. Sure, I'd learned technology and QuickBooks and such with my bakery, but Doval didn't need that type of depth yet. When his business grew, and I had all the confidence in the world that it would, we could introduce production saving and tracking technology. But for now, paper and pencil worked just fine.

"We started small. I mean teeny weeny, miniscule. Just fifty loaves," I said. "Could we quadruple that? Two hundred loaves? Could we do five hundred?"

Doval's eyes lit up, but then his brow furrowed as he looked at the numbers and figured in his head the money needed.

"The sales profit should cover the costs," he said. "I just need to come up with the money to buy the supplies. Cash is tight now, so let's continue slowly, ramping up as we go."

"Good plan."

We spent the next hour filling in the blanks on the spreadsheet. We calculated the ingredients we needed wouldn't be a problem. Doval made a note on the margin to "test the yeast" and I smiled. The biggest hurdle was whether we could ramp up production with the four of us and keep our other commitments to grocery stores and the handful of hotels that bought our products.

Doval bit his upper lip and said, "But you'll be leaving soon, so we may have to consider hiring another baker eventually. Not right now, but hopefully soon."

"Let's continue to talk about that and plan for it," I said. "But we can cross that bridge when we come to it."

"What bridge?" He frowned in confusion.

I grinned. "That just means we don't have to make a decision now."

"Okay, right. Sometimes you talk funny, Paul, but

then you make me understand. I will be sorry to see you leave."

I felt the same way, but I didn't know how to express that. Doval was a smart man, he knew his trade, and he'd figure a way to make it work. Emil and Henri worked hard, took instruction well, and exhibited pride in their craft. I liked the direction the idea of mini-loaves was headed, but how much impact could it have? In the scheme of what Haiti needed, a little extra bread—like money in the pockets of Doval and like food in the mouths of the neighborhood—looked trivial.

Was there something bigger I was missing? Could I introduce this idea to other bakeries in Haiti? Would that betray the trust in me that Doval had shown? Was that even fair to Doval?

I needed to talk with Lew.

That evening: Paul

LEW OFTEN LIKED TO SIT AROUND AFTER DINNER for talk sessions with his guests—now down to six with the exit of Ron Dean—out on the patio enjoying a warm Haitian evening. Sometimes he'd introduce a topic like "when does helping hurt?" But he also liked to talk about success stories—how small strides in caring or giving had helped Haiti in the long run.

This evening he told a story about soap.

"About six years ago," he began, "a ministry group of churches—all the same denomination, all in the same general area of the U.S.—came to Haiti for a mission trip. They visited orphanages, handed out supplies, played games with the children, did a Vacation Bible School, things like that. They stayed two weeks and generally did a wonderful job. I'm sure it was beneficial to the orphans and to their short-term missionaries."

With the way he paused, I felt like the other shoe was about to drop.

"But they couldn't help themselves from doing one... more...good...deed," Lew continued, drawing out the last part of the sentence.

I leaned forward in my chair in anticipation, and so did the others.

"They noticed a lack of hygiene in many of the orphanages they visited. And a lack of soap. A good observation, technically," Lew said. "So, they mounted a soap drive. They tapped into their vast network of churches—and this was a big, big denomination in the States." Lew described the way the visitors sent photos of poor Haitian orphans, mostly dirty or living in squalor, with a plea to send as many soap and hygiene products they could to the home church, who was going to coordinate delivery to Haiti and help in the distribution.

"Sounds like a noble project, doesn't it?" Lew asked the group.

Nobody offered an answer.

"They sent pallets and pallets...and pallets of products to Haiti. The church distributed to all the orphanages and set up a network to send products to sites across our country. Well, most made it, but some products ended up in the marketplaces. It happens. This soap was sold well under the market value of soap manufactured in the country. The soap manufacturer couldn't match the price. Their sales plummeted." With a sigh, Lew's story ended with the inevitable outcome that eventually local soap producers went out of business, taking a viable manufacturing entity off the landscape and putting thirty to forty Haitian employees out of work.

We absorbed this story, but I looked away from Lew, as did others in our group. It was as if we had something to do with the outcome and felt somehow responsible, if not guilty. I remembered seeing many soap dispensers in Haiti, but rarely any soap. I suspected it was all connected somehow.

"That's totally sad," Ashley said in a barely audible voice.

After a minute, Lew said, "But not all stories have such a sad ending. All helping doesn't hurt that bad."

"Paul, why don't you tell us what you've been working at over at Doval's bakery?" Lew suggested.

"Sure, for what it's worth," I said.

I described the work Doval and I had been doing over the past few weeks. I kept the technical details to a minimum, but I mentioned that we'd tested the yeast to make sure it was fresh. Then I briefed them on the experiment we conducted with the first fifty mini-loaves and how quickly they sold. I concluded by outlining the plan to gradually ramp up production of the loaves.

The folks nodded along, understanding the plan, but apparently admiring it, too.

"I know it'll make a difference in Doval's bakery," I

continued. "But in the scheme of things, is it all that big of a deal? Really? Big whoop, right?"

Lew jumped in. "But you also said that if he can keep his quality up now with the yeast problem solved, he could start to win bigger contracts. Perhaps with grocery stores and restaurants, right?"

I nodded sheepishly. "He can do that. And I think he will."

"And both the neighborhood and the bakery win if the mini-loaves idea continues to grow, right?" Lew asked.

"Yep."

"Not to mention the guys selling the mini-loaves," Mirlande added.

I smiled at her, and she smiled back.

"So, win and win and win," Lew said. "I don't see the problem that's showing on your face, Paul. It's a business that grows. It's a neighborhood that gets more food. And it's several workers that distribute the loaves and make some money. What's not to love?"

"I don't know. I just thought we could scale it up. Invite other bakeries to participate. In other neighborhoods, but is that fair to Doval and his crew?" I wondered out loud.

"Have you asked them?" Lew offered.

"Not yet."

"Okay. So, go do that. And while you're at it, ask Doval if he knows other small food suppliers where the same principle might work."

"Like what?"

"I don't know, but it's a legal, profitable business

model that might work in other neighborhoods with other food products, like...."

Before Lew could fill in the blank, Luke said "Pizza!"

Lew scrunched up his mouth, furrowed his brow, and said, "Might work."

"You know that pizza place we went to the other night?" Luke said. "It looks like it mostly served expats and visitors, not locals. Probably too high-priced. But Paul's idea could work there. I mean, the pizza wouldn't be hot, if guys roamed the neighborhood, but everybody likes cold pizza, don't they?"

"I do," Lew said, "but that's not the point. You certainly could find other products to produce and distribute this way. Of course, you'd have to work with the business like you did with Doval. Find the pressure points and figure out how to squeeze out the profits. Work with the owner on a regular basis and oversee the process. Be a sounding board and an encourager. Everything you did with Doval."

I suddenly saw both the logic and the brick walls of such a suggestion. It took me three weeks to launch a program at the bakery that may or may not scale up. Only time would tell. I thought of the investment of time needed to find other businesses and work with owners that didn't know me from Adam—even if Doval introduced me. Then work to find a similar solution to their product. And find the distribution. And...it seemed overwhelming now.

"How's that sound to you, Paul?" Lew asked.

"To be truthful, overwhelming," I answered.

"Of course, it does. You see—and many of you have expressed this to me—everything seems hard in Haiti," Lew said. "Everything. The unknown, the customs, the history, the hopelessness. Those are the first things you see. You really have to train your mind to escape that perception, because on the surface, it's correct. It's hard in Haiti. That's Haiti. That's simply Haiti. I get it."

Lew's sweeping gesture took in all of us. "Overwhelming," he continued. "That's the way you all came to me. Haiti is overwhelming. But it's not impossible. Nothing is impossible. But, and it's a big but, you must be committed. Maybe even move to Haiti full-time. Give up whatever you had back home and give your life to your new future."

I hadn't considered that and wondered if others in the room had.

"Could you stay in Haiti to realize this...this dream?" Lew asked, focused on me now. "Could you move here? Could you do it living here half-time? For instance, hire and train an assistant, pay him or her a decent wage to run your Haiti operation, and you stay in the States and run your bakery. Could that work? I don't know, do you?"

I didn't know, but it certainly gave me something to think about. Seemed like I had way too much to think about. I shrugged.

Lew nodded, his eyes showing he was discouraged, too. "I know. It's Haiti. It's always Haiti."

DAY 23

Mirlande

I DRIFTED IN THAT DAWN OF NOT QUITE SLEEPING and not ready to get up. I pulled the skimpy blanket up to my chin in the early morning chill. My thoughts drifted to Paul and how nice it would be to have somebody to share the mornings with. A cup of coffee, a light breakfast. I always ate my breakfast alone.

Then I heard a knock on my door. The rest of the day was blurry, like a fog drifting in from the ocean and covering everything. Colors and sounds muted, names forgotten, and conversations clipped and hard to decipher. Like a dream. No, a nightmare.

The man at the front door wore a uniform, white shirt with an emblem, dark blue trousers. Official looking, somber. I think he introduced himself, but if he said his name, it never registered.

Worry etched his face, showed in his eyes, and filled

the few words I could understand. He asked if I was Mirlande Baptiste and to confirm my mother's address. I jumped to thinking something had happened to her, but he assured me it was just a way to confirm who I was. He said he knew my mother and when I asked him to describe her, he did. They knew each other from church.

He hadn't talked to her yet today, he said, but came directly to me. I was known in the church community as level-headed and diligent.

He asked me to come with him because he had an important task to complete with me. I was skeptical. He nodded, acknowledging my hesitancy. The sound and depth of his voice conveyed an importance that submerged my reluctance, especially when he told me it concerned Sonson.

He gave me time to collect a few things, phone Lew at the orphanage, and change my clothes. He led me to his vehicle and opened the passenger door for me. I don't think anyone had ever done that for me, opened a door out of courtesy and then made sure I was seated comfortably before they got in.

Although the vehicle didn't look official, a plastic emblem sat slightly askew on the doors. The same emblem that was on his shirt. My fog was so severe that all I could read was the word AMBULANCE. But I wasn't sitting in anything resembling an ambulance. It was a big SUV with no back seats, a little worn—like any vehicle in Haiti—with a distinctive and putrid smell permeating the interior. Like the mix of a stench I couldn't name and bleach. It turned my stomach, and I put my hand on the dashboard, ready to open my door and wretch. But it passed. He patiently waited for me to regain myself. The SUV's air conditioning cooled me but didn't mask the smell. I pushed my hand toward the windshield, indicating that he could proceed. I couldn't speak.

He drove slowly, much slower than surrounding traffic, ignoring horns honking at him and cars buzzing around him. He said nothing, and I was forced to keep myself composed. I refused to ask questions, not wanting any answers. I would find out soon enough what this mystery ride would reveal. I soon blocked out the traffic, the people on the side of the roads, the destination of the SUV. My vision blurred, zoned out, only the ringing in my ears gave me any sense of the day at all. If I stayed in this trance maybe I could avoid reality for as long as possible.

In ten minutes—or I suppose it could have been thirty—we arrived at a white building with a small, green lawn in front and a red hospital cross on the door. The sign above the door read: Port-au-Prince *Mog Lopital*, Hospital Morgue.

Oh, my Sonson.

I called Lew and told him where I was. He said he'd be there in fifteen minutes and to wait for him before I proceeded. They took me to a small office after I asked them to wait for Lew Dessi to arrive. They seemed in a hurry to move the process along but acknowledged my request. I don't know what happened to the man who drove me there. I never saw him again.

I sat in a plastic chair opposite a bare wall. My mind

drifted to images of Sonson. I first saw a flickering montage of my brother as a baby, me holding him. Trying to soothe his constant crying. We thought he had colic. I saw myself as a three-year old carrying this big baby around our tiny home, bouncing him like Mother taught me.

Then he appeared as a toddler, kicking a soccer ball in the dirt street in front of our home. He tried juggling the ball on his foot and knee and had me count how many juggles he'd done. He was so proud when he hit five bounces on his body. That soccer ball was a worn old relic he'd found somewhere, but it was his constant companion for many years.

Whenever I envisioned images of my father interacting with Sonson, I blinked wildly to try to change the channel. Back to memories of his teenage years, displaying new clothes or new muscles—he liked to flex his biceps and have me grip them—puffing out his chest in his almost-a-man posture. He always wanted to be the man. The man of the family. The man of the neighborhood. Any man, just not a boy. He never liked being a boy, never enjoyed the same things boys his age did. I had no remembrances of him with a girlfriend. We never owned a car, so no images of pride there either.

More memories flickered past, usually with other young boys alongside Sonson. He always had a posse, as he called them. He liked being the boss, almost forcing his will on others, at least as much will as a teenager could force. In those days, I was always trying to make him laugh. I could do it when he was a kid. When he flashed those skinny biceps, I'd tickle him under the arm. He'd shrug it off but couldn't help but giggle. When he grew older, the giggles stopped, and my efforts to make him laugh were less and less successful.

When my memories stopped, tears streamed down my cheeks. I looked down and my blouse displayed the cascade, soaked just above my breasts. A box of tissues sat on the table in front of me, but I had no energy to reach for one.

Oh, my Sonson.

The door opened, and Lew appeared with another man.

The other man asked me a question—something about identification—and Lew took charge. He ordered me to stay where I was, that he'd be right back. They argued a bit, but the other man relented.

After an eternity, Lew returned. He handed me a small, worn wallet, opened to a photo of me and Sonson taken a decade or more ago. He said that whoever discovered the body recognized the photo and alerted authorities.

Body?

What happened to him?

Why had it happened?

If anyone had answers to these questions, I never heard them.

Lew put his arm around my shoulder and asked me where I wanted the body to go. That the morgue had limited refrigeration and that the body should be removed to a local funeral home. He said not to worry about the cost, that he would cover all expenses.

I'd always thought I was a strong woman, born and

bred that way. Oblivious to peril around me, determined to make life work as best I could. But I slipped into a wrenching sorrow, collapsing into sobbing hysterics, my wailing filling the tiny office. I never knew such sorrow was inside me. I wasn't willing to analyze its origin, but released its rage and hoped to God Almighty that it wouldn't kill me, too.

Later that evening: Paul

ANDRELITA PRODUCED ONLY LEFTOVER SNACKS FOR dinner this evening, explaining to the guests that a tragedy had engulfed the *lakou* and if they wanted more food, they were on their own. After avoiding questions from others, she approached me. "Lew and Mirlande would like you to join them at Mirlande's home as soon as you're able," she said.

"Why, what's wrong? Is it Mirlande? Is she hurt?"

"No, but her heart is broken."

I didn't understand, but I wasted no time walking to her house.

When I arrived, a dozen or so people milled around the outside. Most were young men with mean faces and firearms stuck in the waistbands of their baggy pants.

I was intimidated, the only white man in a crowd of angry young black men—and they didn't know me. As I walked to the little house, a few toughs approached me with fists clenched, shouting in Creole. I didn't need to understand the words to hear and feel the meaning. Eventually, Lew appeared in the doorway and quieted the crowd, putting his arm around me, an act of assurance that I was welcome. But the scowls stayed hardened on the faces of the young men.

Inside, Mirlande sat dejected at the small table where we'd shared the lemon meringue pie. When she saw me, she quickly rose but did not approach. Lew whispered the news in my ear. I went to her and pulled her into an embrace, hugging her and stroking her hair. An older woman at the table stared up at me with a look bordering on disbelief.

"Mama, this is Paul, the *blan*," Mirlande said. "Paul, this is my mother."

I grabbed both of her hands but had no words.

Finally, I managed, "Is there anything I can do to help?"

Mirlande shook her head. "Just stay with us for a while."

"Sure," I replied. "Lew, can I speak with you outside for a minute?"

Lew patted Mirlande's mother on the shoulder and followed me out the door.

"We'll be right outside if you need us," I said.

Lew motioned for the young men to back away to give us some privacy. He showed his sway with them because they pushed back into small groups farther away from the house. But their grumblings, barely hushed, persisted.

"What happened to Sonson?" I asked.

"We're getting conflicting reports right now, so we don't actually know the details. Some are saying he was killed by a rival gang. But from the reaction of several members of the *Federasyon*, I'm beginning to doubt that. They've been silent on that scenario. Usually they'd be belligerent, showing signs of aggression and violence. But not now. I've also heard he may have been killed by his own gang, as an example of somebody who either didn't toe the line or put up too much resistance. In the long run, I'm not sure it matters much."

"I feel so bad for Mirlande and her mother," I said.

"I understand. I do as well. But Sonson was a troubled young man. He got himself into circumstances that were dangerous. He was misguided and unable to see a better path forward. Like many young men in Haiti. They're unable to see a future, and when men see no opportunity or hope, they act out. It's frustration, but more. Hopelessness. Despair. Those are emotions not easily remedied. There is no salve."

"When you see what breaks God's heart..." I recited from the sign at the *lakou*.

Lew nodded slowly. "Indeed."

"Do we need to disperse this crowd? Is that even possible?" I asked.

"They are mostly Sonson's friends. They don't know what else to do. So, they are here simply posturing, making threats, pounding their chests. I'm not sure it will amount to anything. But we can ask Mirlande if she would rather they leave."

I went in the house and came back outside with Mirlande, whose eyes were swollen and red from her tears. She went to the different small groups of men, holding my hand with Lew on the other side of her. He talked to each man in a low, soothing voice. I didn't understand the words, but the looks on the faces of the men changed. One by one, the groups quieted and then she spoke aloud to everyone.

Lew whispered a translation in my ear.

"Thank you for coming. Thank you for caring. It means so much to my mother and me. I understand your anger and frustration. I feel it, too. Many more times than any of you. But we must not fight hatred with more hatred. Let us mourn our brother, our son. Give us time to bury Sonson and to grieve. Please give us that. We will let you know when and where the service will be held. And we will see you all there. To pay respects. To show our love."

Mirlande took a deep breath. "But for now, please go home and ask God almighty to calm your hearts. Please, please, no violence, I beg you. Not now. Now is the time to grieve. Thank you. Go home, go home."

The young men ambled away, leaving the three of us outside.

"Some days," Mirlande said in a whisper, "the burden of Haiti is too much. I want to leave. To be anywhere else in the world."

Lew nodded his understanding, but I had no words to offer.

"Tell me of this Ohio you call home, Paul," she asked me. "Is there violence? Do young men die?"

"I suppose young men die, but I don't see it often," I replied. "I see green hills and tall oak trees everywhere. I see quiet neighborhoods and ice cream trucks in summer. Young men playing basketball or baseball. Riding the school bus to school every day. A bright, yellow bus full of talking kids, joking with their friends."

She looked at me, and the tears stared to trickle down her cheeks. "That sounds so nice. I would like to see that one day."

I didn't know what to say to that. Had I made Ohio something it wasn't? We had our problems in Ohio, too. But Ohio was nothing like Haiti, and I wanted to convey some of its serenity, even if I over sugarcoated it.

"It's not perfect," I managed to mumble.

"Sounds perfect to me," Mirlande said, moving closer to me.

DAY 24

Paul

I MADE IT THROUGH THE DAY, BUT ALL I THOUGHT about was the death of Sonson and how Mirlande felt. She didn't appear at the orphanage or show up for dinner. The mood at the bakery was sad, too, since all the guys knew both Mirlande and Sonson. All day I noticed Emil and Henri periodically shaking their heads. Even the ebullient Doval had no smiles.

After dinner, Lew asked Luke to tell the group about his project, helping to build an addition to a school. I suspected he was diverting attention away from Mirlande—and Sonson.

Luke recapped the first few weeks in two or three short, clipped sentences. He'd been working with an unseasoned crew to build the addition and had been joined by several younger Haitians who just showed up to help. Then he talked about these two young men and one young woman that he'd met working on this job.

"They're all hungry to learn anything they can about construction. Not all people are. Not just in Haiti, but other places, too. Some people really like building stuff, and some don't. I never hold that against them. But this crew here, they're into it. Always asking questions, letting me critique their work, looking over my shoulder when I'm doing something. They're good builders, too, naturals, all of 'em."

"What do you propose to do with that, Luke?" Lew asked.

"Well, now, that's a good question. Alan and I have been talking about that," he began, nodding toward Alan Waterman. "I'd like to stay on in Haiti, maybe finish up this project and look for a few others."

"That's interesting," Lew commented. "How would that work?"

"Not quite sure yet."

"But I'm willing to bootstrap the endeavor," Alan said. "We're putting together something like a business plan. Not too detailed. Just basics including supplies and a place to store them."

"So, a construction team?"

"Right," Luke said. "We'd take on small projects. Stuff I'm good at. Like small building projects—maybe even putting in concrete floors for people. Carpentry, electrical, and maybe even solar. That could be big here. That's my business at home, all those types of projects. Think I can make a little money doing that? Don't need much."

Lew's expression turned thoughtful. "I'm not sure, but it's certainly possible. I have many contacts in this area of Haiti. I could open some doors."

"Not too many doors. We'd have to start slow 'cause the crew isn't up to speed yet. But I think they'll learn quick. We just need a project or two to keep us busy while I train 'em."

I could see the minds of the others working, seeing possibilities.

"Luke, let me ask one vital question," Lew said.

"Yeah, sure. You're good at that."

"What do you need out of this?"

Luke shrugged. "I'm not sure I follow."

"What's your objective? How do you win? I get that you train them and maybe they eventually get jobs on their own. But what about you?"

"Hey, like I said, I don't need much. I like these people. They're real friendly—and they seem to need my help. You know, I pretty much work alone at home. Got a nice little handyman type business and I make decent money, but it's not real rewarding. Like remodeling a new bathroom. Big deal, huh?"

"You'd like to live in Haiti?" Lew again.

"I would, yeah. I like it here. I feel like I'm in my element, you know. I don't mind the chaos, I kinda like it. And...well...I think these people need me. It's nice to be needed."

Now Lew turned toward the room. We all knew what was coming.

"What can we learn about Luke's experience?"

Alan got to his feet. "One thing I've learned is that

you don't have to change the entire country overnight. You can make a small difference in a few lives, and it might have a lasting effect, over time. Over lifetimes."

Annie spoke next. "But it seems, at least for Luke, that you have to be willing to live and work in Haiti."

"I'm not willing to do that," Alan said. "I'm too old and maybe frail for that life. But I can contribute in some way. Luke and I haven't figured that all out yet, but I'm on his team, even if I live in another country. Like Texas."

"All the Texans I've met seem to think they live in their own country anyways," Luke said.

Everyone laughed.

Lew went to Luke and put his arm on his shoulder. "Luke, are you poor now? Is that why you've been able to carve out a plan here?"

"Nah, I'm not poor. I just dress that way."

Luke wore an old tee shirt, cut-off jeans, and worn-out construction boots. I had never seen him without a ratty hat on his head.

"But you could go back to Michigan and travel to Haiti a few times a year. Or you could stay here for a month or so and then go back and see how much you'd miss it. Why are you ready to jump right in?"

Luke looked down at his hands and rubbed them together, cracking a few knuckles. "The crew I've been around the past few weeks are proud people. Poor but proud. I can tell they aren't content to stay poor, but they're content in life. They want to improve their skills and learn a trade or get a job, but still, they're content. They don't bitch and moan. Most people I'm around complain about everything—the weather, the past, other people, everything. These guys, they don't. That's why I like being around them."

Lew smiled. "The poor are not always poor in spirit."

"For sure. Amen to that," Luke said.

Lew asked Alan to add anything he wanted, but before he could speak, Luke quickly revealed something he'd found earlier that day.

"Remember that little shaker we felt here a few days ago?" he asked but didn't wait for a response. "Well, when we got back to the school the next day, I started walking around inspecting what we'd built so far. Looking at the concrete block—that's about half done, about two walls. And guess what I found? Cracks in the mortar. Which is not so unusual in an earthquake, except that I did a little research, and that tumbler was only 3.3. Barely registered."

Everyone glanced up at the corners of the room.

"Nah, don't worry. I inspected this building. It's cool. But I don't know about the rest of Haiti."

DAY 25

Mirlande

I told Lew I wouldn't be at dinner this evening. What I didn't tell him is that I'd invited Paul to share a pizza with me.

I knew Lew wouldn't have a problem if Paul didn't show for dinner. Into the fourth week of their service, guests had often fended on their own for dinner. Andrelita's limited menu and a bent toward chicken with rice drove people to new and different options.

Paul and I walked to a small pizza restaurant located down a dirt and gravel alley, hidden away off the main street. You wouldn't know to look down this alley for a restaurant—it was the only one on the block. I think it was mostly frequented by expats and visitors, but I knew a few pizza-loving Haitians who liked to linger on the outdoor patio into the evening. The place provided a nice escape from everyday life, even though the view only consisted of other buildings and the road.

After we ordered at the counter, Paul and I took our beers outside and although it was still warm, neither of us seemed to mind. The restaurant didn't have air conditioning anyway. I gave him a quick update on the arrangements for Sonson.

"But I don't want to talk about my brother this evening," I said. "I want to forget the past few days, at least for an hour or two."

"I understand," Paul said. "What do you want to talk about?"

"Tell me about your life, Paul, back in Ohio. Tell me about your bakery. Your family. And you can even tell me about your Abby if you want."

"Uh, sure. I just have to figure out where to start. My folks wanted me to be a doctor, but I didn't have the grades—or the desire—to do that. When I started my business, I could sense my dad's disappointment. Even after I started making some money, I still had the feeling he didn't respect my decision. It's always been a source of conflict between us."

"Fathers can be such jerks," I said. "I know how that is." After a pause I added, "But you enjoy being a baker, don't you?"

"I do. It's a nice business. I have a few employees, we work hard, but it's gratifying. I make a little money, save some. I'm thinking of opening a second location eventually. Maybe next year if things work out."

"And in less than a week you'll be returning to Ohio to be a baker, right?"

He hesitated. "I suppose."

"What do you mean, you suppose?"

"I've been thinking about that every day. There seems so much I can accomplish here. And so little left to accomplish there. It's not really that extreme. I just have visions of how I might help Haiti that I didn't have when I came here. I don't know what to do with that."

"You also want to return to your Abbey," I said, a statement, not a question.

He didn't answer. He put down his pizza slice and took a long swig of beer. Finally, he said, "It's not serious yet. I haven't thought about her much since I've been here."

I wanted to say that was because I'd have occupied his senses, blocked out his vision. I wanted to tell him I'd made him forget—at least for a few weeks—his Abby. But that wasn't true. Besides, he'd have to say that himself. I had no right to put those words in his mouth. But I didn't know how to make him say it. I had always had to be a strong woman. I never wanted to be a woman who could make a man say things. To lure a man in that way. To seduce a man to bare his heart and soul. To be soft and gentle and alluring. I didn't know how to do that.

So, I said, "I'm glad that I have met you." As I said it, I thought it sounded terrible.

Paul looked at me with a quizzical gaze, like he didn't understand what I meant. I didn't blame him.

"What I meant to say," I continued, "was that you have been very nice to me, and I am glad we have spent time together." That was true but was that enough to explain what I was trying to say? I didn't even know what I was trying to say.

His gaze didn't change.

I tried again. "Spending time with you gives me great pleasure." His eyes opened wide. Oh, God, I was so bad at this.

Then he smiled. "Do you mean you like me?" he asked.

"Yes." But I didn't know how much. We were so different.

"Do you mean you don't want me to leave?"

"Yes. I mean, no, I don't want you to leave." But if you stayed, what would I have to offer you? Would he stay in Haiti because of me? I'm not sure I wanted to stay in Haiti anymore. Maybe I'd enjoy Ohio—about as far away from Haiti as I could imagine right now.

"Do you mean you don't want me to go back to Abby?"

"Definitely, yes." Was that selfish of me? Shouldn't he make that choice? Why would he want to stay in Haiti?

I hadn't touched him since we sat down—no hand holding, no shoulders leaning against each other, nothing. Should I reach out and grab his hand? Lean over to kiss him? I hadn't kissed him yet and didn't know if he wanted to kiss me. If he did, wouldn't he kiss me first? Is a woman supposed to do that first? I was so bad at this.

"Well, now that that's cleared up," I said, "I have much more to think about, don't I?"

"Me, too."

Later that evening: Paul

I CAME BACK TO THE *LAKOU* STILL WRESTLING WITH the uneasiness I'd had for weeks. Lew and I talked most every day about it, but he couldn't help me decide my future. I had to do that myself. Now with the insertion of Mirlande into the recipe, I was even more torn between two lives.

Could I live in Haiti? It really came down to that, didn't it? Abigail and Mirlande aside—over time I suspected that triangle would work itself out—the question became: what was I willing to give up and what was I willing to grab onto?

So many questions. Could I give up my bakery? Could I grab onto a life of service?

What about my comfort? Could I enjoy a life without it? Or would I eventually find comfort in other ways?

What about a life without a secure future, or at least one I could predict? Could I grab onto that uncertain life?

As I sat on the patio deep in these dichotomies, a commotion coming from inside the kitchen snapped me back to the present. A large truck pulled out of the driveway as I went inside.

The guests had re-gathered after dinner and were rejoicing. Annie ran over to me and handed me a packing list of what the truck had delivered with a hand-written note attached.

The note read: *From Ron Dean. For the kids.*

"What was delivered?" I asked.

"A whole huge pallet of food!" she replied.

"Well, that didn't take long. Do we know where he got it and how it was delivered so soon?"

"No telling," Gloria said. "He's a man of many means. I suspect he strong-armed somebody with skill and limited self-restraint."

I found Lew out in the driveway examining the food, but without obvious enthusiasm. He counted each item and scribbled a list on a piece of paper attached to a dilapidated and gnawed clipboard.

"Hey, you don't seem as happy as everyone else about this," I said.

"It's really remarkable, that is for sure."

"But...."

"But later this week we are expecting an order of food from a Haitian distributor. Paid for, in part, by the tuition all the guests have contributed to their month here."

"I don't see the problem. You'll have plenty of food."

"I suppose I could accept the order and try to store the food, but much of it may spoil without refrigeration. Or I could cancel the order or delay it for a month or so."

"And if you cancel or delay, the Haitian company loses a sale. That's what you're concerned about, right?" I asked.

"You learn quickly, grasshopper."

"You watched *Kung Fu?*"

"What can I say, I succumbed to the vast wasteland of western civilization."

"What are you going to do about the food?"

"Accept it gracefully. Ron Dean's heart really was in

the right place. And maybe we should just contribute this next shipment to another orphanage—out of the goodness of our hearts. That seems right, doesn't it?"

"It does indeed."

We quickly finished making the list of supplies received from Ron's shipment and returned to the kitchen.

"How was your evening with Mirlande?" Lew asked when we were seated at the table sipping on iced tea.

"How did you know?"

"It's my business to know, isn't it?"

"To answer your question, quite confusing."

"Aha, the dilemma intensifies, huh?"

I took that last statement as rhetorical. I couldn't have answered it anyway.

We sipped more iced tea.

"I would rather have the world look at me strangely when they see what I have done here on Earth than have God look at me the same way when I meet him in heaven," Lew finally said with an air of having contemplated that dilemma over the course of a lifetime.

DAY 26

Paul

WITH ONLY FIVE DAYS LEFT IN OUR STAY, FINISHING projects in our work areas took precedent. All the guests started out early in the morning and usually returned by dinnertime. We'd been gathering in the evenings at the *lakou* to share our stories for many days, and we all had candid, honest discussions with Lew and each other about our progress. Lew had easily transitioned from skeptic to optimist, knowing that encouragement at this stage was most beneficial. He kept it real—he never slipped from his tendency of brutal honesty—but he also helped foster ideas. I was amazed at how he cranked out possibilities for extending guests' work on the island. And his connections here and in the States always hinted at an extended network willing to chip in and buckle down to get things done. He wasn't simply an idea guy; he knew how to spin ideas into action.

Tonight's conversation centered on Ashley and Annie. I'd seen remarkable changes in both young women in the last three weeks. Ashley Tanner had been bubbly and energetic, ready to tackle the world when she arrived. She never lost the energy, but the bubbles had popped. I could now see determination in her demeanor, and it showed on her face. Gone was the wide-eyed idealist, and in its stead, reality had made her focus on possible solutions she could make happen. But it hadn't dimmed her spirit, which was great to see in somebody else. You always think your spirit will only grow, but deep down, after a defeat or three, you simply hope you don't lose heart.

Annie Segura had begun her journey at the opposite spectrum from Ashley. Almost defeated before she started, she'd projected a dismal, dark-side outlook. But she'd changed. Not a complete turnaround, but somehow, someway she'd embraced the idea—mostly instilled by Lew Dessi—that change was possible. Now Annie was less likely to look upon other guests with scorn or disgust, nor did she heap those emotions on herself, anymore. Maybe she'd gained a bit of self-confidence as she'd worked with the girls at the orphanage. The encouragement she gave might have rubbed off on her. Nice to see. She smiled more now, too.

The two were working on a plan to collaborate on ways to help the orphanage. Annie was married and had more leeway to stay in Haiti for long stretches at a time, or at least visiting Haiti more often. Ashley was single, had a full-time job, and needed the income.

'What if I become the main fundraiser," Ashley

offered around the table as their idea came together. "I don't know how to do that yet, but there's gotta be models out there that I can learn from."

"I can provide a few examples that might work," Lew said. "You might first start by raising money for each child we house here. Put a name and face to a funding goal."

"I can take the pictures and send them to you," Annie said, "and then you can take it from there."

"Do we need to become a non-profit company, like formally?" Ashley asked Lew.

"Not to begin with, but I'll refer you to literature that you can download that'll give all the specifics you'll need to know. You could start that ball rolling as soon as you get home, because it will take much longer than you anticipate."

"In the meantime," Annie said, "can we have people contribute to your organization directly? I'm sure Ash can figure a way to track them, so we don't mix our contributors with yours, if that makes a difference."

"Sure," Ashley said, not knowing how to do that but willing to find out." With her huge smile, her enthusiasm was contagious.

"Talk with other non-profits, Ashley, so you can learn their systems. Any organization is only as good as their systems," Lew offered. "Learn the software that works, invest your time to interview those groups that have a clear understanding of who they are and what they want to accomplish. It might take some time to decipher that, but I can help steer you to ones that I think work efficiently."

Both women nodded, and Ashley took notes.

"And remember, Rome wasn't built in a day," Lew said. "Your life may take a dramatic turn toward a life of service in a day, but you won't arrive at the final destination so quickly. It takes time."

"I'll start with making a list of things the orphanage could use," Annie said. "Toothbrushes, toothpaste, clothes, things like that. Maybe we can use the money raised to improve the life of the girls. And we can buy locally—to support local merchants. So, we can't just have supplies shipped in. That won't be so good."

I could see Lew's face and he had the look of a father who had just seen his child put a lesson taught into practice. He beamed in his low-key way.

"Hey, Luke," Annie said, "maybe with your help we could single out a few girls that could get paying jobs in construction, like logistics or supplies, so they'd have something to look forward to once they time out of the orphanage. Think that would work?"

"Could be. I bet Alan can help figure that out. Right, partner?"

"Absolutely, I'll add it to my list. But let's not limit them to office skills. I'll bet many could become skilled builders—with the right training."

"Like my dad always used to say," Luke said, "a hammer doesn't require strength, just accuracy."

Everyone smiled except Gloria Dean. Her shoulders dropping, she looked a little lost and forlorn.

DAY 27

Paul

WHEN I ARRIVED AT THE BAKERY, THE MOOD HAD shifted. The men still mourned their friend Sonson. I knew this by several hushed conversations when we took a mid-morning break. But day-to-day reality helped move them away from lament toward the business at hand. And business boomed.

We'd been tracking sales of the mini-loaves for twelve days and every single day they had increased. Emil and Henri's two friends proved to be tireless and relentless. Every day when they reported to work to pick up the loaves, they asked for more. We never required that they return in the evening to drop off their hauling trays and we'd heard rumors that they often would roam the streets in the neighborhood after dinner selling the final products that hadn't sold during the day. Every mini they sold was money in their pockets, and they never returned with unsold product.

We had started by making fifty mini-loaves that first day. Now we produced three hundred loaves a day with no indication that the market was saturated. The two sellers had even suggested that they hire two more "loaf sellers" as they called themselves, to expand our territory. Doval and I had calculated the increase in supplies —mostly flour—and found that the more we purchased, the better price we received from the distributor. We'd more than quadrupled our flour consumption in less than two weeks. We weren't making much profit, but for every mini-loaf sold, we made a tiny bit.

Emil and Henri had no problems producing the mini-loaves. They'd developed a system and worked hard and efficiently to consistently bake the bread on time each morning. Their capacity for production was a sight to behold. Then Doval confided that he was sharing some of the profits with the two bakers and it made much more sense. Capitalism at work, and in its finest.

Now the question became: could we sustain the quality and production? And secondly, could we somehow expand it?

Doval had worked out the issues of the non-fresh yeast—for the time being. When he'd said nothing is forever in Haiti, he meant that things always seem to slip into chaos. When situations seemed to be going well, look out. We'd set up a schedule when he would do our test to ensure fresh yeast. We also came up with a way to sell fresh, packaged mini-loaves to local convenience stores. We had logistics and packaging to figure out and it wouldn't necessarily be easy, but at least Doval and his team had raised the bar and set their sights higher than before. They had a goal, they'd seen success, and they began to project into the future, seeing themselves grow and expand. It was sweet and satisfying for me to witness that. I felt like I'd contributed something. And I had. No question about it. Yay for me, yay of Doval and his team, and yay for a small swatch of our Haiti neighborhood. Yays all around.

Both of those tactics—a bigger, expanded territory and sales into local stores—would help our branding and possibly lead to opening doors in larger grocery stores, restaurants, and hotels. Like Lew taught us, it was a process. We needed to take it slow, but now we had a plan. Whether I stayed in Haiti to see the plan through or not had yet to be decided.

And there it was, the big question. It kept me up nights and dominated my days. Would I stay in Haiti? Even for an extra month? I could accomplish much in that time. Expand the bakery idea, take it to another business, like the pizza restaurant. Settle my mind about Mirlande. She kept popping into the question as a part of the equation that was missing. When I first starting learning algebra and had to find the value of X, I had many of the factors. Were they called factors? I wanted to call them ingredients, but that was the baker man in me. But something was missing—the X factor. Mirlande fell into that realm, something that was missing from the equation.

I didn't understand—or wouldn't admit—my feelings for her. On the one hand, I had a nice life in Cincinnati, a good, solid business, and a beautiful woman I liked. I had family and friends. I was settled, content.

On the other hand, something internal had changed in the last thirty days. Before my time in Haiti, I wanted to know how everything would work out. My life, my future. I wanted a plan and I wanted to stick to it, with no major excursions and only slight variations. That's how I was taught to succeed.

But now, although I didn't crave the unknown, I'd at least accepted the fact that the future was not planned out. Sure, sure, I believed that God had a plan for my life and that if I kept in touch with him, he'd reveal what that was. But maybe God's plan could change, too. Why not, right? I mean, if I let my heart be broken for the things that broke his, then wouldn't he want me to change course, change direction? Take up his cause. After all, I had free will and if he affected my will by exposing me to his heartbreak in the world—and certainly Haiti was one of them—wouldn't it follow that I'd shift my direction?

And where did Mirlande figure into all of this? Was I thinking about staying in Haiti longer so I could get to know her better? Could I even envision getting close to her? I'd never been attracted physically to a black woman before her. Then again, I'd never met a black woman like her. I'd stayed in my lane my whole life. Not the slow lane and not the fast lane—the middle lane. Was it time to move to another lane? Part of me felt encumbered by a need to stay the course, but another part of me was being pulled off course, redirected to something different. But different didn't necessarily mean better or truer to who I was and who God wanted me to be.

I had to ask if I could separate my purpose in Haiti from Mirlande, and if so, was that possible? I didn't think it was entirely necessary, but it might make my decision clearer, even if I didn't see how to do that. That was part of embracing the unknown.

But time was running out, and I'd need to decide soon.

DAY 28

Paul

MIRLANDE AND I SAT OUT ON THE PATIO AFTER dinner talking about nothing and everything. She told me about her mother and how she survived after her father left the family. With admiration in her voice, Mirlande told me that her mom took any job that she could find at the beginning. Waitress, maid, clerk, anything. That lasted for years until she got a full-time job as a maid in one of the bigger hotels, which meant decent pay, regular hours, consistent work. Her mom still worked, cleaning in that same hotel and adding a few others, too, along with picking up part-time cleaning jobs in other businesses when the opportunity arose.

We avoided the topic of Sonson and his death. I had to let Mirlande grieve that mostly on her own. I had broached the topic before, but she hesitated to convey much depth in her feelings. Maybe she didn't know them all yet—or know how to express them. Grief was hard to compartmentalize, and it never was the same for each person. I recalled my mother's reactions after her mother died. Her grief took many forms. Sadness, isolation, silence, anger. I never figured out how to talk to her during that time. I'd try to be available if Mirlande wanted to talk, but time was running out. At least I thought so.

Although Mirlande seemed happy to have Annie and Ashley working beside her in the orphanage, I wasn't sure she put too much faith in their ability to supply extra funds and supplies in the long run. She was certainly willing to let them try, though, and if they were successful, all the better for her girls. The notion that Luke could take one of two under his wing to teach construction was a longer shot, but it also opened a new way of thinking. When the girls "aged out" of the orphanage at around age twenty, many were unprepared for life even if they had extended family to depend upon. If Mirlande and Lew could find a way to get them trained in anything—and I know they'd tried with limited success over the past years—the girls had a better chance to rise above the lowest level of poverty on the island. Like I said, a long shot.

The one topic that Mirlande and I avoided was my future. Or her future. Or our future. I didn't know if any of those were intertwined, connected in some way I couldn't see. She'd stopped asking me about Abigail, but that didn't mean I stopped thinking about her.

We continued talking about nothing and everything.

Then Gloria Dean opened the door from the kitchen and saw us sitting there.

"Oh, excuse me. I didn't know there was anyone out here. I'll leave you two alone." She began to close the door.

"No, no," I said, Mirlande and I said almost in unison.

"Please join us," I said.

Gloria looked hesitant and a little weepy, but she nodded and found a chair beside us. She took in a deep breath and let it out as a big sigh.

Since Lew was nowhere around, I took it upon myself to be the Lew Dessi in the room.

"So, Gloria," I began, "what are your plans once our thirty days are up?"

She immediately grabbed a tissue from her pants pocket and began to cry. I looked at Mirlande with a shrug— I guess I'd seen that coming—and we both waited. As I observed Gloria, I saw a change in her from almost a month ago when we met. Her hair now was hidden by a bright blue and red bandanna, tied in the front, barely containing all that it was meant to hide. Her pretty nails, brightly colored before, now were stripped of any vitality and she continually wrung her hands, hiding one hand, then the other. Gloria's makeup failed entirely to mask the puffiness under her eyes and a deep sense of worry that spanned her forehead, eyes, and downturned mouth. She seemed unaware that the ways she'd previously projected an image to the world had faded away. Or maybe she knew but didn't care.

When no answer was forthcoming, I prodded.

"What have you been thinking about?" I asked, priding myself at being slightly less confrontational than Lew.

"I could go home to Ron," she said without the least bit of excitement or commitment. "Or I suppose, someway, I could stay?" She asked that second part as a question, with an eye toward Mirlande.

"Have you talked to Lew about that?" Mirlande asked her.

"A little. He said it might be possible."

Mirlande looked at her with sympathy, but could Gloria make it long term in Haiti, I wondered? Short term, maybe.

"I love Ron," Gloria said, "don't get me wrong, but lately he's been hard to live with. He always wants action. And I want peace. It seems we often don't see eye to eye."

I didn't think marriage counseling—considering I wasn't and had never been married—would be a strength of mine, so I stayed quiet.

"Go on," Mirlande finally said. Why didn't I think of that?

"He still wants to work long days and long weeks, and I want him to cut back. We can afford it. But he won't even consider it. I tell him I need more of him, on a daily basis, to just be together, and he just looks at me like he has no clue to what a woman might need. He's been that way forever. Oh, sure, he gives me anything I want, showers me with gifts and takes me across the globe. But sometimes, good Lord, he's clueless."

Mirlande couldn't help but smile. "I noticed that right away."

Now Gloria laughed, the first time I'd heard her laugh for weeks. The two of them just kept laughing, and when one would stop, the other would smirk and start laughing—and both were off again. Giggling, guffawing. Then I started to laugh, too. It felt good.

When the laughter subsided, Gloria said, "Oh, deary me. What am I going to do with that man? He's hard to live with but easy to love. I've been in love with him for almost forty years."

"Maybe you should go home to him," I offered. "Keep him on track with his need for supplying food to the orphanage. There could be a way to expand that idea and supply much more food to the island."

"If there was a way, he could think of it. And make it happen," she said, a note of pride creeping into her tone.

"Then you both could travel back to Haiti to see how the plan was working. You could stay longer to be with the kids. And he could go home and get back to work." Sounded like a plan to me. Mirlande perked up a bit, too.

"That might work," Gloria said.

"It would be your job to keep his energy up on food security in Haiti. He sounds like a man who could get distracted by many things," Paul said.

"Oh, once he puts his mind to something, he's relentless." More pride in her voice.

He didn't sound like such a bad guy anymore.

"But he does need his sharp edges buffed occasionally. I could do that," Gloria said.

We all smiled again, and she seemed a little lost in space.

Finally, she said, "I need to find more ways to love him. It might not have been enough to be *in* love with him."

"Then, maybe, Gloria," Mirlande said, "you need to learn to love your husband first. You have a huge capacity to love others right now. I bet that once you learn to love Ron—with all his faults—it'll be much easier to love others who are even harder to love. Do you know what I mean?"

"I think," Gloria said. "If I can love him, I can love almost anybody."

"Well, I'm glad I didn't put it that way." Mirlande smiled broadly at her. She returned it. She then looked at her watch and rose to go. "I told several of the girls I'd read them a bedtime story. The younger ones. But I bet the older ones will want to listen, too. Thank you both. I'm glad we talked. It helped, a lot."

We silently waved goodbye.

"I do declare, Mr. Whiteside, you're beginning to sound more like Lew every day," Mirlande said to me.

DAY 29

Paul

DAY 29 OF OUR JOURNEY WAS TO BE A DAY AT THE *lakou*. A celebration of sorts, but also a reflection of where we'd been—and where we were headed. Lew had given us an assignment several days ago to reflect and come ready to report. I'd spent several days reviewing my notes in the little journal he'd given us when we arrived. I had much reflection to report, but I wasn't sure of what it meant or where I was headed.

When we arrived for breakfast, Andrelita had prepared something special—scrambled eggs, bacon, and fresh strawberries. The smell of the bacon frying in the pan filled the *lakou*. The coffee today was rich and strong, grown in the mountains in western Haiti. Andrelita told us Lew bought it especially for today from a merchant in the local marketplace. I had a second cup. Before Haiti, I drank my coffee with half-and-half or milk, but I'd gotten used to black coffee now, although I didn't suppose that was the kind of change Lew was expecting me to report.

"Remember when we first met," Lew said, "and I gave you those six rules?" Here he pointed to the sign from the living room that Andrelita brought into the kitchen. I read it silently to myself again.

1. Don't complain.
2. Take notes.
3. Let go of wants and needs
4. Don't rush it or control it
5. Ask if God is present
6. Don't drink the water

"How did everyone do with the rules?" Lew wanted to know.

"When did we stop complaining?" Ashley asked.

"About the same time that Ron left," Gloria said, with a shimmy and a smile.

"I didn't take a lot of notes, but I'm hoping Alan did," Luke said, pointing to his partner ever present.

"Done and done," Alan responded.

"And I did drink the water. Nasty at times," Luke added.

"I had to let go of wants and needs many times," I said, "although I still want a cheeseburger and I need more protein." I tried to be funny, but nobody smiled, except for Mirlande.

"You just might be surprised by what we have

planned for lunch," Lew said, trying to mask any give-away in his expression.

"Number five has been hard for me," Gloria said. "It's sometimes difficult for me to see if God is present here."

Andrelita stepped forward, away from the kitchen and toward the table. "I have lived here all my life," she began, "and I've learned that I need to see God in every situation. Not just in the good times. But every time. It is not easy. You must train yourself to do that."

The room grew silent. I hadn't heard her say so many words at one time since we'd arrived. Ashley started to clap quietly, and the entire room joined in. Andrelita flushed, but I could see a sense of pride beneath the amber patina.

Lew shifted gears.

"The next set of questions," Lew began, "comes from the brochure." He held a copy of it in his hands. "And I quote, 'How can God fill you with all He wants for you...if you are already full and satisfied?' The question is: Has your visit to Haiti disrupted your idea of full and satisfied?"

Alan Waterman was the first to respond. "Later in my life, after I retired, I tried to convince myself that I was satisfied. I'd worked hard all my life. Had much success in business, but I paid a price for that. It killed my marriage and almost destroyed my relationships with my children. At some point, I had to give up my unre-lenting quest to keep going, to keep achieving. In other words, to keep making money."

He took a sip of water. "Now I realize it's quite alright not to be satisfied. I can be content with my achievements, but unsatisfied with the state of the world. Or the state of Haiti. I believe that once we get totally satisfied with life, we either give up or fade away. I'm content, but unsatisfied. I'll keep on working, but rather than making money, I'll make progress. Or, a better word, impact. I want to make an impact for the world. When once I was full, now I will only be full after I make an impact."

I looked at the group, and they were all lost in the wisdom of that heartfelt speech. Several scribbled notes in their journals.

"Very nicely put, Alan," Lew said. "I suspect you put a lot of thought into that. And you will continue to make an impact. It's been a pleasure seeing you evolve over this past month. I hope you'll come back often and report the progress you're making."

He smiled and nodded once.

"Anybody else?" Lew asked.

"Well, I don't know anything about being full," Luke Himes said, "but I have noticed that since I've been in Haiti, most of what I thought I needed—to be full, to be satisfied—seems not to matter much anymore. It's all switched around. I think I could live here and work here and go home a couple of times a year to see my sisters and my folks—and that would be a very good way to see if God is satisfied with me. I mean, right? You want him to be okay with what you're doing. It's not the other way around. I really don't know what God's up to most of the time. I just need to know he's good with what I'm doing. Like I said, that all switched around since I've been here."

I caught myself smiling. I noticed everyone in the room was either smiling or nodding in recognition. Luke did have a way of saying things down home and direct.

"Thanks, Luke," Lew said. "Here's the next question: 'How can God use you for his plan for your life...if you're so busy with your plan?' How has your plan changed—if it has?"

"I can answer that one," Ashley said. "Before Haiti, I had a plan, sort of. I want to work in childcare, get married someday, and start a family, have kids. But now I'm including God more in my plan. I'm not saying I'm giving up on my plan to do his plan. But at least I'm asking for his input. That's praying, although I don't think of it that way. I mean, I don't sit around and pray that exact prayer and then wait for his answer. I could do that, but I really don't know how. I could learn the praying part, but I'm not sure about the listening to God part."

"That's always the toughest," Lew commented.

"I mean to say, you know, that I'm changed. Being here changed me. That's all," Ashley said.

"That's enough," Lew said. "Now we'll see where it takes you. I hope you're open and ready for the journey. It can be exhilarating."

Ashley beamed.

"Annie, what about you? Has your plan changed at all since you've been in Haiti?" Lew asked.

"Well, obviously it's hard to compete with Ash.

Good grief, look at her, all smiling and effervescent," Annie said.

I noted Ashley had stopped smiling.

"I don't know, to tell you the truth," Annie continued. "I feel a little lost. One reason I came here is that my marriage is collapsing. Lew know that but nobody else did. I was hoping to find another future. But it doesn't work that way. I know what you're going to say, Lew, that it's a process and don't rush it. I'm so unsettled right now, though, I want to rush it. I want to hear God say, 'just stay' and then maybe I'd do that and figure it all out. I don't know."

Lew walked over to Annie and gave her a hug, his arm wrapped around her shoulder as she sat. "You can stay. Just stay. Here at the orphanage. Until you figure it out," he said in a low voice that we all could hear.

I saw tears running down Annie's cheeks, unchecked and undone. She turned to him and buried her face in his chest. He stood still, stroking her back.

We passed around a pot of coffee—the good stuff— as we took in what had just happened. Annie had made a commitment to stay in Haiti, at least for the short term. And Lew had invited her. Would that happen to anybody else?

"Paul." Lew called my name and I startled, although I didn't think it had to do with what I'd just asked myself. "You've been mostly quiet. What have you learned since your journey began?"

I took a deep breath. I'd been reading the brochure again and again for the past two days. "There's a statement in there—a bold one really—that goes like this: *If*

you were to empty yourself of all the junk in your life—
pride, pain, scorn, hate, ego, grudges, regrets, trivialities—
what good could fill up those empty spaces?

"I've noticed that some of that junk has disappeared. Not all of it but some," I said as I scanned the list. "Experiencing the poor here, I've let go of pride and ego and especially trivialities. There's just no place for those. I see the pain here and my pain doesn't seem so bad. It disappears. I'm not sure I have much hate in me or that I hold grudges, and I'm doing my best on not concentrating on regrets. That's easy to do I suppose. Regrets live in the past. I'm trying to live in the future, but it's mostly murky. But sometimes you need to clean up your past before you can plan your future."

I looked at Mirlande, but she was deep in thought and not looking at me.

"And have you noticed what good qualities have filled you up?" Lew asked in a calm, metered tone.

"I have. I came up with contribution, grace...and...and...love. Yes, love. Love for these people. Love for what they're going through. A need to love and help them."

Now I had Mirlande's attention. I hadn't meant it to be a statement of my love for her. Just her people, her country, her predicament. I think that's what I meant. I'm not sure.

"What, if anything, will you do with that revelation?" Lew asked.

"I'm not sure," I said in a whisper.

"I think it's wonderful, Paul," Gloria said, "that you've discovered that. Maybe I can give you back similar advice that you gave me yesterday. What I heard you say is this. Make both your contribution to Haiti and your life in the U.S. work. Travel to Haiti to get done what must be done, but don't neglect the main person you're in love with back in the States. Would that work?"

"It might."

What I didn't say was that I wasn't sure the main person I was in love with was in the States.

"Once you see what breaks God's heart, you can't ignore it." Andrelita pointed to the sign above the door she'd quoted.

"Good segue, my dear," Lew said. "You may pass out the presents."

Andrelita grabbed tissue-wrapped presents from a box in the kitchen and handed one to each of the guests.

We hesitated to unwrap them until Lew said, "You may unwrap them. Go ahead."

I carefully undid the wrapping and looked at a homemade wooden sign with finely-painted words that read:

Once you see what breaks God's heart, you can't ignore it.

Each of us held up a similar sign, some with different colored writing and others using different wood.

"These are handmade by a friend of mine in the marketplace. I hope they'll find a suitable resting place when you all return home," Lew said.

Smiles all around.

"There is one more conversation I want to have with

you. It centers around Moses as we see him in the Bible, in Exodus. I'd like to read from chapters three and four to give you a context of what I want to emphasize. Is that alright with everyone?" It didn't sound like an actual question, and no one objected.

"This first voice is God speaking to Moses...

"'*And now, behold the cry of the people of Israel has come to me, and I have also seen the oppression with which the Egyptians oppress them. Come, I will send you to Pharaoh that you may bring my people, the children of Israel, out of Egypt.' But Moses said to God, 'Who am I that I should go to Pharaoh and bring the children of Israel out of Egypt?'*

"'*He said, But I will be with you, and this shall be the sign for you, that I have sent you: when you have brought the people out of Egypt, you shall* serve God on this mountain.'"

"But Moses fought back," Lew continued.

"'*But Moses said to the Lord, 'Oh, my Lord, I am not eloquent, either in the past or since you have spoken to your servant, but I am slow of speech and of tongue.' Then the Lord said to him, 'Who has made man's mouth? Who makes him mute, or deaf, or seeing, or blind? Is it not I, the Lord? Now therefore go, and I will be with your mouth and teach you what you shall speak.' But he said, 'Oh, my Lord, please send someone else.'*"

Lew walked around the kitchen in a patient stroll. He let the words of scripture settle over the room.

Finally, he said, "Moses does what most of us do when asked to respond to God. He says he's not worthy, not ready, and to send someone else. He's almost pleading—please send anyone but me! Moses misses the main point of the whole conversation with God. It's not how difficult the call or your perceived ability to answer the call. It's not the size of the situation or the size of your wisdom or strength. It's that the God of the universe, who call us to do his will here on Earth, always goes *with* us as we obey his calling."

"He never sends us without coming with us. He doesn't only give you stuff—like a staff and snakes and curses like he gave Moses—he always gives you himself because he is what you need. You can tap into the grace and love and heavenly power that is God himself. Every minute of your journey. Let me repeat, he is what you need. Hope is never found in your personal strength and ability. It is found in him. He is all you need."

"Amen!" Andrelita said with enthusiasm.

We all repeated the refrain.

That evening: Paul

SINCE SEVERAL OF THE GUESTS HAD EARLY MORNING flights out of Port-au-Prince, we said our goodbyes after a dinner of...cheeseburgers. Lew had a sense of humor. They were delicious, especially after eating chicken and rice for a month. He put out a few Red Stripe beers, but they went untouched. Nobody was in a party mood.

My flight wasn't until late afternoon the next day because I had plans to spend the following day in Miami visiting friends. I didn't have much to pack, so I knew I could get that done in the morning.

After visiting everyone's room for a final hug, Mirlande and I settled into our familiar chairs on the patio.

"Now what, *blan?*" she said with a smile.

"We're back to *blan* again?"

"You are the one going back to *blan*, aren't you?" The smile had faded.

I had never kissed Mirlande or held her hand. Never touched her, except for the hug after Sonson was killed. I reached out and grabbed her hand, running my thumb along her fingers.

"What are you doing?" she asked.

"Reaching out."

"Why?"

I looked into her eyes and saw sadness.

"I don't want to leave," I said.

"But not all of you wants to stay either, right?"

I shrugged. "Maybe that's true. I don't know." I leaned toward her, letting my head touch hers. I inhaled the scent of the lotion she always used, not quite perfumy but with a distinct coconut aroma.

"That's Haiti," she whispered.

"What do you mean?"

"It lures you in. You want to help because it needs so much help. We are desperate for help in many ways. And yet...it is so hard. Hard to live here. Hard to enjoy life here. Hard to see happiness."

I nodded because I knew what she meant.

"Why don't you leave?" I asked.

"Because it's my country, my birthplace," she replied. We still held hands; we still touched foreheads.

"And yet, I want to leave all the time. I want to escape. I want to live in a home with air-conditioning. And carpet. Sometimes I wake at night, and I can feel the soft, plush carpet with my toes. I want to feel that. I want to go to a grocery store, walk the aisles, and buy anything my heart desires. All of it. I want a stocked pantry, a refrigerator full of food. And sometimes I want a nice glass of wine, not just Red Stripe beer."

"I have all that," I said, not an invitation, but a declaration.

"I know you do, Paul." Her voice wasn't a whisper, and she pulled her head away from mine.

I gripped her hand more firmly. Now I saw more than sadness in her eyes, more like oncoming anger.

"Sometimes I want what you have," she continued. "And I think I want you along with it. But do I want you —or just everything that you have—everything that you represent? Freedom. Air-conditioning. Carpet."

She rose and paced the patio. She wrung her hands together, then rubbed her face, and stretched her neck from side to side, trying to ease the tension.

She turned and looked at me. "But what do you want, Paul?"

There was no easiness to the question. It seemed like a demand.

"Part of me wants to stay in Haiti. Part of me wants to leave." I thought about my family and my business.

She still stared, wanting more.

"Part of me wants to know you better, but part of me is...not scared, just unsure. Do I want to spend time with you because you are Haiti and I want to help you? Or do

I want you and to take you away from all this and showing you a better, easier life?"

She walked over to my chair, grabbed my hand, and helped me stand. She stood close, inching closer, our bodies touching, chest to chest. She leaned in and kissed me. We lingered in that embrace. She grabbed me behind my head, her hand running through my hair, pulling me into another kiss.

"There was a time," she whispered into my ear, "about a week ago, I wanted you to invite me to this Ohio, to come home with you. But then I didn't know if that was right to ask. That seemed very unfair of me, putting pressure on you, on your do-good heart, to save me...from all this. Now, I'm not so sure I want that. How could I leave? Why would I leave? Would I just be abandoning my country? My work here in the orphanage? I am torn between two worlds—and one of those worlds I don't even know."

"I know. I feel the same way—but opposite. I want to stay here in a country I don't really know. To see if God can use me. And yet, I long for the comfort of home. My home, my family, my people."

"Your Abigail."

I shook my head. "If this month has taught me anything at all, it's that she's not my future. I know you better than I know her."

"And I just told you I wanted to use you to get me out of the country. That's not your best interest, is it?"

"I don't know. It doesn't feel bad. It feels right." I grabbed her hand again and held on. "But I'm not sure."

"That's Haiti. For sure."

———

AFTER MIRLANDE LEFT, I LAY AWAKE ON MY COT. I bunched up the small pillow and felt the scratchy sheet on my chest. Both of my feet were outside the covers. My flight left the island in a little more than twelve hours. I still didn't know if I'd be on it.

I could stay a little longer and see if I could get my bakery idea to infiltrate other industries. If I went home now, I could come back in a month or so and try to sign up the next industry—pizza maybe—to jump on the mini-loaf brigade. But most of the ideas Lew and I batted around were short-term solutions. The next six months. And I could think six months out. But after my talk with Mirlande, I had a longer view.

I'd turn thirty-eight in two months. Well before I came to Haiti, I had talked to my bank back in Cincy about taking out a loan for a second bakery. I was confident I could do that. But was that what I wanted?

Was Haiti my future? What about Mirlande? Was she more than a lure to keep me here? Was she a woman I could make a future with?

I lay awake long into the night. Waiting for a sign—a God sign—for what I should do. Could I step out, in confidence, like Moses? Could I put my confidence in God, regardless of all the reasons I didn't want to?

I finally fell asleep thinking, oh, Lord, please send someone else. Please send anyone else but me.

DAY 30

Paul

MOST OF THE GUESTS WERE LEAVING BEFORE EIGHT this morning. Lew had arranged a van to take them to the airport. We hugged in front of the *lakou* and promised to stay in touch. They piled into the van without much merriment. I knew most were ready to return home, but all of us shared a melancholy mood over leaving. The van driver told me he would be back to pick me up at four o'clock for my seven o'clock flight that evening.

Lew and Andrelita waved as the van pulled away. Mirlande was nowhere around.

I decided to walk over to the bakery one more time. As I meandered through the now familiar streets, I had a sense that God wanted me to stay in Haiti, but I tried to justify my indecision by somehow conjuring up in my head that I wasn't sure that's what he meant.

Doval wasn't expecting me. We'd cleared up everything the day before. I had finalized schedules, yeast tests, cost analysis, and made a nicely printed copy of all the convenience stores, hotels, and other outlets that might use his bread products. A database of sorts.

"Did you forget something?" Doval asked me as I walked in the door.

"No, I came by mostly out of habit. And I wanted to say again what a privilege it was working with you. I wanted you to know how I feel."

"I understand that, Paul. And Henri and Emil do, too. We're going to miss you."

Just then, Emil tapped me on the shoulder and handed me a small plastic bag full of mini-loaves.

"For your flight home, so you don't go hungry," he said, smiling broadly.

I gave him a big hug and tapped myself on the heart to let him know how much it meant to me.

Doval and I shared a last cup of coffee. I told him I hoped to be back soon, but there was no real conviction in my voice. He nodded knowingly.

"One visit to Haiti is enough for most people," he said as he leaned closer to me.

We said more goodbyes, and I walked out the door. I turned to look at the bakery one more time. I took it all in. It had become a second home, a second business to me.

I had more time to kill so I took the long way back to the *lakou*. I passed the marketplace, a hub of busyness that only intrigued me now. I nodded to several people that I knew by sight, and they nodded back. I circled back and walked past the bright blue home where I met the lady sweeping off the porch. She wasn't there, but I went up to her door and laid the small bag of mini-loaves at her doorstep. It didn't matter if she knew it came from me, only that somebody was looking out for her.

The driver of the van taking me to the airport arrived just a few minutes late—not bad for what we came to call "Haiti time." All the other guests had left by then. I hugged Lew and Andrelita one last time, but Mirlande had not come to see me leave. I couldn't blame her. I didn't know what to say to her and figured the same was true for her. But I had her cell number and would call her when I got home.

Sitting in the back seat of the van, I kept my eyes on the surrounding neighborhoods. It was only a few miles to the airport, but traffic could be an issue in the heart of Port-au-Prince and this January afternoon was no different from any other day.

Suddenly, the van lurched to the side, like we had a flat tire. We were bumping along as if we had no shocks on the van. Then I noticed various items on the dashboard jumping and rattling like the van was being shaken from somebody jumping on the rear bumper. I heard a scream from the open window.

"What is going on?" the driver yelled.

I saw a telephone pole fall over—and I knew.

Earthquake!

The road in front of us shockingly opened up—and we plunged into a four-foot gap in the roadway. I slammed against the far wall of the van and felt a pain sear my right shoulder. Then it all went black.

I don't know how long I was out, but when I came to, all I could hear was screaming amidst an eerie quiet. No traffic sounds at all. The van shook again. An aftershock. Was it over? Good God, was this over yet? My heart thundered in my chest. I had to get out of the van before it fell farther— I had no idea where—hell?

My right eye stung, and as I swiped at it, my hand came away bloody. Tentatively, I touched the huge gash above my eyebrow. The van was lying on its side at about a forty-five-degree angle. I struggled to reach the far door, but as I stretched my right hand to grab the seatback in front of me, I yelled out in pain from my shoulder.

The driver was gone.

I managed to slide the passenger door open and after several tries, it stayed open so I could crawl out. I slid down into the roadway gap and hauled myself up to the road surface. I was injured—and probably badly—but I could walk. For a few seconds, I contemplated returning to the van to get my backpack which held all my valuables, including my phone.

I needed that phone. I had to call...somebody. Who would I call? My legs were shaky, unsteady, and I was so lightheaded I sat on the pavement but glanced overhead to see if anything could fall on me. I was safe in that spot, at least for the moment. I wrapped a handkerchief around my head to try to stem the loss of blood. I said a quick prayer for my grandmother who told me a gentleman always carried a handkerchief in his back pocket. My right arm was almost useless. I probed the collarbone and although no bones were protruding, I felt a lump and shooting pain. I'd probably cracked it when I slammed against the van door. The pain stabbed but sitting here on the pavement that seemed like the least of my worries.

I needed that backpack. Not only the phone, but it also carried a bottle of water, and my throat was parched. I had to go back down there, into that van.

Another shake rattled the road, and I heard screaming from all around me. It wasn't just a reaction to terror coming from the voice box. This sound was part wail, part cry, with a huge *noooo* attached. It sounded like it was coming from women, like at the death of a child. *Wha, nooo, whawhanooo!*

Even engulfed in a cloud of smoke and dust, I looked around, aware I should move, get the backpack, and find safety somewhere. But frozen in place, I was bewildered by what I saw and couldn't see but only imagine. This was a huge earthquake, not the little trembler Luke had felt that day in the *lakou*. Many people had died in this one. I was sure of it. To my left, dust was settling over a home that had flattened upon itself. I didn't know what had been there before, but I was quite certain that if anyone had lived there, they lived no more. A lone car tentatively came up the street, and I shifted closer to the van. It passed along the grassy area to the left of the road, which had now been severed almost in two.

I covered my nose from the debris in the air. I slid my body closer to the van and peered inside. I saw the pack lodged against the far door, the one I'd slammed into. It looked a mile away.

With my left arm I braced myself against the top of the roadway and slid my foot down to the next step below, a jumble of rocks that didn't look at all like a foothold. I stepped gingerly down—and it held. Then I lost my balance and instinctively grabbed the doorframe of the van with my right arm and felt like I'd been shot in the shoulder. I let the arm down slowly and regained my vision after the black and white lightning bolts against my closed eyes subsided.

Bracing myself against the floor of the van with my good arm, I shifted my right leg up and over and onto the floor. Then I had to pull my other leg in because I couldn't reach for the pack with my right arm. I was now entirely inside this death trap. I reached over and grabbed the pack, but it didn't budge. One of the straps was lodged between the seat and the door.

Are you kidding me?

I pulled and pulled, so hard I could feel the van shift every time I yanked. I crawled on the floor of the van to see what was holding the pack so tightly. The seat I had been in had come loose from its bolts and was now crammed against the door. No way in my condition could I dislodge that seat. I finally realized that I could undo one of the straps from its buckle and slide the strap away to free the pack.

Once I had the pack, I retreated as fast as I could, retraced my techniques, and exited the tomblike trap for freedom. I was drenched with sweat and reached into the pack for the water bottle. It felt heavenly going down, but I'd see enough Western movies to know that I needed to preserve some water for later. I crawled away from the van and the crack in the road to the grassy area.

Now what? I tried to calm my brain and think rationally. I was alive, badly injured, but still alive. It made little sense to try to make my way to the airport, which had to be close. If this road was any indication, the runways were in shambles, too. I coughed up something odd from my throat—a combo of dust and dirt—and took another swig of water. I kept hearing the wailing and tried to say a prayer for those crying out and for the dead. Then I thought of my friends at the *lakou*—Lew, Andrelita, Mirlande and the orphans—and I knew where I had to go.

But I was in Port-au-Prince, and I had only a vague idea of how to get to Lew's compound. My watch still worked. It was nearly five o'clock and close to dark. I'd have to make my way to the *lakou* without light. I knew electricity—sketchy much of the time in Haiti—would be down and out. Somehow, I urged myself to a standing position, took a few deep breaths, and looked around. I knew the way back down the street where the van had come from, so I turned that way. I reached into my backpack and grabbed a sweater and jury rigged a sling for my right arm.

I took a few tentative steps in the direction of the *lakou,* at least I thought it was the right way to go.

I recalled seeing a large, white building at the corner of the street in the direction I was headed. We'd passed it on the way to the airport, and I thought then it might be a hospital. I stumbled toward it, but it was nothing but a pile of rubble. A dust cloud was still settling. The second floor had fallen on top of the first and now only a jumble of concrete, half walls, and a single door surrounded by six feet of stucco was recognizable. Several people lingered outside. Muffled voices were coming from somewhere. Maybe inside the rubble.

I approached the people outside and said, "Lew Dessi? *Acul Lakou?*"

They stared back at me with mix of confusion and terror in their eyes. They had no idea what I was talking about. I searched my injured brain for another landmark that was close to Lew's.

"Doval Bakery?" I shouted, too loud now, but I had to make myself heard. Nothing. They ignored me.

Now I condemned myself for not learning more about the towns surrounding Port-au-Prince. Then I remembered the GPS on my phone. I checked my power and signal. Not much of either, but maybe I could bring up the area and map out a route, then shut the phone down to preserve power. I wandered the street looking for a better signal, but I suspected that cell towers were down. Suddenly, I had no signal at all. I yelled my frustration to the heavens.

I knew the *lakou* stood west of the capital city because I'd seen a map of the area. I followed the sinking western sun in that direction. An hour later, stumbling through what looked like war-ravaged neighborhoods, I was struck by a sense of controlled confusion.

Since the earthquake hit at rush hour, cars were everywhere, moving in random directions. Traffic lanes were obliterated, and the roads in upheaval. Excavating equipment—probably on site for a building project—was now being used to dig through the rubble. Gingerly at times but always with determination, this equipment was supervised by many different people at sites needing immediate attention.

A young man carried an injured woman in the opposite direction I was going. As I got my wits about me, I realized people were carrying the injured all around me. A hospital must be nearby, but the only one I knew about was destroyed. Reality stuck hard. I was injured, but not so badly that a hospital would tend to me immediately. They'd be swamped trying to treat and move those badly injured and dying.

Now I walked faster than the car traffic. Drivers were shouting at oncoming cars. I couldn't understand what they were saying, but they shouted frantic questions, probably about what was ahead.

Some people hurried along, but others wandered aimlessly. I caught the eye of one older man, his features taken over by grave concern. We stared at each other but didn't need words to acknowledge we were in the midst of a disaster we still didn't grasp. What would happen as darkness came? Would this determined collective trance descend into chaotic fervor as the impact of the quake became known? The sun had already fallen into an eerie orange band at the horizon, shrouded by the ever-present dust cloud. In an hour, it would be dark.

I tried to concentrate on finding landmarks I might recognize. I'd once read a survival book about people who got lost in the wilderness. The ones who'd made it out alive had found a way of retracing their steps from landmarks they remembered. Now I wished I'd paid more attention on the way to the airport.

Much of what I saw bore no resemblance to what it probably looked like hours earlier. Haiti had struck me as a social country where people milled around on the streets in conversation. Now even more people flooded the streets, in front yards, in vacant lots. Men stood on dilapidated walls, pulling debris aside. Women did the same, but some stood sentinel outside of homes. Or what used to be homes. Dread took over. How long it would take to rebuild this city? Even with my untrained eye, it was clear that everything was destroyed. Everything.

That thought didn't help my mood. I'd slipped from determination to find the *lakou* to a mental state verging on panic. I'd never been in such a hellish situation. I was the baker man, not this man, stranded in a foreign country. I knew my way around a bakery, but not Armageddon. Other people had been taking care of me. Lew, Doval, Andrelita, and Mirlande. I saw a part of the country, I'd experienced it, but this was way different. I'd have to survive on my own. Panic rose inside of me, closing my airways, strangling me.

I struggled to breathe and coughed from the dust and cloud of dirt the air had become. Coughing brought up bile and mixed with other tastes I couldn't and didn't want to identify. Over and over, I told myself I couldn't panic. Absolutely not. I muttered every thought out loud to keep my focus. I needed a cool drink of water and a place to rest. My water was over half gone, but I still searched for a quiet spot.

When I came across an old metal chair by itself in

the rubble, I dragged it back from the road and out of traffic. I checked my phone again for a signal. Nothing. I dug around inside my backpack for an energy bar. Thank God. Victorious, I gobbled half of it down and took another sip of water. While I waited for my energy to perk up, I surveyed the surrounding area to determine the direction of the setting sun, but since dust covered everything and permeated the air and sky, I couldn't figure it out.

How strange, I thought, that I had no one to talk to. Any other time in my life, hitting a roadblock meant turning to other people to listen and offer advice.

"Does anyone speak English?" I said to a group of young men rushing past me. One man shook his head and moved on.

"Do you understand English?" I asked an older woman holding the hand of a young child.

She stopped. "*Oui.*"

"Merci," I said, quickly describing the place I at least hoped I was headed. She listened attentively, nodded her head often, and finally, when I described the marketplace near the bakery with the hibachis cooking, she pointed in a direction to my left. West. I was on the right track.

"Merci, merci," I said again. I wanted to hug her. Instead, I gave my half-eaten energy bar to her. A tear form in her eye as she handed the bar to the little girl. She tapped her heart with her free hand, and they walked away.

With renewed determination, my panic subsided, and I moved in the direction the woman had pointed.

My guiding angel. She'd only said one word and used hand gestures to point the way. But she gave me reason to move again.

At some point, I thought I glimpsed a wireless signal, but as I zigzagged in my pursuit, it vanished.

I came upon a small crowd surrounding a young child on the ground. As two men parted a bit, I caught a look at the boy, a large wound on his head and a brown puddle of blood on the ground. I looked away and tried not to vomit my energy bar. I stumbled away.

Twilight deepened, but I could make out whole office buildings crumbled into the street. Telephone poles slumped drunkenly, leaning down almost to the ground. Long electricity lines were splayed haphazardly along the roadside like long black gigantic snakes. More people roamed the street, and I wondered if looting had begun. I could see bulges under shirts but maybe those were loaves of bread for tomorrow's meal. The bright blue house where I left the mini loaves came to mind. Was it still standing? And what had happened to the sweeping woman?

I wandered in the direction of the marketplace, searching the ruble around me for landmarks. But my eyes took in the people in the streets or in front of crushed homes because they were everywhere I looked. A young girl stood in front of a crushed Toyota Civic. She wore a bright yellow blouse, blue jeans, and sandals with hardly any dust on her. The car was parked in front of an apartment building, once many stories high, flattened to a mountain of ruins.

The girl stared at me.

"Do you know someone inside?" I asked.

"My whole family," she answered in perfect English.

"Do you hear anything?"

She shook her cocked head slowly.

"I'm so sorry." I had nothing else.

I kept walking.

I stopped in my tracks farther down the same block. Under a flattened home, a single hand reached through a gap in the rubble, barely moving.

"Hello, can you hear me?" I yelled at the hand. I went closer, afraid to touch it, terrified that I could offer no hope of rescue and comfort was completely inadequate in this situation.

No answer. I crept closer and reached out to touch the hand. It shook but not like it knew I was there. I tried not to put a face or body with the hand. I began to cry.

I looked around. Several people approached me. I didn't know if they were in some way official, like emergency workers, or just neighbors. I pointed to the hand, and they yelled to more people—and now a crowd gathered. They spoke quickly in Haitian.

"Do you speak English?" I shouted above the clamor.

"Yes. Do you know this person?" a fierce young man asked. His eyes were bloodshot, his clothes covered in dust, with sweat pouring down his face.

"No. I was just passing by. I saw it, I saw..."

"Move, move. We have to get him out."

I moved away, and they started working. I took slow

steps backward, away from the hand. I couldn't bear to watch. I didn't want to know if they got him out alive.

I kept walking down the same block, but without being sure I was headed in the right direction. How would I find a landmark if all the landmarks were gone? I stopped again, seeing a body on the side of the road. An older man, arms splayed outward, not moving. A crowd approached him from the other direction. Ready to move the body off into a safer spot, they began to lift the man when he punched out his left arm. He shouted at them as they placed him back on the ground. He wasn't dead, but maybe dead drunk. Who could blame him?

When I came to an intersection I turned left, but it was only a guess. It was dark now, except for rigged lights, likely from a generator, that illuminated big swaths of the block. Several bodies were neatly placed in a row in the grass. I asked anyone that I saw where the marketplace might be. I only got vague guesses.

Looking to my right, I noticed something familiar. I rushed across the road—traffic had come to a standstill because of a huge crack in the concrete—and saw the pizza place where Mirlande and I had dinner. I saw the sign on the ground, anyway. The building looked like something out of a Salvador Dali painting. Skewed, slanted at an odd angle, like it had been pushed down from above by a Herculean master of the universe. At least it wasn't flattened. I stared inside, looking for signs of life. I shook my head, realizing I finally knew where I was.

I could find the *lakou* from here.

I still had almost a mile to walk—and the sights I saw slowed my progress because I couldn't look away. My mouth was parched, my skin crawled with dust and sweat, my nose cringed with each breath, but I was headed in the right direction and that alone gave me encouragement.

The next half hour blurred into a stressed trek. The sounds of the earthquake made me want to shut out everything within earshot. Wailing, sirens, shouts of anger and horror, screaming. I tried not to imagine all that had been lost. I didn't know the epicenter of the quake, but this area of Port-au-Prince and its surroundings were devastated. My mind wanted to run to what might be total destruction of the country, but my hopes held me up. I remembered the big earthquake in San Francisco, the one during the World Series. Late 1980s? I couldn't think straight. I saw the bridge collapsed and the freeway smashed and at first thought the whole city must have crashed into the Bay. But it hadn't. It was bad, but not devastating. That helped me hang on to hope. Maybe the *lakou* survived, maybe the orphanage was untouched.

I passed the bright blue house where I'd left the mini-loaves earlier in the day. No one would ever live in that house again, I thought. It wasn't a house, just a pile of wood and stone. I hoped the nice lady sweeping the porch had made it out alive.

I passed the bakery and ran to the door. No lights were on, and it was locked. I banged my fist, but no answer. I looked in the window but without light, I couldn't see. The building still stood. God had spared it, but many around weren't so fortunate. I said a prayer for Doval, Henri, and Emil. Maybe I'd see them all again one day.

Now I ran toward the *lakou*. I jumped over crevasses in the street. I ignored pleas for help. I sprinted past dead bodies, smoldering fires, and frantic people.

When I reached the back entrance to Lew's property, I couldn't see the roof of the orphanage. The one-story orphanage building made of concrete block with a tin roof had been leveled. The roof sat askew at a deadly angle. I heard nothing but saw a few children wandering the property. I saw Gloria at the picnic table, surrounded by a group of girls.

"Gloria?" I managed to croak.

She just stared at me, tears running down her cheeks.

"Are you okay?"

She shook her head.

"What? Say something."

She opened her mouth, but nothing came out.

I repeated it. "Say something."

One young girl grabbed my arm and turned me toward the back wall. I saw Annie laid out on the ground in a line with several others.

"Mirlande?" I asked. I almost couldn't get it out.

The young girl said, "She wasn't here today."

That gave me hope. A little. I remembered I hadn't seen her before I left for the airport. Could this possibly be the same day?

I ran to the *lakou*, and although I could see damage

—the doorframe to the back door sat at a crooked angle —the building still stood. Maybe Luke was right, and all the improvements Lew had made over the years paid off.

I entered the kitchen, our home away from home for the past month. Lew sat at the table, weeping softly. A single candle lit the room. He didn't see me at first. I looked around. Dishes were smashed on the floor as the hutch had fallen over. Lew's signs—his philosophy on a plaque—were crooked on the walls. Lew sat in the only chair still upright.

Then he wailed. The same wail I'd heard from dozens of men and women over the past six hours. It started low in his gut, made it up and out his throat, and drowned the room with sorrow. My heart broke. I could feel the heart of the country break. Lew had channeled the Lord God Almighty as he cried for the people of Haiti.

I staggered over to him and put my arms around his shoulders. He gripped my hands, turned, and looked up at me. I saw the horror of sadness in his eyes. Then he wailed again, and I joined him. I only hoped I wasn't wailing for Mirlande.

Lew finally stopped. He stood and grabbed my hand and led me to the back patio. I shuddered before he opened the door.

Lord God, I prayed...

A body lay on the lounge chair, covered with a table-cloth. I froze. My heart pounded in my chest. I couldn't breathe.

Finally, I grabbed the cloth and uncovered the head.

Andrelita. I carefully covered her back up and knelt on one knee.

I turned toward Lew who had slumped into one of the chairs.

"Lew, where's Mirlande?"

He looked up with vacant eyes. He shook his head.

"Did she come into work today?"

Another shake.

"Have you seen her?"

"No," he said in a whisper. "Go find her, Paul."

"I will. I'm so sorry...for everything."

"That's Haiti. That's just Haiti."

"I'll find her. I will."

"I can't lose her, too."

Me neither, I thought.

"Your head," he said with a look of concern.

"I'm fine."

I grabbed one of the thin, kitchen towels I found on the counter. I removed my head bandage and with my one good arm, I fashioned a new bandage with the towel. Then I took two more towels and rigged a better sling for my arm. I drank two glasses of water.

Without looking back toward the orphanage, I set out for Mirlande's home in a slow jog. I knew where I was going but was also aware I couldn't do much for all the people on the streets. I had a single focus to find Mirlande.

What if she were dead? What would I do? Would I leave Haiti, never to return, silently wailing for the rest of my life?

What if she was alive? Would I stay in Haiti and

help rebuild the orphanage? Luke and Alan would help. A plan was already developing in my foggy head.

She was alive—she had to be alive. Please God, don't let her die. At that moment, running now toward her home, I realized my heart broke for Haiti. It broke for its people, its plight, the devastation, the past and now the future. My heart broke for Sonson. For Annie. For Andrelita. For Lew and what his life would be like going forward.

I would never forget the last thirty days. I didn't want to. Ever. My entire past—my bakery, my parents, everything—faded from me. Lost in the landslide that was Haiti. Lost to the work to be done. I felt new, like something in me had died. My head ached and my arm sent shivers through me with every step. But it was pain I could deal with. It was pain that I cherished, like a badge of courage, a badge of honor, a badge of survival, of coming through hell's fire to the other side, no matter what the other side looked like or held for the future.

Then I saw a little boy by the side of the road. Shoeless, wandering in the street, seemingly no family around. He immediately reminded me of the little boy in the brochure. The boy who broke my heart. The boy who led me to Haiti.

He looked directly at me, with his big belly extended, dirt on his face, fear in his eyes. He clutched a little stuffed animal. I wanted to run to him, grab him in my arms, and tell him everything would be better. I knew it would. Then he turned away from me and ran toward a voice calling a name. I hoped it was his mother or his father. I hoped he'd grow up. Survive.

I sprinted. Her home was close, only a block away. I wailed as I ran, wailed for all that was lost, for all that would never come again, for everyone who'd died, and those who suffered the terror of not knowing. For lives lost, for loves lost, for futures deprived. For Haiti.

I rounded the corner and saw her house. Most of the house lay on the ground. The cement blocks knocked over, the roof gone.

I stopped. I fell to my knees, exhausted. I wept.

Suddenly, she came around the corner, limping. A smile spread across her face.

"I prayed that you would come," she said.

"I did. I came for you."

She limped over to me, knelt, and touched my head. She touched my arm ever so softly.

"Now I pray that you will never leave."

I kissed her.

"I never will."

The darkness covered us, blocking out the rubble and destruction. Sounds and smells faded from our embrace. We clung to each other. I didn't want to think what we would face in the coming months. Right now, her touch was all I needed.

The morning would come soon enough.

The End

Thank you for reading *Anyone But Me*. If you enjoyed this book, please consider sharing a review at your favorite online retailer, BookBub, or Goodreads.

DISCUSSION QUESTIONS

1. Have you ever been on a mission trip to a foreign country? Describe the trip to the group. What made you uncomfortable? How did the customs and culture of the country differ from yours?

2. Describe Paul's feelings of making a difference in the world. How do you make a difference?

3. In the example of soap being collected and distributed in Haiti, how did that solution hurt the country? Can you think of similar examples that you've either experienced or heard about?

4. Did you ever disappoint your parents? How did your parents view your career choices? Were they demanding in helping you select your career? How were they supportive of your life choices?

5. Describe Mirlande's dilemma—to stay in Haiti or to leave.

6. How do you listen to God? Do you hear him speak to you?

7. Do you feel unworthy of God's plan for you? How do you resist or follow God? Where is he leading you now?

8. Can you relate to the character of Ron Dean? Are there times in your life when you cannot wait to do something? Give examples of how that turned out, both good and bad.

9. Describe Paul's change of attitude and demeanor during the book. What specifically changed him?

10. Describe Mirlande's change. Why do you think she changed?

11. Most of the characters in the book were learning a lesson. Describe several lessons learned. What lesson are you learning now? How are you learning it?

12. Lew Dessi served as a mentor to many of the characters in the book. Have you ever had a mentor? Do you have one now? If not, who could be your mentor and what would you expect to learn?

13. In reviewing the characters of Ashley and Annie, to whom do you relate? And why?

AUTHOR'S NOTE

Each character and every event in this book are fictional. I made it all up. But I have traveled to Haiti several times and those experiences influenced this writing. For example, I know of a bakery that put something similar into the marketplace like the mini-loaves of bread. The soap example that Lew Dessi talks about happened, but much later in history, several years after the earthquake when a cholera epidemic broke out. I've visited an orphanage of girls in Haiti, where the children pulled water from a well with a coffee can. I stuck my head in the door like Paul Whiteside.

Those experiences in Haiti changed my life. After twelve years of service to Haiti, I'm not done yet—serving or changing. You can visit the non-profit organization in which I serve by going to www.extollo.org. I'd be happy to answer any questions about missionary work in Haiti or offer quantity discounts of this book for your non-profit. Please reach out via my website, www. bkirkpatrick.com, or my email address, bruce@bkirk patrick.com.

ACKNOWLEDGMENTS

I don't bake, I barbeque. My wife is the baker in the family. So, when I had baking questions, I went to my wife, who said, "I have recipes, but I mostly do it by feel." That wasn't quite enough for the story, so I went to the next best solution. I found Bettie the Baker on YouTube and thoroughly enjoyed her "Understanding Bread Making Step by Step." Any mistakes in the story are mine, not hers.

Thanks to my wonderful team. Virginia McCollough, my editor, finds all the holes in the manuscript and makes me fill them in. Julie Moore of Moore Design makes the book cover come alive. Maria Connor of My Author Concierge performs all the production work— proofreading, line editing, formatting, and preparation for distribution.

I hope you read the dedication page. Cheryl and Sherman Balch have influenced my life for thirty years. For the past twenty, I've served on boards of directors for their non-profits, including in Haiti. They inspire me to do the good work in the world. I don't have Hollywood stars or sports figures as heroes. I have Cheryl and Sherman.

ABOUT THE AUTHOR

Bruce Kirkpatrick writes to inspire people to discover their full measure of God-given gifts and talents and their true purpose in life. A Pennsylvania boy, he now writes from Southern California. He spent over thirty years in Silicon Valley as an executive and entrepreneur.

Bruce now divides his time between writing and serving on non-profit boards of directors, including Extollo International, a ministry that is helping unleash Haiti's potential to build a strong future by training a construction workforce of character and capability, while adding strength and safety to Haiti's infrastructure (Extollo.org). For more information about Bruce and his books, visit bkirkpatrick.com.

To join his email list, please visit https://bkirkpatrick.com/gift/